$400 ✓
YA

# What they're saying abou

MW01107287

*"To Follow the Moon* is a sist
*Child,* and *The Forest Wife.* This book creates a vivid sense of what it
was like to live in the past and shows European Americans how to
reconnect with their rich Earth-based cultural heritage." **—Sarah Pirtle**
Author of *An Outbreak of Peace,*
winner of the Olive Branch Award

*"To Follow the Moon* gives the reader a revealing glimpse of history not
found in school texts: women coming to the New World on their own,
having to struggle with a hollow interpretation of women's place in the
world. Reading this book is richly rewarding." **—Antiga**
Feminist, crone, author, workshop
facilitator, and outrageous woman

"I was enchanted by the Willow People's concord with nature. Would
that all faiths were grounded in the health, strength, and mystery of the
physical universe as this Pagan religion! Great good luck with this
lovely story!" **—Faith Sullivan**
Author of *Empress of One* and *The Cape Ann*

"This appealing YA novel counters stereotypes about Pagan communities,
in lyrical, fast-paced prose. The characters are women old and young who
fear, love, and dare to defy convention. Svien is a fresh, talented new
voice. Highly recommended for YA audiences and classroom use."

**—Jane Katz**
English teacher and author of *I Am the Fire of Time* and
*Messengers of the Wind: Voices of Native American Women*

*"To Follow the Moon* by Kaia Svien is a novel which gives some historical perspective to the earth-based spirituality about which I wrote in *The Girl Who Kept Her Magic*. Beginning in 17th-century England, *To Follow the Moon* weaves together the lives of Basuba, a forty-five-year-old midwife and healer; her niece, Marion, who has just reached the time of her first menses; Fiona, a twenty-year-old woman who is trying to save an ancient grove of trees; and Matthew, the man who loves Fiona. As the religious environment in England continues to narrow, the group finds their individual fates pointing them toward the New World. With this as the backdrop, we are skillfully led through the cycle of the year, learning about various seasonal celebrations as well as such time-honored traditions as "drawing-down-the-moon," welcoming first blood, and honoring last blood. For adults and young adults alike, this book is a great addition to the slowly growing library available to people who celebrate the Earth and their connection to Her. I highly recommend it. Blessed be.

**—Laurel Reinhardt**
Author of *The Girl Who Kept Her Magic* and *Seasonal Magic*

# To Follow the Moon

# To Follow the Moon

### Kaia Svien

1999
Galde Press, Inc.
Lakeville, Minnesota, U.S.A.

*To Follow the Moon*
© Copyright 1999 by Kaia Svien
All rights reserved.
Printed in Canada.
No part of this book may be used or reproduced in any manner whatsoever
without written permission from the publishers except in the case of brief
quotations embodied in critical articles and reviews.

First Edition
First Printing, 1999

Cover art by Nancy Svien

Grateful acknowledgment is made to Antiga for sharing "Charge of the
Darkness of Winter Solstice"

Library of Congress Cataloging-in-Publication Data
Svien, Kaia
    To follow the moon / Kaia Svien — 1st ed.
      p.  cm.
    ISBN 1–880090–82–1 (trade pbk.)
    1. Great Britain—History—Charles I.   I. 1625–1649—Fiction.
I. Title.
PS3569.V55T6    1999
813'.54—dc21                                                    99–18848
                                                                    CIP

Galde Press, Inc.
PO Box 460
Lakeville, Minnesota 55044–0460

*To all of us who dream of living in harmony
with Mother Nature, may this book awaken your
memories of the Old Ways. And deep gratitude
to each of you who carried the vision with me as*
To Follow the Moon *was birthing.*

# Contents

# *Preface*

*To Follow the Moon* is an exciting journey into history, imagination, and spiritual transformation. As you read this book, experience seventeenth-century England through the lives of wise women and their people. Journey with them into the enchanted realms of Nature and learn about timeless ways of working with herbs, trees, creatures, and the Land. Attune with the wise women to the ancient rhythms of celebrating the cycles of the Sun and of the Moon. Deepen your understanding of the challenges wise folk of Nature experienced in practicing the sacred ways of their ancestors in an age of social turmoil and religious persecution. Attune to the courage and wisdom that the wise women central to the story summon forth from within themselves through their deep resonance with the spiritual dimensions of Nature. And, as you complete your journey through this book, reflect on your own life processes of personal growth and empowerment as well as your own relationship with the larger natural world of which we all are part. This book not only is an entertaining adventure, but it can be personally transforming as well.

*To Follow the Moon* is an inspiring tale for our time for people of all ages. Kaia skillfully weaves together her research and knowledge of spirituality, folkways, and history. Set in the past, this story embodies lessons in strength, perseverance, intuition, courage, and collaboration which are greatly needed for this present time as well as for the future. This tale is a enriching mythic adventure especially relevant for women of this era who endeavor to live full, holistic lives that balance feeling and thinking, reflecting and acting, and service to others with self-care, healing, and empowerment.

My own journey with *To Follow the Moon* was a powerful one. I strongly connected with the practices as well as struggles of wise women past and present and I resonated deeply with my own ancestors from England, Scotland, and Wales who came to America in the seventeenth century questing for religious freedom. It is my hope that all who read this book will not only enjoy their journey, but come away personally enriched and with a better understanding of the sacred ways of Nature as well as the importance of honoring cultural diversity and upholding religious freedom for all.

Well wishes as you embark on your own journey *To Follow the Moon.*

Blessed Be,
SELENA FOX
Priestess and Psychotherapist
Circle Sanctuary Nature Preserve
in the forested hills west of Mt. Horeb, Wisconsin, USA
New Moon, July 12, 1999

*Chapter 1*

# All Hallows' Eve:
# Marion & Basuba

EASTERN ENGLAND, OCTOBER 1640

*The veil is lifting, return, return.*
*Boundaries are shifting, return, return.*
*Spirits of loved ones, return, return.*

Something was bothering Marion. Basuba had first seen it yesterday in the way her niece ignored Gray Cat when he poked his paw out again and again to get her to play. Then she had heard it in the heaviness of Marion's voice when they were chatting in front of the fire last night. Now this afternoon, watching her come in from the garden, thin arms stretched wide around three pumpkins, it was there in her gait and in her gaze.

Usually her niece, just back from Ely, would be darting all over the grounds to find everything that had changed while she was gone. The pumpkins would be half-forgotten by now, plopped down somewhere on the grass. She would have clapped her hands together and jumped as high as she could when she saw how huge the cowslip patch had grown, would have stuck her nose in the mint for a good whiff, plucked a couple of dill sprigs to chew on, and "tsked" over the disappointing show from their first crop of carrots.

Not today. Instead, Marion Carryer walked directly towards the cottage, keeping her eyes locked on the path she knew by heart. Without one glance over her shoulder at the ducks splashing in the pond or at the blackbird calling from the ash tree.

"It's not her health that's the problem," mused Basuba. The girl's cheeks were ruddy. Her wavy shoulder-length chestnut hair shone, and her hazel eyes were clear. Her body, a bit too long for the brown woolen shift she wore, looked strong.

Thirteen years old. "An unusual woman-child she is," thought her aunt. "Why, sometimes she stands right out in the busy Ely market, and other times a body has to search long and hard to find her in a crowd. A stranger passing by might figure her to be a young woman of sixteen one day, but then guess that she was no older than eleven on another day."

In a flash Basuba realized that something or someone had frightened Marion. "That's where the trouble lies. How long before she'll be willing to talk about it?" she wondered.

Basuba Hutchinson, plump as the apples she had plucked earlier this morning, stood just outside the doorway of her thatched-roof cottage that lay on the edge of a marsh about twelve miles west of the English city of Ely, famous for its cathedral, for its mutton and its malt. She glanced at the weak autumn sun, wishing it would put out a bit more warmth to share with them on this last day of October 1640. Instead, the air was as cool and crisp as the sky was blue with just a few clouds starting to mass on the western horizon.

Basuba tugged at her homespun tan shawl and knotted it tighter around her thick waist. She rubbed her hands together briskly to get the blood coursing in them.

As Marion neared the simple cottage, raucous cawing pulled her eyes to the sky above. There, twenty or so black large-winged birds spiraled up, up, up on a rising current of warm air. When they reached the top, they cawed even louder and flew off in twos and threes, then careened down to catch the current for another lift.

"Oh, I want wings like those next time around," cried Basuba. "Look how they ready themselves for the great migration. Come tomorrow or the next day they'll be off, flying day and night without a stop."

"Blessings on your journey, you Black Beauties!" called Marion loudly to the feathered ones.

Basuba muttered in a whisper, "Thank Mother Nature those birds have the power to bring her out of herself. Let's hope I can build on that."

She raised her voice and addressed Marion gaily, "Look at the grand size of your pumpkins. And their fine color! They'll make a cheery welcome for the Spirits tonight. Put them down by the door and come warm yourself with some cider."

Marion entered the thick-walled cottage and shivered from the cool dampness created by its clay walls. A relief in the hot summer, but unwelcome today. From the rafters of the single room hung bundles of drying herbs and roots, some so large a person had to duck to get under them. Signs of a full harvest.

The straw ticks they had slept on last night were stacked against the back wall to make more walking space. The single window in the northern wall was still covered with oiled paper, but the shutter Basuba sealed it off with in the colder months stood below it, just waiting to be hoisted into place. There were two benches with storage space side by side along the southern wall; Blackie, a standoffish tom-cat, was waking up from a nap on the one closest to the hearth. Gray Cat, scarcely more than a kitten, pawed expectantly at the tall basket that held newly spun yarns on the floor near the door. When Basuba saw that Marion was not going to pick out a ball to toss to her furry friend, she motioned for her niece to sit at the wooden table in the center of the room.

Basuba limped slightly as she returned from the hearth carrying two mugs of cider she had tucked between the last coals of the dying fire. She was a solid woman of forty-six who wore her raven-colored hair in a single long braid. A fine network of lines was just beginning to lace her face; they showed when she laughed or squinted to follow a bird's flight far off in the sky. Her voice was deep and strong as if it had roots that went way down into the Earth. She loved raising cats, grow-ing herbs, and bringing in babies as much as anything else. Because she lived alone on the marsh and knew a great deal about healing people with potions and teas, some folks were afraid of her. Basuba put her hands over her round belly and laughed hard when the fowler's wife said as much, for she herself was not afraid of many things nor had she ever attempted to scare anyone.

Marion gulped the warm cider without saying a word. She avoided looking her aunt in the eyes and had hardly cracked a smile since her arrival last night.

"I'll have to bide my time," thought Basuba. "Mari's not ready to say any-thing about what's on her mind yet."

"I'd like you to be the one to set the pumpkins out this year, Mari. You'll have to start soon. Your grandmother's Spirit often comes early, and the sun is already beginning to bed down for the night. Grandfather'll be pleased with us. He wor-ried about leaving only daughters behind. Feared none of us'd be able to till the land well. The sight of these fine pumpkins'll set him at ease."

At Basuba's words, Marion sat up straighter, turned her green eyes that were dotted with flecks of brown directly towards her aunt, and nodded. Being chosen to set the path for the Spirits on All Hallows' Eve was not a right given often to a person her age. It was important work that had to be done carefully. The Spirits must be sure they were truly welcome at a hearth or they would pass on by.

Was she really ready to be the one in charge? She took a deep breath and willed herself to relax. If Basuba thought she could handle it, why should she doubt it? Except for one thing: she knew the truth about the broom, and Basuba didn't yet. Would Basuba have given her this honor if she *did* know about what had happened?

"But it wasn't my fault," she wailed silently in her head as a huge lump swelled in her throat and took up all the room she needed for swallowing.

Pushing as hard as she could, Marion shoved away thoughts of the broom. She turned her attention to the laying out of the pumpkins. She would work as carefully as she could and do everything she remembered. Then she'd ask Basuba for her opinion. When things were just as they should be, they would make the prayers together. Marion tipped her mug to drain the last of the cider and left the cottage.

She surveyed the pumpkins and the path that led to the door as she wondered which one to put nearest the cottage. With the memory of her father bright in her mind, Marion touched each of the pumpkins. Her hands came to rest on the biggest one. Yes, that made sense; of all the folks she knew who had died, he held the largest place in her heart. She cleared a spot for the orange ball amongst the fallen leaves. Her eyes blurred with tears as she held it close to her chest for a minute.

"This is for you, Papa," she whispered. "I miss you so much. Sometimes I do feel that you are close by, but other times you seem so far away." Her throat ached. She settled the pumpkin into its new home.

She saw a good place for the second pumpkin about two feet out from the first one. She closed her eyes and brought to mind her grandmother's face. She looked over the two remaining choices and made a selection.

"This very round pumpkin is for you, Grandmother. I remember you. A little, anyway. The way you smelled. Me very tiny and your lap so big and soft. You'd rock me and sing, 'I see the moon, the moon sees me…' There, this pumpkin's all set."

Now for the last one with its speckled burnt-orange hue. She rolled it around a bit before it slipped into a resting position. This one was to honor her grandfather. He had passed over before her birth, so all that she knew of him came from the stories told around the evening fires and from these visits on All Hallows' Eve.

Thinking she was finished, Marion looked up to see Basuba standing over her, holding out a fourth pumpkin. As she reached for the golden orange globe, the girl wondered who it would bring to them tonight. Her hands trembled as she took it. She had heard of folks who refused to put out an unnamed pumpkin for fear it would call in a troubled Spirit.

When she had asked Basuba about that once, her aunt had replied firmly, "I expect I can hold my own with any Spirit that feels called upon to visit me. Most times I'm honored to be remembered by them. And I often learn something. Much of what I know about two of my favorite herbs, lavender and St. John's wort, I've gleaned at this very hearth on All Hallows' Eve. Passed on to me by a Willow

Woman, a lady of the herbs who lived in these parts more than a century ago. And if there's any soul with unfinished business between us, I'd rather he or she come tonight than surprise me in my dreams."

Marion bounced the pumpkin once or twice in her hands to get a feel for it. It was smaller than her father's, not as perfectly rounded as her grandmother's, and lighter in color than the one that would call in her grandfather. Curiosity slowly edged out fear.

It was when she was ready to clean out the hearth that Basuba realized that she had not seen a trace of the All Hallows' Eve broom yet. Odd, it should have arrived with Marion last night. Perhaps the broom was hidden outside. If so, it was past time for its presentation. Somehow the broom must be at the bottom of Marion's sorry mood. After a moment's pause, Basuba made a hasty prayer of apology to the Spirits for using an ordinary broom for holy work, and set about tidying up.

She carried the last pile of cold ashes outside to toss over the rosebushes that grew to the left of the cottage entrance. With such a short distance to travel, she could use both hands for carrying a basket or herb bundles and leave her walking stick tucked by the door. She threw the ashes out with a little prayer.

"Thanks, Roses, for the beauty you brought to our door this summer. May these ashes blanket you, Bushes, and protect your roots from the harshness of the coming winter."

Her eyes followed the soft grayish flakes as they sifted through the bare branches of the plants to the ground below, and she wondered, "Is this to be my last winter in England?" Sadness pierced her heart with that question. Marion's question was a welcome interruption.

"How do you fancy these pumpkins, Aunt?" she asked, dusting the earth off her hands as she stood up.

"Inviting, indeed. If I were a Spirit, I'd come right in, even if I'd been planning to travel on to St. Ives," said Basuba with a grin.

She looked warmly at her niece. Yes, it was time to turn this important rite over to Marion. The older woman gazed down at her own hands for a moment. Still strong and sure enough to turn a baby during its birthing they were, and yet small brown spots of age were beginning to collect on them like the falling leaves of autumn.

Basuba was one of the oldest Willow People, a small community of women and men who worshiped Nature and believed that every living being was sacred. When it was time for Marion to be initiated into the women's circle at Candlemas, four months from now, she would become the youngest Willow Woman. Now Marion was laying out the pumpkins this All Hallows' Eve, setting in motion a series of changes. From now on, traditions and powers would be passing from Basuba's hands into Marion's.

"Bittersweet, it surely is," thought the older woman. And, she reminded herself sharply, a moment for great gratitude. Why, in these days, not every wise woman had a young maiden willing to learn the ancient ways.

"What's left for us to do before prayers?" Marion hoped her voice didn't sound as uneasy as she felt. The story of the broom would force its way out before much longer.

Basuba said evenly, "Setting the food out on the table, decorating the broom, and placing it right out here by the door. The vines with which to wrap it are in my big wooden bowl on the bench where Blackie naps. Make sure lots of those bright berries show."

Basuba looked closely at her niece. "By the way, Love, where is the broom? I was so happy to see you last night, I don't remember spotting it."

"I don't have it, Aunt," cried Marion, turning her head quickly to hide the tears that spurted from her eyes.

Basuba frowned. "Strange. That's not like you to forget something so special…"

Anger and pride outlined each of Marion's words as she said stiffly, "I would not forget the broom, Basuba."

Her aunt's voice slowed and softened, "Tell me then, Marion, about what happened."

Just like a pot of root stew boiling on the fire, one scene after another of harsh memories bubbled up to the surface of Marion's memory.

She could see the cruel faces, hear the mean, hard voices as they taunted, "Ride your broom, Hag. Ride your broom, Hag. Ride your broom." Louder and louder. More and more of them joining in. A sharp, sure rhythm, steady in its own way as a heartbeat—but the heartbeat of a many-headed monster.

"I wasn't going to tell you. It makes me feel so bad. Like, like I'm dirty."

Basuba stepped forward to put her face close to Marion's. She cupped a hand gently under her niece's chin.

"You are always blessed. Start from the beginning, child. I've known that something was amiss since you crossed my threshold last night."

"It was on my way here. I was late leaving Mother's, so I took the shortest way across town. I had to pass the Cathedral School. Some of the choir boys playing in the courtyard spotted me carrying the broom." Here her voice broke. "Oh, Basuba, I had decorated it already to please you. It was so pretty! So some of those boys could tell the broom was for All Hallows' Eve. They came running to the fence and poked their faces between the iron rods. They pawed at me, calling me terrible things. Shouting as loud as they could. More boys came. They grabbed the fence and started shaking it so hard, as if to tear it down. They jeered at me and All Hallows' Eve..."

Tears sprang to Marion's eyes again. "And, Basuba, I got so scared I couldn't move. Just like in a nightmare. They made the Hanging Sign. A man dressed in black came over. He told the boys to stop, but then he held his cross up against me. So most of the boys copied him, making the cross with their fingers, calling 'Fie! Fie!' Then the man told me to get out of their sight as fast as I could. And 'Be damned.' That's when I could run again."

"Child, yes, yes, I understand."

"I was running, but I was so afraid someone else would see me and that there wouldn't be a fence between us." The red drained from her cheeks, leaving them pale. "Basuba, I feel so bad." She stared at the ground for a minute before she spoke again. "I threw the broom behind a hedge; it's still there now."

Marion looked down at the ground of the cottage floor as though she would never be able to lift her head up again. "I wanted to tell no one for feeling so unclean and so unworthy. Such a coward. I almost didn't come here, but there was no other place to go." Now she was sobbing.

"I understand all that you did," Basuba spoke softly and put an arm around Marion to rock her gently as she talked. After a silence, the older woman continued, "Yet it is right that you came here and that you are telling me what happened. In a short time, you will know that. You will feel safer to have your story shared by two. You have shrunk its shadow by half in the telling already. We'll figure out something else for the broom, don't worry. Now tell me, what did they call you?"

"Aunt, I cannot say it."

"Child, you must. To keep such things secret is to say yes to their curse. Each name will come unstuck from you as you speak it to me. I promise. Go ahead. One at a time."

Marion took a deep breath and began. She squeezed her aunt's hand tight while she spoke. The name burned its way out her throat. "'Evil...Evil Eye!' first one of them shrieked. 'Look! She's got green eyes. She's one for sure.' Then they were all stamping their feet and calling out, 'Evil Eye, Evil Eye, Evil Eye!' at me."

"Go ahead, now. Just spit it out."

"Evil Eye," said Marion weakly.

"Say it again now. Louder. Louder. And spit it all out of you."

"Evil Eye," the girl whispered. "Evil Eye," she repeated more forcefully. "Evil Eye!" she screamed.

"Yes. Just like that. Spit now. As far as you can. Send any bit of the name that lingers in your body out with your spit."

"Devil's Handmaiden!" And louder, "Devil's Handmaiden!"

"Stamp your foot hard while you say it."

Louder still and coming down swiftly with her foot, Marion cried out, "Devil's Handmaiden!"

"Good. That's the way."

Marion spat and went on. "Baby-Eater! Baby-Eater! Baby-Eater!"

"Breathe, Marion. Breathe deep. Take your time. Come back to yourself after you spit out each name. Come back fully to yourself before you go on to the next one," coaxed Basuba.

The woman placed one of her hands squarely on the girl's mid-back and the other on her solar plexus to hold her steady. "Remember, I am right here with you, and we are both Willow People. I call on the Spirits of all our foremothers and forefathers to be present with us, too." And she added with a grin, "Since it is All Hallows' Eve, that will be very easy for them to arrange."

Then Basuba saw that Marion was crying. "So, my brave maiden, there's more. The hardest one. What is it? Get it out."

"I hate Christians. I hate them."

"Stop there! Your mother is Christian, Nick is Christian. Most Christians would treat you well. These are simply little boys wanting to tease and poke and make someone cry. Back to the word, Fierce One."

"They weren't so little, Aunt. And the man joined in with them. It's 'witch.' They called me 'witch.'"

"Ah, so. And why does Witch make you cry so?"

"You know. It's because it's who we are. None of the other words can hurt me for they do not speak the truth of us. But Witch is our name. And so it cuts into me like the sharpest blade."

"Yes, Love, the Witch they call us comes from our name, Wicca. But it has no more power to hurt you than the other names. For when they call out 'witch,' it does not signify to them what Wicca does to us."

"I don't understand you, Aunt."

"The root of Wicca, Witch, wicker, and willow means 'to bend, to change shape.' So, we dance with Life; we change and flow as it calls us to. But when people who fear us call us 'witch,' they are thinking of an evil person who has supernatural powers to use against them."

Basuba picked up her walking stick and said to Marion, "Go in and pull two handfuls of straw from that tick. Take it from under where your feet lie when you sleep. They won't miss it. And bring us a piece of yarn, too."

When Marion returned with the straw, Basuba had her hold it firmly around the bottom end of the stick while she secured it with the string. "There, that's starting to look like something already," she crowed.

Then Basuba took a piece of greenery and began to wind it the length of the cane, saying, "Think about this Hallows' Eve broom of ours. We make it pretty with greenery and ribbons, and then clean the hearth with it on the one night of the year when we let our fire go out. Next, it goes outside the cottage as a sign to the Spirits of our loved ones that we are ready for their visit. The sun goes down and darkness comes, bringing them with it. Since they no longer have bodies, we sense their presence more easily when we do not depend on our eyes to see them. So the broom is a gateway between our world and Spirit world, is it not?"

"Yes."

"Now, the folks who are scared of meeting their dead kin, they avoid the darkness for the same reason that we seek it. It frightens them to know that we make a holy time out of sitting in the dark. So they take our little broom here and turn it into an evil creature of tremendous—"

"But why should they fear their dead?"

"Because their priests teach that most folks are sinners who burn in hell when they die. If we want to visit with the dead, then they know that we are not afraid of hell. If we are not afraid of hell, to them that means that we must be friends of their devil who rules hell. They hope that hell is far away from here, and so they believe that we use our blessed brooms to fly there," explained Basuba.

"So those horrid boys were actually afraid of me?"

"That's what I'd guess. And it was their fear that made their actions hateful. You'll see that whenever you look into the roots of hate, you'll find fear."

"So you are saying that the meaning of Wicca has been twisted the same way the meaning of our Hallows' Eve broom has?"

"Yes, this exactly."

Marion felt the strength leave her thighs. She sat down fast on the cottage doorstep.

"Enough of that for now," Basuba said softly. Her voice perked up as she handed the cane to Marion. "Make this very special broom as pretty as you can.

It will work just fine for us." After a pause, she cocked her head and said, "Listen, Mari. Hear that owl? It's called twice. Right at sunset. It won't be long now. The Spirits are on their way."

When the table had a plate of roasted pumpkin seeds, a plate of raw pumpkin seeds, and a dish of cider placed in its center in the shape of a triangle, Basuba stood back a ways, hands spread wide on her hips, and surveyed the scene in the dimming light.

She rubbed her hands together happily. "Let's see. We've got food and drink for them with the roasted seeds and the cider. And the seeds for next year's pumpkins for them to bless. Good thing our relations are not gentry, or we'd need a separate dish of cider for each one of them from what Martha, the serving maid at the manor, says," chuckled Basuba. Then she added briskly, "Mari, we're wanting some barley and gourds for table decorations. Run out to the garden for four of them, will you."

"Can I finish my porridge first? I'm really hungry."

"Sure. But since it's pease porridge, you better gobble it right down and clean your bowl out or your grandfather will most likely snub us. Mother could never get him to eat a spoonful of pease porridge, even when there was nothing else in the larder," said Basuba, tossing Marion a grin.

Returning from the garden, Marion leaned against the door to shut it tight in hopes of leaving the cold behind her. Basuba had shuttered the window closed and put a candle in the very center of the three plates.

"This tiny bit of light may give us some clues about their arrival," she said as Marion joined her on the bench. "It's a pity we can't use the light of the Moon since She's nearly full, but without a fire it's a cold, cold night and we're better off well-tucked-in."

"Basuba, how do you know for sure when they are here?" asked Marion.

Basuba sniffed the air. "Can you pick up that trace of lavender out there? Your Grandmother's just come. Arrived first, of course, even though you put your father's pumpkin closest to the door. Lavender's her favorite scent, wore it all the time. She had us put lavender water on her wrists the day she died."

Marion took a deep breath and nodded slowly. "I can just catch it now, but I wouldn't have noticed if you had not pointed it out." There was a touch of disappointment in her voice.

"Don't worry. This is how our lore is passed on. I learned all this from my grandparents the same way I am handing it on to you. Open up your imagination and let it play with what I tell you. Now let's greet Grandmother."

"Oh, yes. Excuse me, Grandmother," said Marion, embarrassed at having made her Elder wait. All at once, she was a toddler, running in and out under Grandmama's long skirts, pretending they were curtains on a stage. Then the skirts became theater curtains and she was a grown-up actress taking a bow in Drury Lane in London. A moment later, she was back in the cottage, listening to Basuba chat with the old woman. With the old woman's Spirit, that is.

"Will I ever really learn all that you know, Basuba?" asked Marion the next time her aunt turned to face her.

Basuba shook her head slowly and seriously and said, "No, you will not learn all that I know." Then she broke into a wide grin and pinched Marion's cheek playfully. "You'll learn all that comes up for me to teach you, but you'll know it in your own way, because we are different. And you've no doubt learned things already that I don't know from Nature, from animals, from other folks."

"You mean, you don't know everything?"

"Oh, First Robin of the Spring, I will keep on learning 'til I die, and I still will be far from knowing everything. That would be impossible. It's part of the Mystery; we each know some things and are blind to others. That makes us seek the holiness in each other."

"What's one thing you don't know ?" asked Marion.

Basuba opened her arms wide. "Let's see," she said, looking up at the ceiling of the cottage. "What's one of them? Oh, yes. I'm ready to learn from Moon about Change. You know how steady Sun is, a full golden ball every day, whether there are clouds or rain. Meanwhile, Moon changes every night. She grows larger 'til She's full and then smaller 'til She disappears. And then She does it again. This is the first season I've planted flowers that bloom at night. They're my sign to Moon that I want to learn that secret of hers…"

Suddenly the candle flickered and Basuba's hand jumped out to cup the flame. She laughed and said, "Oh, Father, up to your old tricks, are you? This time I was ready for you. I knew you'd be right on Mother's heels."

"That's right. He always does try to put out the candle. I remember that from before. Why does he do that?"

"Ask him."

Marion paused and then said, with an awkwardness in her voice as though she were talking to someone who was not really there, "Greetings, Grandfather. Why do you insist on putting us in the dark?"

She tightened up her face, especially the muscles around her ears and listened hard. After two minutes she whispered, "Basuba, I can't hear a thing."

"You're trying too hard, I suspect. Relax your body, remember your connection to him and to Nature, and pretend you are getting a message from him."

Silence. "All right. It's coming. I see him when he was alive, walking through a cottage without a candle. Now he's walking in a woods without a light. So are all the others. It seems he's saying that we must stay comfortable in the dark. Not get so that we need an outside light to move through the darkness."

"Good. That's the same message I've been getting from him. Niece, it's wonderful to have you old enough to scry like this, and trust the messages that are coming to you from the Spirit world. But it's always better when two or more folks can talk together about what they are gleaning from the other side."

Then Basuba turned away from Marion to address the darkness, "Father, as soon as everyone's here, we'll blow out the candle. Meantime, we need that little bit of light to help us know who's arrived." She paused, then went on half-serious, half-playful, "Don't sneer at me, Old Man. It's not as easy as it was in your day. Things are changing."

Blackie rubbed against Marion's right leg and began to purr. Next he was settling into her lap.

"Hi, Papa," she called out tenderly, looking around in hopes of sensing her own father more fully.

"Ah, so you know," crooned Basuba. She reached over to stroke Blackie. "Yes, this fellow showed up as a tiny bedraggled kitten one rainy night. The night we'd buried your father, Jimmy. Odd it is. Friendly as Jimmy was, this old cat comes over to be stroked only on All Hallows' Eve." Basuba peered into the shadows. "You've got a sprightly daughter here, Jimmy. With your blood coursing through her."

"And, Papa, I miss you so much. Thank Nature I've got your sister here to guide me." Speaking aloud about her loneliness thinned it out some.

As Basuba and Marion chatted with their relations, Marion felt the darkness changing. In place of the emptiness out there in the shadows before, she sensed a gentle comfort enfolding her. "It is as though a veil that separated us from you who've passed on has been lifted," she sighed happily. "You're not so far away after all."

The candle flickered again and Basuba cupped it just in time to save the flame. "Patience, Father. We're waiting for one more."

A bit later, an owl called from nearby. "That's coming from the willow, don't you think?" asked Basuba eagerly.

"Yes," said Marion, irritatedly.

"What's wrong?" asked Basuba in surprise.

"Just when I've got my family back, some stranger's going to drop in on us. It's the Spirit that the fourth pumpkin has invited here that's calling now from the willow, isn't it?"

"You can leave whoever it is up to me," said Basuba matter-of-factly. "But I do need to center my mind so the Spirit won't pass on by."

After a few silent moments, Marion said in a puzzled voice, "Basuba, it seems I should tell you that I feel tears in me even though I am not in the mood to cry."

"That's it. Thank you." She rose, made her way to the window and called out through the shutter in the direction of the willow, "Little Willow Sister, come in. Feast with us. Take some pleasure with us. We are friends."

Something stirred from the direction of the window and the darkness grew fuller. The candle went out and Marion and Basuba laughed.

## *Chapter 2*

# All Hallows' Eve: Fiona

*Ancient tree, ancient tree*
*You who've known one hundred years.*
*Please, won't you tell me*
*All that you see, all that you see.*

That same day, west from Basuba's cottage, over the marshes and into the meadow lands, the All Hallows' Eve sun treated Fiona Carter to one of its most gorgeous settings. As it sank through a broken bank of clouds, the fiery ball sent red tendrils out to nestle along the horizon line. It wrapped the oaks on the hill where she stood in its last intense glow, lighting up her brown eyes, turning her cheeks rosy, and burning her copper curls pure red. Then, to say goodbye, it touched a few of the haystacks out in the fields with pure gold for just a moment. The silence left behind was sliced by seven geese honking loyally to encourage their leader as they winged their way south.

Fiona called out to the sun as it dropped into the waiting ocean of sky, "I cannot enjoy your beauty when these oaks here may be turned to stumps and timber in a few days' time." She reached out a hand to the nearest tree and pressed her palm against its fiercely gnarled bark and added, "But we will never let that happen. We will find a way to protect you from the sheriff's saws."

In the distance, Fiona could make out some of the straw and mud cottages that dotted the land. Closer in, her eyes scanned the wheat and hay fields that she had worked in since she was eight years old. She knew just which family rented each section of land, and she remembered how much bigger their strips had been before Lord Nash tripled the size of his sheep herd four years ago. Jamie Gate's family had to move on then, and Sally Bolt's left last summer. They could not force enough produce out of their sections to feed themselves and pay their rent. If what

15

Fiona's older brother, Patrick, told her was true—that the Bolts had joined the squatters who lived in lean-tos in the woods—Sally must be very unhappy. She had always fancied herself a serving girl at the manor house.

That was one thing Fiona would never do: serve at the manor house, curtsy to Lord Nash, say "Yes, ma'am" to the Lady, and the rest. After all, the Nashes were the root of all the cottagers' troubles: giving over good crop land to sheep, draining the marshes to make for more grazing, ditching and hedging in the free land where her people had always hunted and roamed. "Come now," the wealthy folks said, "any fool can see that the future is in wool. They're crying for it in markets all over England and on the continent."

"Too bad for the Bolts and the Gates and the rest of us that we don't eat wool porridge, I suppose!" yelled Fiona to the fields as though they had ears to hear her.

With anger tearing through her body, she searched the nearby forest floor for the largest available dead branch. Determined to break it, she jumped on it, she bashed it into the ground twice, but it would not snap. She ground her teeth, hoisted the branch high above her head, and flung it as far as she could. When it landed with a thud and split in two, she cheered.

"Oh, that we may be rid of you, Lord Nash, and you, Sheriff Worthington, so easily!" she yelled to the lifeless oak limb.

Fiona turned around to face the forest of giant oaks that stretched out for a mile or so. Not too long ago she had believed that these trees went on that way forever, to the ends of Earth. She winced. Now, this very night, in fact, she and her people had to figure out a means to protect what little was really left of the oaks.

Time to head home. Darkness was falling and bringing a chill with it. Fiona tied her cape around her neck, and after a moment's hesitation put up her hood. Since she was the only redhead around, and proud of this sign of Irish blood in her veins, she hated to cover her hair. Hated to hide it even more than before, now that Matthew Fields had told Patrick how winsome she looked. She had her grandmother, Alyona, to thank for these curls that the other girls envied. Alyona had come south from Ireland years ago with her folks, peddling everything from potatoes to mending pots and magic spells. Their wagon broke down just long enough for the young woman to fall in love with the farmer who was to become Fiona's grandfather.

Besides her hair, Alyona had given her granddaughter buckets of freckles that played on her face, arms and legs. Her strength was a gift from her grandfather. She had outwrestled boys her age from five villages around. At eighteen, everyone supposed she had given up all interest in such activity. However, Fiona knew in her heart that if she had been allowed to keep on she still would be winning those contests.

If people did not think of Fiona as the tender sort, perhaps it was because she directed all her soft feelings to plants and animals, especially to trees. Ever since she could recall she had loved trees best. As soon as she toddled, they became her playmates. She would pull up flowers in the summer to scatter around the base of her favorites. All the straw dolls Alyona made her passed their time sitting in the forks of branches or talking to trees. And before too long, Fiona spent much of her time hugging trees. She started out with saplings with thin bark. When it grew easy for her to sense the rhythm of the fluids moving through those trees, she practiced on trees with thicker trunks and heavier bark.

She assumed, of course, that everybody listened to trees with their hands the way she did. How could a person not want to? The sap sang songs of years gone by; it held the weather stories of the lifetimes of her parents, her grandparents, her great-grandparents, and many generations before them. She smiled when she realized that these same trees would be telling the weather stories of her life to her children and their children, all the generations yet to come in the remainder of their leafy life-spans. Besides, the rhythms she could sense beneath the bark were so different from the way people moved. They were different from what she knew about cats or cows or wheat, or anything else.

Fiona had been fully surprised to find out at age nine that most folks did not spend time with trees in this way. She had been puzzled when Alyona clucked at her and told her to be careful about mentioning what she knew to others.

"But you, Alyona, you know what I mean. You talk with trees, too. You must."

Alyona thought for a moment and shook her head. "No, granddaughter, I do not. My people say that in the Old Times most folks did. But there are not so many like you now." She shook her head sadly. "It's easier for folks to cut 'em down in droves when they refuse to believe that trees speak."

When she saw the little girl's face so crestfallen, the old woman quickly added, "Fiona, you talking with trees, that's a special gift from the Spirits. We each are born with gifts, but many folks forget theirs as they grow up. The difference for you is that you will remember this gift. Just be careful about whom you show it to."

Alyona started to walk away. She stopped and turned back to Fiona and said, "Granddaughter, I want you to tell me what the trees teach you. Always."

Word was out that Sheriff Worthington would arrive tomorrow morning, All Saints' Day, to fell some of the ancient oaks. Possibly had his eye on the same spot where Fiona had watched the sun set. He and Lord Nash dared to think they could turn these 150-year-old giants into ship planking!

"Must he always pick our feast days?" growled one of Fiona's younger brothers when he first heard the rumor.

"Yes, Brother. He's smart enough to think that's when Pagan folk would be least likely to notice."

The lad snorted, "Well, he's surely wrong about us."

"And not smart enough to realize that a holy day makes us even stronger."

By the time Fiona reached Blue Fens, her village of fourteen cottages, a crowd was gathering and the moon was rising. Word of the tree-felling must have spread quickly; most of the twenty or so cottages in the outlying area were sending someone. What would happen tonight?

The first time Worthington came to the woodlands with six sawyers in September the cottagers had held him and his crew off with pitchforks and soldering irons. The hired hands had balked, deaf to Worthington's ridicule of them as cowards and "women," and that had been the end of it.

But Ashby, the friendly cabinetmaker who worked at the manor, had stopped by Blue Fens yesterday to say that he had heard the sheriff tell Nash that he had hired war veterans this time. Some folks were sure to be frightened by that news.

A large fire, big enough to warm the thirty or forty people gathered around it, was burning in the central fire pit when Fiona returned from her cottage with a hunk of brown bread and some goat's cheese in hand for her dinner. The men moved in close to talk as usual. Women hung back in the shadows to listen and nudge and plant ideas. Fiona found her brothers and father and stood behind them, whispering her opinions in the ear of one, then another, at various times.

Halfway through the night Fiona knew that nothing would come of this meeting. Just as a cold north wind rushed the fire, she saw the jugs of malt liquor come out. A sign that folks were surrendering to defeat. She would not allow that, even though it meant breaking rules.

She stepped forward into the circle of men, all eyes upon her.

Fiona quickly pictured her favorite oak, a furled giant of a tree she passed each day that she walked out to work in the meadow lands. She pretended that she had the age and strength and height of its body inside her as she summoned her courage to speak out in front of the others. She did not know all that she was going to say, and she prayed fast for the oak's ancient wisdom to guide her.

Just as she finished her silent plea, Fiona sensed her grandmother, Alyona, behind her. The old woman reached forward and thrust a tall staff into her granddaughter's left hand, the venerated talking staff of the Elders.

Brave now, Fiona looked across the fire into the waiting faces. Her gaze landed on a friend of her brothers' from another village, Matthew Fields, who was giving her his full attention. That helped. She tapped sharply on the huge hollow log at the fire's edge so that everyone would stop talking and listen to her.

"Our Rights of Common are in great danger. We at this fire can remember the stories the old ones tell about the Rights of Common. It's the King's gift to the people, to us—commoners, tinkers and squatters. His thanks for our loyalty on the battlefield. The great forests should stand for all to use until the day his royal flag flies no more. You've heard these stories. I am calling now for you to rise to defend the ancient grove."

Fiona paused to get a sense of who was with her. The Elders, those whose duty it was to pass on the stories of the Rights of Common to the youth, were gathering to stand with Alyona. Matthew, her brothers and cousins and their friends were rising to their feet, or at least stirring, nodding at her words. But most folks in the middle of their lives, her parents and their neighbors with children, sat stone-faced.

Suddenly one of those brooding men jumped to his feet and yanked the talking staff from Fiona. He said angrily, "You know what's happening all over England! We'll have to fight to keep the woodlands free. I've lost three sons to the King's War. Those trees will fall if they must before I'll give up another lad to the sword."

He knelt and slowly lay the staff on its sheepskin cover and began to roll it up. As though he could feel Fiona's rage searing a hole in his back, he stopped just short of tying the skin closed. When he stood, fists and "ayes" and a couple of liquor jugs went up around the circle.

Her neighbor was right about the dangers. Fiona knew that as well as anyone else. Tales arrived every few weeks from the West country about fights over land enclosures. Cottagers with their pitchforks and homemade axes were no match for the muskets and pikes with which the gentry could supply their hired hands. Through it all, the tree-felling continued.

There had to be another way.

Fiona bent down swiftly and rescued the staff from the sheepskin. It was still warm from the heat of the mourning father's touch. She swallowed hard. She was defying tradition with this action. Her Elder had laid the topic to rest when he put the staff in its covering; the Blue Fens custom stated that one should wait until at least three other folks had spoken before taking the staff again, and only men were expected to address a fire council.

She called on Oak's Wisdom to steady her and began to speak. "When people have been defeated, it's because they didn't work together to protect the forests. We cannot be stopped if we join together. All of us in every village in Norfolk County! Whenever we see a sheriff on the move, we'll spread the word. Let's take our lessons from the ants who work for the good of all."

Matthew Fields, stocky and muscled with a shock of blond hair and blue eyes, reached out a burly arm from across the fire to take the staff next. Many heads jerked up in surprise. An outsider from ten miles to the east, who was he to be addressing their gathering, let alone cutting in ahead of the Elders? Still, no one stopped him; they were either too discouraged or too hungry for action.

He spoke up, "The woman's right. Folks in my village are tired of being bullied by the gentry. Just as you are. They're waiting for a good plan, that's all. I'm sure it's the same for others." He sensed some eyes on him and broke into a smile and continued confidently, "There is a way to spread the word when we see the sheriff: we'll post lookouts. That's an easy task for any of the herders when they're out with their animals. When we know where the troublemakers are heading, we'll light signal fires on the knolls to point out the direction. Once the other commoners know what to look for, it'll be easy to alert them all."

Matthew stepped back and looked around to see how folks were responding. More people were looking up at him instead of gazing dismally at the ground as they were before Fiona spoke out. A few men were beginning to talk amongst themselves in little groups here and there.

Something was coming to life.

Quickly another young man reached for the staff, his face bright with excitement. Then another and another. Spoke after spoke in the wheel of a great plan was forged.

Finally, only the skeptics were left. Peter Brown, the manor's ironsmith, scowled and whined loudly, "Bah! So, you'll let a wench of eighteen or twenty years talk you out of your good sense, will you? How'll you get folks to look out for each other? Scratch the surface of any of us, and all we care about is our own hide, maybe the skin of the children we've raised. The first shot Worthington fires will send everyone running for cover."

"Besides, he's arriving on the morn. You don't have enough time to make anything happen," said a birder who kept Lord Nash's dining table full of plump plovers and curlews.

That moment gave birth to Fiona's victory. She took the staff again and lifted it high to the sky. In a loud voice she said, "Then it's with women and children that we'll greet the sheriff and his men. There we'll be, our arms stretched around the trees they try to cut. We'll refuse to move unless they strike at us. They won't be expecting us at all. They'll have to stop. That gives you men enough time to alert the others."

Silence. The men looked into the faces of the women. The women looked around at each other, nodding. Heads moved slowly at first, and then women reached out for each other's hands, most of them stepping forward to the fire circle together.

"Yes!"

"But we mustn't bring the bairn with us."

"We can. It will help us to have little ones there. We'll put the older lads and lasses in charge in case something happens to us. They'll know how to run off with the little ones."

"Nothing will happen to us, though. It's the sheriff who's in for the surprise."

In the end, it was the youth like Fiona's brothers who bickered most loudly about sending the women out.

"They won't be strong enough."

"They couldn't possibly be as brave as they'll need to be," they complained.

It wasn't until the Elders helped the young males see how important their signal system would be for future successes that they stopped grumbling and settled down to work out the details of the plan.

Folks picked up their blankets and jugs and ambled off to their homes. Four lads, working in teams of two, wrestled the sitting logs back into their places around the fire pit. Alyona patiently secured the sheepskin covering around the talking staff with a long piece of rawhide. The fire keeper bedded the fire and put his rake away, wishing the others a "good night" as he passed by.

Matthew Fields seemed to be the only person standing around with nothing to do. Fiona guessed that he was waiting for her. No good; she had to have time alone to take in all that had happened. She signaled Matthew a "good night" with a nod of her head that came off a bit sharper than she had intended. How awkward. She turned away into the darkness before he had a chance to react.

Fiona walked the perimeter of the village to slow her heartbeat. When she neared her own cottage, she knew that she still had far too much energy pouring through her to think of putting her head down to rest. Her heart was pumping in her chest and her blood was racing through her veins. Blood coursing through her the way sap moves through the tree trunks.

She walked back behind her thatched-roof cottage to her favorite tree from childhood: a beech planted to celebrate her birth. It towered over her now. She wrapped her arms around it tightly so that she could feel its life force through her arms and chest as well as in her hands.

"Teacher," she said softly, "you were the first tree I learned from. Be with me tomorrow. Show me how to guide the women so we can protect your sisters and brothers." Fiona stood there for a long time, letting the slow, steady rhythm of her rooted friend bring her own pulse back to normal, return her mind to a state of calm. "Thank you," she sighed. "Now I can sleep."

When the sheriff caught sight and sound of some twenty women and children playing hide-and-seek in the oak grove he came to fell, he reined in his high-stepping bay mare and sat there tight-lipped.

He had counted on All Saints' Day being just another holiday that lazy country folks used as an excuse to avoid working. They were sure to be tired from staying up late the night before, dancing, praying to some idols, and who knows what other godforsaken things. The malt would have been flowing fast and free since sunset. All in all, an easy time for him to slip in, timber some trees, and get out with no one the wiser. Instead, here lay half the village, right in his path!

The sheriff called out gruffly in a loud voice to the tattered, ill-kempt men following along behind him, "Men, take your places and begin to cut. We'll start with those three trees in front."

The villagers continued at their game until the hired hands got quite close. Then they calmly stopped, hushed the children, and sent them off with their older siblings to wait further back in the woods.

When the women looked out at the disheveled mob of fifteen or more men, fear raced through them. They were staring at vagabond veterans from King Charles I's army. The Blue Fens folks, like other cottagers, dreaded meeting up with misfits like these who, half-crazed from their war experiences, wandered the countryside in small gangs, robbing and raping and demanding to be fed and housed by the locals unlucky enough to be in their path.

Three women, too afraid, made a dash for the sidelines, covering their faces with their aprons when they got there. The remaining women came forward to take their places by the trees. They stood with their backs against the oaks so they could keep their eyes on the men and stretched their arms out until their hands met and clasped. The effect of their actions was immediate: the veterans froze in their tracks.

Fiona seized the opportunity to get the sheriff's attention. "By the Rights of Common, you cannot harm these trees, Sheriff," she called.

"The Rights of Common be damned!" he replied, bristling that such defiance would come from a female voice.

"We will stop you. We will petition the King if we must."

"Go ahead." He aimed a big wad of spittle onto the ground near her feet. "Your King cares nothing for the likes of you. You people count for nothing. Besides, his days are numbered. He'll not be bothered with helping your kind."

The women began to chant, weakly at first, until the singing began to feed their courage back to them. Some of the hirelings hung back for a few moments, then, loyal only to a wage, most came forward and carried the women forcefully away from the trees they were protecting to the edge of the forest.

Refusing to move one step further from where they were dropped by the soldiers, the women watched their every move.

"We are bearing witness to what you do," promised Fiona grimly as the women formed a circle around the tree-felling.

And so the women behaved as they did when attending a death. Some turned away from the massacre in sorrow; others sobbed with their faces in their hands; still others stood motionless and silent, the way the great trees themselves would have done. At times they chanted songs from wakes and funerals. The sheriff rode into them occasionally and flicked his reins halfheartedly as though to shoo them away, but they would not leave. They simply stepped aside at the last minute to let him pass through.

Sheriff Worthington won the round, and four green giants of the forest, who had watched the tender arrival of more than a century of springs, shook the Earth around them mightily as they fell by day's end. When the first one crashed onto the forest floor, the sheriff flung his arms in the air and cheered wildly, but his cries fell away rapidly when he realized that not one veteran had joined him. He was silent until the women headed for home. Then he called after them, "I've got you now. We'll fell five more by nightfall tomorrow."


The blood of the Blue Fens women was stirred up. They were not through yet. They put their heads together and made their plans. They rallied their menfolk.

When the council around the fire ended, Blue Fens was ready for the sheriff's rough, ragged band on the morrow.

The cottagers arrived at the fatal spot just before dawn. Fiona especially was comforted by their having some time alone with the fallen trees. When the sheriff and his men got there, women accompanied by a few children encircled the tallest oaks. And as before, the soldiers jerked on their arms and struck at their clasped hands, causing many a bruise and outcry, handling the children with no more gentleness than they did the women. After carrying the defenders away from the trees, the men picked up their axes, ready to chop, when a chant came to them from the treetops. Looking up, the men were shocked to see women and children sitting in the upper branches of the huge trees they were about to strike, their knotted climbing ropes pulled up behind them.

From behind nearby trees, cottagers from miles around stepped out to witness this confrontation. Led by their Elders, they began to sing songs that they hoped the sheriff and his motley band had known in their childhood. They sang sea ballads, lullabies, and love songs, praying that the tunes and words would make their way into even the hardest heart. The soldiers cursed and grumbled, they threatened the folks in the trees, and shook their fists angrily up at them.

Then one of them who wore the remains of a tattered officer's coat flung his ax against the nearest tree, spat at it, and strutted off, calling out loudly, "There's easier work than this to be had, Sheriff."

One by one, in twos, and then threes, the others followed his lead, dropping their saws and axes as they walked off.

Realizing the power he had, the first man grabbed the bay's bridle and said, "I'll take my wages now, Worthington. You've cost me a day in bed, and we'll not be going until you've opened that leather bag that bulges at your waist."

With that, the other veterans swarmed around the big mare who shied in alarm. They growled and muttered and a few reached up towards the sheriff's person. Frightened and cursing, the sheriff opened his pouch to give a coin to each man. With angry hands grabbing at him from this way and that, it was impossible for him to know which fist he had fed and which he had not. The moment someone crowed about getting two coins, demands for the same rose up from everyone else.

The ex-officer, fueled by his two successes, pulled hard on the bay's bridle and spoke again. "Now, Sheriff, how about your tenants? They've lost their day's wages and sung for us all as well. They must be paid, too. A coin for each of them, down to the babes who stood 'round the trees."

The sheriff snorted, sat up as straight as he could in his saddle, and sent a loud "Never!" ringing out through the woods.

"Never?" questioned the tall soldier, jerking quickly and harder than before on the bridle. "You're in no position to cry 'Never,' Lord Sheriff."

With that, others among the swarm took up the demand. "Coins for the cottagers, Sheriff. Coins for the cottagers!"

The sheriff took a moment to study the malcontents who surrounded him. Some were chanting with the tall one; others stepped back a bit, saying nothing. He saw his chance to shove a wedge between them all.

"So, you would have me give coins to these landless wastrels, eh, fools? What have they ever done but curse you and wish you away as fast as you came? They bring you their food and their daughters, but only because you force them. Meantime, they hate you with all the bile that's in 'em. And you would give 'em coins now?" Quickly the magistrate tossed a handful of silver to the far side of the feisty mob.

That was all it took. The men turned upon each other at once, fists now raised up, now falling, as they argued over the money. The tall spokesman was forced to let go of the bridle to defend himself, and the sheriff deftly edged himself out of the mêlée and gave his nervous, sweating steed all the rein she wanted. Meanwhile, the cottagers slipped back into the forest, not wanting any more contact with their self-declared champion or his fellow marauders.

When the sheriff was out of earshot, Fiona raised her freckled arms toward the sky and let out a loud hurrah. Children scampered out from behind nearby trees as the twenty-odd women joined Fiona in cheering, stamping the ground and mixing their giddy shouts with laughter and whistles. They raced back to the trees that held their friends. Knotted ropes snaked down from the trees followed by their climbers and more cheering.

As the adults and weary children headed back home, Fiona yanked off the white cap that completely covered her hair. Her tight copper curls tumbled to her shoulders. Early this morning two of the older women had pleaded with her, "Hide every last wisp." A lone redhead amongst the others would be too easy to identify. Well, an odd way to pass All Saints' Day, but worth it. And, no doubt, the Spirits had helped them rout the sheriff.

Fiona could not wait to make sure her brothers understood how wrong they had been: women were brave enough to stand up against men with arms. Not only had they stood up to Sheriff Worthington and his men, they had defeated them. With her plan! And so saved the trees. Thank Nature, dear Mother Earth, for that plan!

By the time the women and children drifted into Blue Fens, the Elders had food and drink ready for them. Matthew Fields made his way through the crowd to stand close to Fiona. She felt his eyes on her as she talked with a neighbor woman. How strange! On the one hand, she liked knowing that she could draw a man like Matthew to her; on the other, it brought to mind how much the frisky mare the Nash's stabler sometimes let her ride hated having the reins tightened on her. She turned to face the young man.

"Well done! Well done! We've stopped them, Fiona, I mean, Mistress Carter. It wouldn't have worked without you," he said eagerly. "I know…"

He was staring at her, not saying a thing. His face flushed red and he scrambled quickly for more words. "Fine work you and the others did today."

He gestured widely towards the byway that led out of the settlement. "When this story gets around, folks everywhere will want to join us. When there are enough of us, the sheriff and the nobles will have to listen. Our day will come. I know it will."

The youth's words rushed through Fiona like a current of wind coursing through tall shafts of grain.

## *Chapter 3*

# December 22, Winter Solstice

*Go into the long night*
*Seek your fears, seek your fears.*
*Go into the long night*
*Seek your tears, seek your tears.*
*Go into the long night*
*Seek your rage, seek your rage.*

Basuba awoke, tired and sore, to the new day. She lay still for a few minutes on the makeshift straw mattress pulled up near the fireplace in the central room of Marion's mother's house in Ely.

"It must be this tick that's the cause of my problems. It still lacks the proper stuffing to suit my aging bones. I'll get Mari to help me knead it some more," she thought, tugging at a piece of straw lodged in her hair.

Then an image from last night's dream surfaced in her mind, and she knew immediately that the dream was the source of her fatigue. In the dream, fragments of familiar objects were strewn across a forest floor. Pieces of clay pots underfoot, remnants of carefully tied herb bundles tossed hither and yon. A curved plank from a butter churn, or maybe it was part of a spinning wheel, blocked the path in front of her. Lost in the shadows of thick tree branches they were, hidden by roots twisting around them. One part of a bowl cracked as she stepped on it in the dark and disintegrated into a dusty powder at once, a disturbing powder that ran through her fingers faster than the finest flour she'd known. The edges of the fragments were blurred, perhaps blunted, unlike one of the other dreams where they'd been sharp as knife blades, cutting her fingers each time she bent to pick them up. Some of the destruction seemed old; some reeked fresh.

Like the first two dreams, here was a sense of urgency, of the chase, the charge of having to find all the fragments and piece them back together before Time runs out. Too late for what? She couldn't tell. The finality of being too late stalked the forest as it had the other dream spots where she'd been forced to hunt for fragments.

Basuba shuddered as the full force of the dream settled in on her. Winter Solstice, falling on December 22 this year, was just around the corner. This difficult vision must be one of its gifts to her, she mused ruefully. The harsh lessons of the darkest night of the year seemed to come to her in dreams. It had been like that for years. So what was the meaning these dreams carried? She shrugged. She had thought about the first two of them so long it made her head ache. It was time to turn to some means of divination. Maybe something would be revealed at Solstice.

Basuba sipped a dish of steaming oatmeal at one end of the roughhewn table, the largest piece of furniture in the cottage, while Marion sat at the other end, putting a comfrey poultice carefully on the old family cat. "Poor Granny," the girl crooned as she held the cat's spotted paw firmly on the wooden surface. "You curled up too close to the hearth and got yourself a good singeing. You must be taking cold on these winter nights, old woman."

The herbalist beamed as she watched her niece at work. Marion had learned a lot under her tutelage in the six weeks since All Hallows' Eve. She had gathered, sorted, dried, and labeled a substantial crop of herbs, applying herself to the detailed work with relish. She had put together the special packet that Basuba would need when she attended the birth of the neighbor child in a day or so. And comfrey was not the only plant the girl could poultice.

"So which will come first, the baby or the Solstice?" Basuba wondered. She prayed they would not arrive together. Her loyalty would be to the birth, but the heaviness of her dreams told her that she needed the purification that the Winter Solstice ceremony promised.

"It's best for us to stay the night with my friends, Rosemary and Elinor, after the Solstice celebration," said Basuba. "That way we won't barge in on your mother in the middle of the night. Your mother'd prefer not to have to think about what we are doing on Solstice. You agree?"

"Oh, yes. She'll either rant against my going with you for the night or say that I should leave with you for good. She needs my help since her husband gets her with child each year, but she wants naught of me."

"You are so like your father in your looks and your ways. I suppose she thinks of him whenever she sees you."

"With full respect to you, Aunt, if she loved him so much, I think she'd treat me better."

"Couldn't tame him; can't tame you. Theirs was not a simple love, Marion. I remember that she couldn't keep her eyes off him. He was the same about her. But they were as different as night and day in their thoughts and desires. Your mother loves God in His church; your father worshiped the Great Mother in nature. And they fought as though no dawn or dusk could bring them together. Your mother sees all this when she looks at you."

Marion shrugged. She was tired of trying to figure her mother out. Tired of being left out of her love, pushed aside by the new babies and the new husband who insisted that she call him "Mr. Edwards."

"I'm ready for her," said Marion matter-of-factly. "I'll bundle a blanket around my drum and hide it out by the shed. She'll be too busy as usual to notice that I'm fasting. When the time comes, we'll just be off."

The baby came early, swimming into the world a few days before Solstice to find harbor in Basuba's waiting arms. When his dreamy gaze found hers, she felt, way down deep in her belly, the honor of being the first person he looked upon. She cooed a prayer of thanksgiving to the Great Mother, a blessing of the Spirit and matter come together to give life to this little child. Then she gently delivered the babe to his mother's breast and sat down on a nearby bench to wait for the umbilical cord to stop throbbing before she severed it.

Good to relax after all the bending, the standing, the holding and encouraging the birth had called for. She sighed in relief. Plenty of time now to make sure that the mother's milk came in and to rest before she greeted the Longest Night.

Basuba and Marion set off for the Solstice ceremony when the sun sat three fingers' width above the horizon. Marion's mother did not say a thing to them but rolled her eyes and threw her hands in the air when they told her that they would be spending the night with Rosemary. It was all Marion could do to keep from slamming the door hard behind her as she left. Aunt and niece walked silently down the city lanes, neither one able to find anything light to chat about.

Marion pulled her shawl tighter around her shoulders. Weakness from a full day of fasting let the damp cold of the evening cut easily through her body. She distracted herself from her discomfort by imagining all the people throughout the city who were also stealing away from their neighbors at this very moment to celebrate Winter Solstice. In small groups of adults and older youths, she saw them heading for the beloved ceremonial sites so carefully hidden away in the groves and fields of Ely's outskirts.

Gwyneth slipped out of her door as soon as Basuba and Marion rounded the corner on her street. Pausing for just a second on the front step, she looked quickly to the right and to the left and then suddenly was at their side. Her brown eyes darted quickly about her narrow face that was framed with strawberry blonde hair. Just like the first time they met, the girl's swift, smooth movements and her small nimble body brought to mind for Basuba a fox, or perhaps a mink.

After greeting them, Gwyneth said, "Mary and Elinor passed by just a moment ago. I wanted to call out to them to wait for us. It would be so much fun to go all together." Her voice dropped a little when she added, "But I remembered not to."

Basuba shook her head, annoyed. "It hasn't always been like this. Before the witch hunters came to England, we had no need to sneak around this way. Many's the place where the whole village would turn out for a ceremony." She straightened her spine, tightened her grip on her walking stick, and said proudly, "As it should be. As it will be again. In your day, if we're lucky."

"Perhaps in your day, too, Aunt," Marion hastened to add. She hated it when Basuba spoke as though she were not likely to be around for long.

"I wish. But the signs are against it." Basuba paused. "Mary and Elinor don't like me saying as much to you, but you've both come into your bleeding time, and so, to my thinking, you're women enough to learn about this troubled age we're living in."

"Tell us more, Mistress Basuba," begged Gwyneth, hungrily. Her mother guarded her from the news of the marketplace, so she was always on the lookout for adults who would tell her what they knew.

"Keep in mind, you maidens, there has been no witch-hanging in Norfolk County for a hundred years. But the wind carries evil mutterings these days from the northern counties and from the land of the Scots. And there's word of a witch hunter come to London from the continent to start training Englishmen in his deathly trade."

Basuba dropped into silence to get a sense of how her young companions were handling what she had to say. She could feel that her message had set the air swirling dizzily all around them and turned it dense and heavy as lead. Perhaps her message was too severe. "Remember, I don't say this to frighten you but to explain why I don't think I'll see the day when we can worship freely."

"Aunt, what makes you think Gwyneth and I will see it then?" Marion's voice trembled. "What will make the Christians change their minds about us?"

"My Winter Dove, Life does go round and round. Like the seasons. Just when we cannot bear to have the day die into night one moment sooner, it is Solstice and the Sun King is born so the light can return. It will be the same for Wicca."

The three reached the ceremonial grove just at dusk. A cold breeze stirred around their feet, bold enough to lift their heavy skirts a bit.

Gwyneth saw Marion shiver and grabbed her friend's hand, saying, "I'm glad we came out here with Rosemary to build that lean-to. Looks like folks'll need it for a windbreak after all."

The girls stopped to survey their handiwork. They swelled up when Basuba praised its sturdiness. Marion remembered how she had grumbled about all the branches they had to haul across the clearing in order to build it. That was Tuesday. Now on Friday evening she felt proud of what she and Gwyneth had accomplished. As her eyes moved over the structure, she glimpsed a corner of something protruding from behind it. Something about a man's height and covered with a gunny sack. She nudged Gwyneth, "Look! That's where they've hidden the Sun King." Another good reason to build a lean-to. They looked at each other and laughed.

"Did you ever convince Nell to tell you what he's made of?" asked Gwyneth, her eyes brimming with eagerness at the chance of uncovering a secret or two.

"No. She almost broke down once, but she said that Preston would dunk her in the stream with Elinor's approval if she opened her mouth about it. All she'd tell me was 'You'll be so surprised!' But I already knew that since the Sun King has to be different each year."

"Oh, Mari, I wonder when we'll get to make him. I hope they ask us to do it together. Otherwise, I'm sure to end up getting dunked, for I could never keep a secret that grand from you." Gwyneth grinned as she stomped suddenly on Marion's left foot and said, "And I'll make sure you can't keep it from me if you're building him."

Basuba laughed at them as she rubbed her hands together. How the cold stiffened them. "I'm off to the warming fire. Lots of folks there I haven't laid eyes on since my last visit to the city."

Soon Basuba was toasting her hands over the crackling flames of the small fire built off to the side of the ceremonial circle. The dark that was settling in around her and her five long-time friends made a silhouetted wreath of their gnarled hands spread out over the glowing orange circle to capture its warmth. Only Mary was so cold that she preferred to sit on her haunches to get even nearer the heat. While the Elders caught up on news, the younger people walked back into the trees towards the east.

The sound of chanting, beginning in the distance and making its way ever closer, was the signal for Basuba and her friends to quickly finish off their last pieces of gossip, pick up their music makers, and make their way to the ceremonial circle. The old folks stood about five or six feet away from each other, positioning themselves around the dusty ring that had been etched into the Earth by many nights of dancing.

As people had done for centuries before them, the Elders greeted the chanters by turning to face them and beating hand-held drums or playing fifes. When the initial torch appeared at the edge of the woods, it lit up the first figures following behind it. Marion and Gwyneth were at the end of the procession since they were amongst the youngest folks there.

"Welcome to you, Willow People!" The loud call boomed out into the darkness, a wedding of two strong voices, one female, one male. The woman and man who spoke each wore a coat made from dark curly bearskin and carried a large tambourine. They greeted every chanter by shaking their tambourines three times as the person passed in front of them. When everyone had entered the circle, the rhythm of the chanting changed with some people picking up one beat, some another, some another still. A few moments later, a third rhythm emerged to set new words dancing through the air. Then, again and again, another chant surged to rise, hold forth and finally fall away. As though the chants had a life of their own, they moved seamlessly from one to the next. Then, just as organically, the sounds died away.

An Elder stepped through the shadows into the center of the circle. He turned his wizened face to the huge night sky, and everyone watching him followed his gaze upward. Everyone watched as the enormous black cavern was anointed with twinkling stars. The old man had come to address the Darkness of Winter Solstice.

"Oh, my favorite part of the whole night," whispered Marion to Gwyneth. "When the Elder calls out to the Darkness, it seems to come right into the circle with us."

The man was beginning, "The Dark at the Center swirls and churns. The Dark at the Center is both moving and still. The Dark at the Center spirals in and then spirals out, revealing what's hidden from view. The Dark at the Center is me, it is you. The Dark at the Center is She whose dark power ends what has gone on too long. And opens a way to begin. So swirling and churning, turning and whirling, we welcome the Dark of the year."

People leapt up to echo his words, and their own swirling, churning, and spiraling began. The dance wove the celebrants in and out, around each other. A person here and there would stand in place, circling slowly, as though churning a giant, invisible stick around and around and around. Another person would pass and join in, and the first churner would leave to spiral and whirl some more. This dance had no formal beginning or end; it continued until the dancers stopped moving.

As people reformed the circle, a youth grabbed a torch from where it had been lodged in the fork of a tree. He ran as fast as he could to the large fire pit in the center of the circle and plunged the torch into the middle of a pile of kindling that had been rubbed thoroughly with pig fat. The bonfire ignited at once. Huge flames leapt skyward. The woman wearing the bearskin called out in a strong ancient voice and gestured towards the fire with her right arm, "Time to end All that has Gone On Too Long. Time to end All that has Gone On Too Long. Time to end All that has Gone On Too Long."

People took up her call and accented it with heavy pounding on their drums. A strong steady beat came into being, building a curtain of powerful sound around them.

This was the time for anyone who wanted a certain situation to end to approach the fire. A man came forward and said, "I throw into the fire my anger at my neighbor who stole my rooster and sold it at Sutton Market. I'm tired of having my stomach tighten into knots whenever he goes by. I see now that he was desperate to feed his young ones." With that, he launched a log into the bonfire.

A young woman in a rust-colored shawl went next. When she threw her log into the flames, she called out, "Time for my poor old dog's life to end. He's too sick to go on, and I haven't it in me to take his life myself." Her voice caught as tears threatened her throat. "Nature, call Laddie back to your lap. Please." She raised her arms up into the sky as she finished her prayer.

Basuba was the fifth person and the last, as it turned out, to come forward. She made her way to the pile of wood stacked near the bonfire, and Marion winced a bit to see how heavily her aunt leaned on her walking stick as she traversed the uneven ground.

Basuba searched through the collection of gnarled, twisted and forked branches and logs for the piece of wood that seemed just right. As she pulled it out, Gwyneth and Marion saw that the branch had a long gash that pierced one side of it deeply. The gash was wide enough to have left strands of fraying bark that hung in eerie silhouette against the flames. Basuba walked to the fire and held the branch out for all to see. Marion gasped as she watched.

Basuba spoke in a voice that roared and shook with her rage. "This broken branch, cut to the quick, stands for the children being torn away from us. More and more with each generation. They leave us out of fear for their safety, and who can blame them? Our Tree of Life is threatened. Without the young to carry on the worship of Nature, we will vanish from the face of Earth."

Thrusting as hard as she could, Basuba threw her branch into the very middle of the fire so that it would burn all the faster. "Be gone, evil destruction!" she cried out as others joined her. "Just as Fire becomes Smoke, so must You change form now."

Marion knew right away that her aunt was thinking of what had happened to her outside the Cathedral courtyard before All Hallows' Eve. At the time of the teasing, Marion had felt sorry for herself and ashamed. Frightened, too. She had not stopped to think that this same kind of thing could be happening all around England to children of the Wise Ways.

For the first time in her life, she felt afraid for almost everyone she knew and cared about. Her mother's face popped unexpectedly into her mind, and Marion saw that she could read the fear in it much better than she ever had before. Then, all at once, it was too much to go on thinking this way. She started kicking at a stone that was wedged into the Earth beneath her feet.

Gwyneth tugged hard on Marion's sleeve. "Mari, you're missing the whole thing. Look! The King's entering the circle right now!"

Sure enough, there was the Sun King, as splendid as she had ever seen him. He was a huge wheel whose spokes were made from thickly bundled straw. The circle that formed his open hub was crisscrossed with red ribbons. The two concentric circles that bound his spokes together were also wrapped in strips of red fabric that had once been someone's skirt or shirt. Two youths, Nell and Preston, proudly carried him around the circle, holding him as high off the ground as they could reach. The moon, waxing near to full, rose behind him.

"Oh, he's gorgeous! And all that red cloth, dear as it is!" Gwyneth exclaimed. "We must get some red scraps from them for the pouches we're sewing. Oh, how shall we ever make the Sun King as unforgettable as this one when it's our turn?"

Round and round the circle the Sun King went. Faster and faster. Soon everyone joined in after him, laughing and shouting. Loving his promise that the days would grow longer again. People cheered and hugged their neighbors. They grabbed each other's hands to form a circle once again. With arms raised high, they rushed into the center close to the fire pit, and then rushed back out again. After two rounds, most of the Elders bowed out so the younger folks could move even faster.

When it was time, the two leaders closed the ritual with prayers. They bid farewell to the Spirits of their Ancestors who had gathered to form an invisible sphere around the edge of their own ceremonial circle.

The young folks began to clear the site of the extra firewood and bits of decoration that had fallen from people's clothing, and anything else that might otherwise give away their event to unfriendly eyes. Too often over the last dozen years, the Willow People had returned to a beloved ceremonial site only to find it trampled and destroyed by folks who feared what went on there.

Older folks fell into small groups to chat. But Basuba still had something important to accomplish; it was time to ask for guidance in understanding her dreams. She moved in close to the fire pit and beckoned to three Elders to join her. The cold was intensifying. It would not do to linger in one spot for long; they must work quickly.

The bonfire was ready for scrying. The flames had died away to ember-studded logs and glowing coals that popped now and then. With Basuba's dream stories in mind, the old folks looked deep into the glowing fire pit to see what scenes and images the coals might give them.

"I see a cooking pot, near the center," offered Rosemary, squatting close to the dying fire. "There's a fast-moving river of red pouring out of it, rushing from coal to coal. It says to me that the things strewn through your dreams all come from the same source, the Creator. They are all part of the river of Life. But somehow they have been broken and separated by the time they come into your dreams."

A darkened log, gutted and ridged with gray ash, fell suddenly with a muted thud and a jerk across Rosemary's pulsating river of fire, cutting it completely in two.

Right afterwards, a second dead log landed directly in the path of the molten river, causing it to fork. "And we see here what breaks them," an old man stated certainly as he jostled the two fallen logs with a stick. "It is the church and the law." With that, he pushed one log aside so that the ember river could run more freely again. "There, that's better," he crowed.

The third Elder sat in a silence so profound that it drew Basuba inside herself to put together the clues the evening was giving her. She sighed in a way that made her whole body shift, and she said, "Ah, the Dream's meaning comes clearer now. The River that Rosemary sees is the past when Nature's wisdom flowed easily and steadily to us. The logs that cut right through the stream show what has happened to our people these last hundreds of years. What is happening still. So much, too much has been lost. Only fragments of our knowledge remain."

Basuba stirred some coals on the edge of the fire with a stick. "Thank you, friends."

"Take it further, Sister. What is the Dream's message for you? For us?"

In the hope of finding an answer, Basuba stared into the center of the red, hot coal river that Rosemary had pointed out. She let the words that were flowing into her mind speak for themselves. "What the Dream is saying is true of the herbs. I can sense the force of Life in them, like a heartbeat, when I hold them in my hands. But many of their healing stories died with our ancestors in the Hanging Times. I know something about this plant, something about that one. The rest I have to guess at. Try this or try that and watch what happens."

She stopped to let more words stream into her mind, wondering how they would string themselves together. She waited until they were ready to be spoken. The relentless cold was biting into her, and she knew that it must be sucking at the other old bodies around the fire. Maybe her words were too tender to be uttered, for with the raw tongue of the damp night lapping at them they began to retreat. The rest of the message skittered away, leaving her empty.

"It's the same for planting and harvesting," said the Elder who'd been silent before. "Only bits and pieces of the lore have come down to us. Someone heard this and someone else has heard that, and the third bit of advice goes against the wisdom of the first."

"And so for the ceremonies," added Rosemary. "We have a verse or two of a chant, or all the words but no tune. And," her eyes glittered hard with anger, "sometimes in the market, I catch snatches of a song or prayer of ours that's been made ugly and evil and given to the Christian children to taunt our little ones with. Innocent children, they do not understand the barbs their words hold. But by the time they are grown, they have come to hate us and to fear us."

Rosemary looked over at Basuba, her friend from childhood, with tenderness. "So, Sister, does the Dream tell you to gather up those fragments that are left?"

Basuba shuddered. "It brings me no such comfort as that. Instead, it gives me the feeling that it's too late for gathering." She hung her head and brushed the back of her hand over her eyes. Then, as though to leave those thoughts behind, she jumped up as quickly as her body would let her move, raised her face to the sky, waxing moon overhead now, and called out, "Dream-maker, send the next Dream. I refuse to have our story end here."

On the following Thursday, Marion rose early as she did every week to do Nick's marketing in the central square. Nick, wounded in one of King Charles I's military forays, had been her father's best friend. And Nick had been the one to carry her father's limp body off the only battlefield he would ever know. That was seven years ago.

Nick had returned to Ely, never to regain feeling in his right leg. He found lodging in a brick rooming house not far from where Marion and her mother resided. As a little girl, Marion had passed many hours playing at Nick's feet, pretending that when the kind fellow shaved his blond beard and cut his long locks her own sandy-haired papa would appear. Eventually she replaced that fading illusion with the hope that this man would marry her mother. As she grew older, she put away her fantasies and began to market and cook for Nick. He, in turn, taught her his trade of scribe: writing letters for folks who had no schooling.

Even though Marion also marketed three times a week for her mother, she never tired of the chore. Looking at and touching all the wares, listening to the hawkers' calls, bartering for the prize deals, wandering amongst the artisans and fortune tellers, who could ask for more excitement? To be sure, there were always the drunken soldiers who might suddenly fling themselves, or be flung, out of a stall that sold spirits and slam into an unfortunate passer-by. Or the quick sting of a coachman's whip lashing someone's calf muscle, a signal to move in closer to a stall to make way for the marketing staff of the Duke or some lesser nobility.

The market stretched on for aisles upon crowded aisles. Grains, flours, seeds, fresh produce, yarn, cloth, trestle tables and benches, pots, pans, buttons and the like each had their place. Most of the aisles were marked by a distinctive smell, particular to their wares. The goods were carried in daily by back, pushcart or wagon from all the villages in the region to be exchanged for the mysterious items reaching England's shores from afar: strangely scented spices, brightly plumed birds that talked and shrieked, brilliant shiny silks, delicate laces, pungent teas, peculiar-looking medicines, and sassafras. Fishmongers, carrying their goods on their heads, cried out their wares, dueling with each other over prices. Vendors whose tiny shops fit into baskets two yards across advertised their strawberries, apples or plums, herbs, roots, cucumbers, their nuts, oranges or lemons, in loud voices. Seed merchants spread out their array of products on a ground cloth: in this pyramid, seeds for very wet soil; in that one, seeds for sandy soil; over there, seeds for a slope that faces into the sun all day.

The market also drew all kinds of entertainment: jugglers, street theater, dancers, fortune tellers, and more. Once Marion stopped to look at a funny small hairy creature with a long tail and a wistful, human-like face who skittered about to the tune its owner cranked out of a box. Another time, a dark-skinned man with a parrot on his shoulder caught her attention, and she joined the crowd that gathered around to hear his stories and songs and put a penny in the pouch he passed. And then there was the older woman with three necklaces who read people's futures in their palms.

Marion always lingered until she had at least one good story for Nick. Although the writing and reading he did for folks in the neighborhood brought most local news into his hands, he longed to know what was happening in places he could never visit. He had an appetite for the rumors from London that arrived fresh and hot like the morning's buns and the stories of the continent and Africa that were spun out slowly by sailors and traders used to having time on their hands. Lately, too much of the talk on everyone's lips—peddlers and fishmongers, cobblers and maids, fruit vendors and parsons—was of the possibility of civil war.

Today the girl found her tidbit of gossip for Nick at the tea seller's stall. She included this stall in her shopping plan at least once a week on the chance that the stall's owner would be gone. When his master was out of sight, his young assistant would gaily open two or three of the tea canisters for Marion to smell, knowing full well she had no money for a purchase. Some of the scents were sweet and fruity, bringing her daydreams of foreign lands; others tightened the inside of her nostrils with their stringency; for some, she could not find words to describe them. Today, the miserly tea seller was there, conversing animatedly with a passing vendor. No free whiffs of tea, but juicy conversation instead. Marion stopped to rearrange her parcels and listen.

"Have you heard yet, Mr. Phillips? The King's men rounded up all the folks at Lander's Coffee stall. Yes, early this morning. The criers are reading out a ban all through the market. Says we're forbidden to gather in establishments where coffee is sold."

"Curses on the King. Coffee, is it now? His men are always coming through here with one decree or another. Say, have you heard tell if this ban includes teas? That would be my ruination."

But the button salesman had revealed all he knew and was eager to get on to the next tea stall with his gossip before it became old news. He extended his hand for a tip. Coffee wasn't tea, but it was clear that the news had riled up Mr. Phillips. The tea man grumbled and busied himself with a tea canister; the salesman squared his feet and held his palm out until he got his penny. When he left, Marion hurried back to Nick's quarters.

Instead of finding her friend at the table reading a document to someone or taking dictation, Marion saw Nick and a customer standing at the window of the lodgings, peering out. Moving that far across the room was no easy feat for Nick. Something was up.

"What is it, Nick? Are you all right?" asked.

"I'm fine. But it's the cobbler, Porter, who rents the shed out back. He's just been tarred and carried out of here, tied to a post. Six men showed up with no warning, two preachers with them. They caught Porter and basted the poor fellow with hot tar. His sons and some friends are following after them now. His wife says all he's done is rebaptize the tailor in the name of Jesus."

Nick threw up his hands and glared at his right foot. "Damn this leg! I heard the whole thing from start to finish. Couldn't do a thing to help but yell at them from here."

Marion prayed silently to Mother Mary to help the cobbler. He was one to go on talking forever, always about "the people's god," but he was a kind man. The thought of his body covered with hot tar made her nauseous, almost faint. She had heard enough stories to know that most people survived that torture, but often with terrible burns that left deep scars.

Chopping the onions, cabbage and beets she had just picked up, Marion put together a stew while Nick finished up with the stonemason who was dictating a letter. When Mr. Jordan left, she saw that the blotter Nick had been using was smeared with more ink than one letter merited, a sure sign that he was still shaken.

"Will you eat, Nicholas? Food will settle your mind."

"No, I cannot. I won't have an appetite 'til I see Porter back here safe and sound. But come and sit by me. Talk a while."

Marion sat down beside Nick, ready to listen. Those familiar words, "talk a while," always meant that the man had something on his mind.

"Marion, you're an able student, in spite of what the schoolmasters say about girls. I've taught you almost all that I know about scribing. Oh, there's special wording for some petitions that I haven't shown you yet, and some spellings you still do by ear rather than by sight. But come May, you'll have learned all that I can teach you."

Something in Nick's voice sounded so final that Marion burst in, "And then, I can charge greater fees and we'll be able to eat even better." She didn't really know what she wanted to say, she just did not want him to continue in the direction he was going.

"Marion, listen carefully to me. Soon you will be a full-fledged scribe, able to earn your way in the world. At least amongst those folks who'll bring their work to a woman. When that day comes, you must leave. Leave England, and so, leave me. It will be hard for both of us, but you must do so." He looked at the girl who gazed up at him with huge round eyes, her face blanched in amazement.

He patted her hand and said, "Hush now, Marion. Let me finish. One of the documents you are familiar with is the Notice of Land Enclosure, is it not?" Marion swallowed hard and nodded in silence. Nick went on. "We're seeing more and more of those papers. The plains will soon be fenced in, the trees harvested."

"Your father sang all the time about the land; his songs were love songs for the hills, the wind, the moon. Couldn't keep a job in the city because of his yen for Nature. He'd go off for days to the woods, the hills. That's why your mother was always angry with him. At first she thought he had another woman. Says she could have understood that somehow, but losing him to Nature made her furious. I know she's tried to break you of that same faith. She used to bring you to Church every Sunday. Kept at it 'til when? After her second child with Edwards, wasn't it. But, I know Basuba, too, and I can see it in you; you are your father's child through and through. Oh, I'm rambling like an old fool now, lost in the past. What I'm trying to say, Marion, is that it's time for you to leave here for the New World. The wilderness goes on there forever, they say. If Jimmy were still alive, he'd be there by now, running free with the Nature Spirits he sang to. You must go. There's no question about it."

"Nick, stop. Please. You've never spoken to me like this before. You think I should leave England? And you, not go with me?"

When he nodded, she cried, "I couldn't leave without you. With Father gone and Mother with Mr. Edwards, it's you and Basuba who are my true parents. Besides, there's plenty of common land around Basuba's cottage. If ever a hedge goes up, birders are sure to pull it down by sunset. And the groves around Ely, where we go for Solstice, and…"

"Marion, the places you know are not changing—yet. But, mark my words, with every land enclosure, there go twenty cottages for commoners like Basuba, and who can guess how many Sacred Circles, if that's what you call them." He looked at her with a sad grin and mimed himself, lifting his bum leg with both hands. "I cannot go with you, much as I don't like to think about losing sight of you. There's wilderness where you're going. That's why you're going. I can hardly make it round the cobblestones of Ely; I certainly cannot manage fields and forests."

"I'm not going then, Nick." Marion stood up and put her hands on her hips to bring the conversation to an end.

"Marion, you'll make me use my ace, will you?" Nick reached for her hand, and she gave it to him immediately. "Girl, I love you like you were my own daughter. I would not order you away if I didn't think it the best thing for you. But, truly, I fear for your safety. I do not know exactly what it is that you and the others do in the woods, who or what you worship. It doesn't matter to me. I know that you are good folk, that Basuba is a fine healer. But, we Christians are a varied lot. Look at what's happened to poor Porter downstairs, Marion. Some of us accuse each other of working with Satan; you can imagine what's said about your people."

Nick gave her hand a quick squeeze and let go of it. He picked up his stack of papers and tapped it sharply on the table to even the edges. "Time to prepare for my next customer." Marion knew from the cut-and-dried sound of his words that it was pointless to pursue the topic any further for now. Their eyes met briefly, then Nick lowered his and said softly, "Four months to teach you everything you need to know. Wet your pen, apprentice."

## Chapter 4

# February 2,
# Candlemas

*Candles of St. Bridget*
*Burning, burning bright.*
*Warming Earth, restoring Life*
*With the Sun's growing light.*

Proud as she was of her victory over Sheriff Worthington, Fiona sometimes admitted to her favorite oak that she worried about the future. The encounter with the ragtag veterans had sobered her right along with the other cottagers. It was one thing to make an appeal to men who had families and neighbors of their own; it was another to try to reach through to men hurt and hardened by the vicissitudes of war.

Folks talked about it often through the long dark nights of winter. One night in mid-January, Alyona stirred the embers of the council fire when the women gathered to talk about protecting the forest and said, "It is too dangerous for us— and most certainly for the children—to hold off the soldiers. Most of these broken men have long since cut their ties with the women who once mattered to them. Some of them rape and rob the poor, and even murder. To do that, they must have closed off, perhaps killed, the part of themselves that could let our lullabies in."

"And too dangerous for our young sons and brothers," added another. "Their manhood courses through their veins and will not allow them to pacify these soldiers with lullabies one more time. I could see that in their faces last fall, and I heard it in their muttering all the way home."

After a long silence, another Elder said, "It is time for us to fight in a new way. What other means do we have?"

Fiona, seated across the fire from Alyona, prayed to her oak for help and reached for the talking staff. She answered the Elder's question with thoughts that had been building up in her for a while. "The threat of enclosure is spreading through the land. And word of our tree-circling moves with it. It is time to carry these messages out ourselves. Go to all the villages. Tell people our stories. Listen to theirs. Let all the commoners know we face the same danger. It is by our hands that the nobles and the King have food on their tables each day. We are simple people, but we hold the food of the land in our hands."

"Aye, we are their food baskets. And it's time to teach them to think of us that way," agreed the Elder who had put out the question. Some women picked up the idea and began to knead it with their minds, rolling it out this way and that. A few of the young women crossed their arms and stayed silent, annoyed that it seemed always to be Fiona with the bright ideas.


In a few days' time, everyone in Blue Fens was talking about the possibilities that had come through Fiona with the help of her beloved oak. Already some of the young men were vying with each other for the role of messenger. A few of the older men grumbled about losing hands for the farm work. But when the older folks looked at the younger generation and thought about the coming years, most agreed with the idea.

Fiona and Alyona were carding wool one morning when Fiona said, "Granny, I feel your wandering blood running through my veins when folks talk about who'll be the messenger. Some, like my mother and some of the women my age, say it must be a man. But I know I can do as well." Her face burned bright red as she spoke.

Many of the women spoke up for her, but others looked away when she passed them. She stamped her foot hard and ground it into the soil when her mother spoke of Patrick being the one to go out. She would not be held back.

"It's your safety, Daughter, that worries your mother and me. I know that you can move freely among tinkers and others that live deep in the woods. It's the men coming out of the city taverns with ale in their bellies that bother us," said her father one night when Fiona and her mother had not spoken to each other for two days.

Her mother, listening from her chair by the hearth, blurted out, "Think of the work, too, girl. And be not so stubborn or prideful. How many men will come to the Church or the Commons to hear a lass speak? None that have any standing in their village, let me tell you. And then where's your great plan? Gone to ashes because of your pride."

Fiona felt the truth in what her mother said like an arrow piercing her breast. At first she had no response. Then she approached her father. "Come with me yourself, Father. Alyona's blood runs hot in you, too. I have seen that the road calls you. With Patrick so strong and able, Mother can spare us both."

And so it was agreed, more readily by some than by others in Blue Fens, that Fiona and John Carter would be the first messengers to go out.

Fiona stood at her family's hearth on Candlemas Eve and stirred the tallow again with a long smooth stick. She smeared some of the thick beige liquid against the side of the cast-iron vat to see how well it clung. "It's ready. We can dip five candles at once. That is, if you girls can stand close enough without stepping in the fire itself."

Alyona, an older, slighter, somewhat bent version of her granddaughter, peered over the edge of the vat that hung in the fireplace. "Ah, that bayberry gives a strong, full scent and a touch of color that brings to mind young wheat," she said with satisfaction.

Giggling, five little girls stepped forward and lowered their wicks into the vat. It was the first time they'd been allowed to help with the Candlemas preparations. Outside in the Commons their brothers were learning how to build the altar for St. Bridget that would shine with a mass of candles, one for each villager, on February 2.

An Elder hugged his thin shoulders against the winter cold and said to the fellow next to him, "Thanks be to Nature, we've made it to another Candlemas. Whenever it comes time to thank Sun for brightening these cold days, I know that I can survive 'til Spring. Until we can light all these candles to mark the change in the daylight, I'm never sure," he shook his head ruefully.

His friend laughed and nodded, "Yes, old man, we've made it to the quickening of the season. My old body is as glad as yours."

The first fellow turned to the little boys who played at the base of the altar their older brothers were building. His eyes crinkled as he teased them, saying, "Remember, I give a ha'penny to the first one who can bring me a wriggling seed. No good just to see it wriggling in the soil on the Saint's Day. It must move around in your hand when you show it to me. No one's won the prize since I did as a wee lad. You have to pray to Lady Bridget with the right words."

"Tell me the words, Grandfather. I won't tell anyone else," begged four little voices, one piling on top of the other, as children clamored over him.

"My words wouldn't help you. The Lady needs to hear what's truly in your heart." The old man tossed an imaginary coin back and forth between his hands.

"Keep a sharp eye out for a dancing seed. I'll be back, here on this very spot, on Candlemas at noon." He winked at another old man. What fun it was to pass on to the youngsters the same rituals that had shaped their own childhoods. Then his eyes clouded over as he recalled the Beltane festival last year when the parson had arrived with the sheriff to declare that putting up a Maypole would mean a big fine for Blue Fens. The Elder shook off the memory; he did not want anything spoiling this day.

That night Fiona packed her satchel while her mother filled the cottage with the smell of barley cakes she was baking for their trip. "Thank the Great Mother you and John are leaving us on such a propitious day, Daughter." She added under her breath, "If you must go."

Fiona replied, "Alyona chose it. She said, 'Just as Life quickens in every tree, in every seed on Candlemas, so it quickens in us. Sun brings us more Fire each day.' Father and I will take Fire with us into every village."

There came a bold rap on the cottage door. Fiona opened it to see Matthew. Her eyes widened when she glimpsed the walking stick in his right hand and the pack he carried on his back.

"Plainfield wants to send me with you, too. It is high time to organize the countryside. You'll be stronger if folks see we speak for more than one village. So I'll travel with you…if you don't mind," said the young man to Fiona, watching her face closely as he spoke.

Her father had come to the door behind her and answered first. "Fine with me," replied John Carter immediately, reaching out to greet the youth. "There'll be plenty for us all to do, though three's a handful to find lodging for."

Fiona looked away and fidgeted with her hands. She stood in the doorway without asking Matthew to step in from the cold night. What to do? He was a fine lad to look at—hair the color of autumn wheat, eyes blue as Stony Brook, body supple as one of her father's goats—and her brothers thought him reliable. He had stood up for her at All Hallows' Eve council.

But the thought of him coming along was irritating. Yes, he had thought of the signal system to alert other cottagers, but the original plan had been hers after all. She pictured herself speaking to a village of folks, exciting them with her ideas of what was possible if they united. If he came along, she would certainly be on the sidelines some of the time. Maybe she'd have to fight to make sure she was not on the sidelines all of the time. Which she would most certainly do. That's right, no reason to worry about him. She could hold her own with anyone.

She slowly pulled her eyes back to Matthew. She saw in his face that he was waiting for her answer. A good sign. At least he did not assume that her father spoke for both of them.

Fiona crossed her arms and planted her feet farther apart as she faced Matthew squarely and said, "I say you travel with us until we stand at the steps of Ely Cathedral. Then we'll decide if we stay together or go our separate ways."

"Agreed," Matthew said lightly. Then his face beamed with such a smile that Fiona found she was grinning back in spite of herself. "You'll let me in then? It's cold out here."


In the early gray light of Candlemas dawn, the Blue Fens cottagers gathered at the south edge of the settlement to sing some of St. Bridget's favorite chants. Their breath hung like little cloud puffs in the air as they huddled together to stay warm. They formed a circle around the three travelers as part of their well-wishing, everyone facing the direction in which the journeyers would go.

When the Elders were satisfied that sufficient blessings had been bestowed, a little girl ran up to Fiona with three apples in her hands. Another youngster shyly held out to them a bag of jerky that his father had prepared. Matthew bent down to him, unbuckled his pack, and threw open the cover. The lad quickly stuffed the jerky into a corner without looking up into the faces of the adults. Then, shouts of "Farewell!" and they were off with Matthew's yellow hound at their heels.


Gwyneth and Marion sat together at midday on the bench in Gwyneth's home, their sewing supplies spread on the table in front of them. Gwyneth fingered a piece of red fabric and grinned, "Elinor must have tucked this away for us first thing when she was making the Sun King. She had such a merry look on her face when she pulled it out of her pocket and gave it to me on Solstice. And there's just enough material for the front of two First Blood pouches. We're so lucky."

"Especially you, since your stitches are so neat. Look at mine. They're huge and crooked," complained Marion. "Youch! I just pricked my finger."

"That's what thimbles are for, silly. Here's one that will fit you. What are you going to use for the back of your pouch? This piece of black worsted or…"

"Here's a surprise for you," interrupted Marion. Dramatically, she pulled two pieces of tightly woven brown wool from her pocket and set them in front of her friend. "As the oldest living Willow Woman, Mary has given us each a piece of her hem for the back side. She says we're to do the same for initiates when we're the oldest. Part of the ceremony will be her showing us the bag she sewed when she came of age."

"Do you know much about what will happen to us?"

"I've been to two initiation ceremonies. But I can't remember them. You see, I was so little. I was one of the kids the initiates say good-bye to when they walk over to join the adults. I think I might have been a baby the first time and slept through it all." Marion grinned sheepishly. "And, of course, once I did get old enough to remember, they wouldn't let me come because then it wouldn't be a surprise for me now."

"Oh, Mari, I am so excited. I used to think this day would never get here. Now that it's finally time for us to be taken in, I don't feel like I'll ever be truly ready inside. I'm scared."

"You're afraid, too? I know I am, but you always seem so sure of yourself, Gwyneth."

"We're so lucky to be best friends doing this together."

"Yes, and best friends help each other with their clumsy stitches, don't they?" teased Marion, picking up the shears and the red fabric.

"Another way we're lucky is that we have been bleeding for a few moons now. It's two for me, and you started one before that, right? So at least we're used to that part of being a woman. Not everything will be new for us."

"And besides, we've been going to ceremonies ever since we were tots. The main difference will be what we feel like inside after the initiation. And, of course, we'll start learning how to prepare the ceremonies. And how to grow our talents."

"Mari, remember when you first started bleeding? And I asked you to tell me what it was like. You told me some things, about using cloths and making teas so my stomach wouldn't cramp. But there was one thing you said you would not tell me. No matter what I said, you would not tell. Will you tell me now? Now that we're about to be initiated." Gwyneth's voice was a little shaky.

Marion was silent for a while as if she were asking Gwyneth's question somewhere deep inside herself. She brushed some tears out of her eyes with her hands, and then she stopped crying. Her face got very red and she sat up as straight as she could, pulling her hands into fists. Gwyneth sat beside her and waited, taking some deep breaths and trying to stay calm inside.

At last Marion spoke, "It was Mother. When I told her I was bleeding, she slapped my face as hard as she could. She said it was the gift that mothers hand down to their daughters when they become women. And then, even worse," tears flooded Marion's eyes again, "she told me to stay away from her husband."

Gwyneth's eyes were open as wide as they could be. She put her arms around Marion and waited to see if that seemed to help. When she felt her friend relax into the hug, she held her tight. Finally a few words came to her. "What a cruel, mean thing to do!"

"She said her mother did it to her. She said it is the thing to do when a girl starts to bleed."

"And to say that to you about Mr. Edwards. As though she could not trust you. As though you would think twice about that man who's never shown you any kindness."

"And I don't even like boys yet!" Another river of tears burst out from Marion's eyes, so Gwyneth just held her for a while.

"And, besides, it's not true that that's what every mother does to her daughter! My mother gave me some rags she'd been saving for me to use to catch the blood. And she kissed me on the cheek and said, 'Oh, you're growing up so fast.' Have you told Basuba about this yet?"

Marion cried even harder and shook her head no. "I cannot. Once I told Basuba that Master Edwards walks around in his underclothes when I am in the cottage alone with him. She got very angry with Mother. After their fight, Mother locked me in the shed for two days. Two days alone in the dark in that tiny room was horrible. I did not mean to tell anyone about the slap." She grabbed both of Gwyneth's hands and squeezed them tight. "Gwyneth, you must promise not to say anything about it."

Gwyneth swallowed hard and was quiet. She pulled her hands free, and when she spoke she rubbed them together like she was twisting wool. "Marion, you are my best friend. I would not do anything to hurt you. But to promise not to talk to Basuba about something that is so wrong feels bad." She paused to think for a moment. "I could promise to help you figure out what you can do to feel better about this. Yes, let's do it that way."

Marion said slowly, "But you must not tell anyone until I say it is all right."

After a moment, Gwyneth said, "Agreed. I won't say a word until you're ready. But someday I will do my best to talk you into telling one of the Willow Women. They're our sisters, after all. That's what this ceremony is about."

Marion managed a short smile and stuck out her hand to Gwyneth. "We've got a bargain, then. But now you have to help me with my stitches…and, thanks."

On the days leading up to Candlemas, Marion put in extra hours working with Nick and helping out her mother around the house. She needed to have all morning of February 2 free to help with the final preparations for the ceremony.

That morning, she was up before dawn, did the last of some chores, and left the house just as the sun was climbing into the eastern sky. As rosy fingers of light slid softly across the horizon, she stopped where she was to make a prayer of thanksgiving to the East and to everything connected with that direction—the element of Air, All Living Things with Wings, and the Power of the Mind.

Just then, a merchant with his head cast down from the hard work of pushing a heavy cart full of sacks of grain came hurrying down the street. At the last moment, he saw Marion standing in the middle of his path and swerved to avoid hitting her.

The man complained loudly as he went by, "Mind where you stop, fool. Damn wenches, damn Pagans, too stupid to know what they are doing."

When Marion got to Rosemary's cottage, which was also a candle shop, she saw that the candle making was already under way. Three of the grown Willow Women were standing by the vat chatting. As Marion walked over to join them, a rush of warmth danced through her body; after tonight, she would always belong with them. She smiled shyly as she slid in beside Elinor.

Rosemary, strong and sturdy, wore an apron spattered with candle wax from many dippings. She was showing Elinor how to stir the melting tallow. At the nearby bench, Mary was pressing the sheet mold into a tray of hot beeswax.

"So, Rosemary, was it Candlemas that brought you to sell candles?"

"Yes," laughed the Scottish woman, "since I was a wee girl it's been my favorite holiday. A hill of lovely candles, burning bright in the middle of winter. The promise of spring returning. And, I love the beginning of something better than its middle or end. Even with all my years, I'm still a Maiden at heart," she said with a wink and a nod to Marion. "So, St. Bridget is my guardian. It was her and losing my husband to drink that started me selling candles. And it helped that my cousin is a beekeeper."

"What I love most about St. Bridget's Day is the chance to wonder about what new things are stirring in me," mused Elinor. "I think about the seeds beginning to feel the life in them under the ground, and it starts me asking what is getting ready to bloom in me."

Mary smiled over at Marion and said, "And this Candlemas is a special one, for we'll be making two new Willow Women out of these dear girls. It's been a few years since anyone's come of age."

Suddenly her smile faded and she turned her face away quickly as though she needed to peer hard at the wax press. The old woman was remembering how many more young women were initiated with her. They had been at least ten or twelve. No, it was thirteen. She knew because they had all chuckled to realize that there was one of them for each New Moon of the year. This year, but two maidens.

Marion felt the question that had been brimming in her for a few days rise to the surface and sit on her tongue. She hated to have to ask it. What if she was supposed to know the answer already? But it would be more embarrassing if she were somehow forced to ask it after the ceremony was over. She cleared her throat.

"Mary, does initiation always come at Candlemas?" she asked quickly. She looked around and was relieved to see that her query had not arched any eyebrows after all.

"Yes, the time of Quickening when the seeds first awaken under the soil is the time to bring in new Willows. It all fits together; new life for Nature, life for us." She smiled warmly at her young friend as she thought of something to add that cheered her, too. "This is a very special Candlemas for it falls on New Moon, the time of Increase and Beginnings."

Mary returned to pressing the beeswax, content with thinking that though there were but two maidens, these two were bright and eager and full of Life.

The clear sky gave way to gray clouds that hung low with the weight of the snow they carried. By mid-afternoon the skies began dumping their load on Ely. This kind of weather meant the initiation ceremony would take place in the back of Rosemary and Elinor's shop rather than outdoors where Winter Solstice was held last December.

"But I really wanted it to be outside," said Gwyneth to Marion in a slightly whiny voice. "Oh, all right, Sky, you win. We'll be indoors."

"Yes, I'm sad about it, too. But remember, wherever we gather, we are on Holy Ground. All of Nature is with us anyway."

A cold wind followed the girls down the street, chewing at them as they returned to the candle shop at dusk. "I have to admit, Rosemary's hearth sounds good right now," confessed Gwyneth.

When they knocked on the door, Elinor greeted them and led them to the ante-room between the shop and their living quarters. As the girls had suspected, they would not be allowed to enter the main room until everyone and everything was in place. Marion stole a glance at Gwyneth and both of them started to giggle.

"I can't help it," whispered Marion.

"I can't either," replied Gwyneth, "but I'm so embarrassed."

When Elinor came for them, their giggles died away immediately. The end of childhood was upon them. They had taken a huge step towards womanhood when they started bleeding. Tonight they would be officially welcomed into the circle of women.

Taking each girl by the arm, Elinor guided them into the main room. When they first entered the dark room, they came upon two babies. One was the boy who was birthed right before Solstice; the other, a toddler. Elinor made them stop.

She left them and rejoined the women on the far side of the room. The women stood around a beautiful altar that shone with the light of many candles. It seemed to Marion as though she could not take her eyes from it.

Rosemary, dressed in a red cape, stepped forward and greeted the girls. "Wel-come, Maiden Gwyneth and Maiden Marion to the Circle of Willow Women. If it be right, you will join us tonight."

The candle maker talked about how the girls had belonged to the circle of children until tonight. When she asked them if they were ready to become Willow Women, Marion's heart leapt to her throat. Memories of the angry merchant this morning, the taunting of the choir boys, and Basuba's words at Solstice rushed into her mind. The cold chill of fear ran down her spine and the faces of the women across the room blurred. She could no longer feel Gwyneth beside her. She imag-ined herself turning and bolting out the door.

Then, from somewhere deep inside, she heard a wise old voice whisper, gen-tly and firmly, "Breathe Dear Self. Breathe."

After a moment, the fear fell away like an old coat falling off her shoulders to the ground, and she could see clearly the smiling faces that awaited her by the altar.

Rosemary directed the girls to hug each child as a way of saying farewell to that part of their lives. As Elinor had coached them to do, Gwyneth and Marion gave a small gift they had made to each child. Then they purposefully turned away from the youngsters.

Next, Rosemary asked the girls to tie their First Blood pouches around their waists as proof that they had the right to cross the room because their Sacred Bleed-ing had begun. Even though Marion and Gwyneth had tried the pouches on before to make sure that the cords would be the right length, securing them now to their bodies in front of the others felt so different. With all eyes upon them, they moved slowly and carefully to do the tying. When they had finished, Rosemary gave them permission to come halfway across the room, then stop and sit on the floor.

Basuba, waiting until they were seated, came forward and asked them to say something about what they thought they were leaving behind and what they thought they were moving towards. Gwyneth spoke first, and Marion tried hard to listen to her instead of thinking about what she would say during her turn.

"I've learned enough over the years about respecting others when they speak by listening well to them. I better do it now when I'm about to cross over," she counseled herself.

When it was her turn to talk, Marion surprised herself by having enough to say, even though she had not had the chance to think it out before she opened her mouth. It seemed like the women were listening carefully to her. She could see different ones nod their heads at something or other she said. When she had finished, she realized with a jolt that the women had acted as though they were learning something from her.

Sure enough, Suzanne, a woman in her late thirties, said, "Thank you, Maidens. I had forgotten, or maybe I never was aware of, much of what you've told us. Since I am raising children now, your words will be teachers for me."

Gwyneth and Marion looked at each other, feeling both shy and proud.

Three sharp raps snapped their attention back to the group of women. In her right hand, Mary, the oldest, held a shepherd's crook which she had just tapped on the floor. Marion had admired this crook before when it came out at special occasions. The wood had some figures carved into it and ribbons of many colors tied to it. It was time for the Willow Women story, time for the maidens to learn the heritage of their name. Marion wrapped her arms around her knees to get comfortable for a long tale.

Mary settled into her chair near the altar while someone lit four more candles that stood around the edges of the sacred table. The effect of the additional light made the altar seem to nearly double in size.

The crone began, "We who call ourselves Willow Women go back, back, back in time. We go back long before people lived in cities. We go back long before there were ships big enough to cross oceans. We go back to before the time Christianity was brought to this land.

"Our name has not always been 'Willow.' While we love the name 'Willow' for reasons you shall soon know, we grieve the loss of our original name, a name no longer remembered by us, a name carried only on the winds." Mary's eyes turned from the maidens and she looked off into space for a while. After a few moments, the woman next to her gave her knee a slight squeeze.

Mary shook her head as though to shake off the cobwebs of the past and picked up her story again. She explained her lapse simply, "My young friends, the story about how we lost our original name is a story for another night. Tonight we celebrate Beginnings, and so I will tell you how we came to be so lucky as to come by the name of 'Willow Women.' We took this name in our foremothers' time, perhaps seven or eight lifetimes ago.

"There was a bishop then who made sure that every church, every monastery, every priest had a copy of the witch-hunter's book. In many villages, most of the women were arrested. While they were tortured in terrible ways, they were asked to name their friends, the other 'consorts of the devil.' It was impossible for most of us to withstand the torture, so names were given and more arrests were made. Because there was no one in the church or the court willing to protect us in time to save our lives, we knew that we had to find our own way to survive.

"We believed that these terrible killing times would end someday, and we wanted to be present then, with our lore and our ways still known to us. We went to a grove, thirteen of us, and fasted in silence together for three days. On the fourth day, in the dark, lonely hour before sunrise, we prayed to Nature for guidance. We asked to be given a sign of the plants or creatures whose ways would protect us through the evil times.

"There was one amongst us whose mind was filled with the mighty Oak, but she did say that she had come to the grove with that tree in her thoughts and was unwilling to clear it from her mind during the fast. The rest of us, we were all given various signs of Willow. One of us saw the branches; another knew she was standing, bending over a stream, with deep roots going into Earth; another heard 'Willow, Willow' in a bird's call; and one saw nothing but began to dance for the rest of us in a way that was surely Willow's duet with the wind.

"We came to understand that Willow was given to us so that we would know how to bend, how to flow with the winds, be they breezes or gales. As Willow, we would not break, and we would not be taken for timber or firewood.

"So Willow's suppleness and quiet grace became our blessing, a promise that we would not continue to lose fine brave bodies to people who could not see us for what we were. We feel blessed that our branches can touch Earth when they dance. We give shelter to those who come willfully looking for it. We do not proclaim our healing like huge Elm would, so more of us survive. And though we have not been able to save all the Wise Ways," here she glanced lovingly at her friend Basuba, aware of how hurt she was about the losses, "we have some of the roots and quite a few seeds for New Beginnings."

Saying this, Mary pulled away a quilt to reveal a collection of big knobby roots and a plate full of seeds. She called the toddler to her, and together the two of them, old age and youth, grabbed fists of seeds and threw them into the air to land all over the room. Even Basuba joined in the laughter and gaiety.

When things quieted down, Rosemary beckoned the maidens to come a few steps nearer. She said, "You have heard our story. We give you an invitation to join us. And we ask you to pledge to be faithful to us and to uphold the honor that comes down to us through the Tree of Life from the beginning of time. If you are ready and willing to do so, step now into our circle."

Without hesitation, Marion and Gwyneth stepped up to the empty place the others had left for them when they formed a circle around the altar. Marion couldn't tell if the heart she heard pounding was her own or Gwyneth's. Each maiden put one hand on her heart and the other on her throat as she made the pledge, a sign that their desires and their words were in alignment.

"How do I know for sure that I am strong enough to be a Willow Woman?" The question blazed into Marion's head. It echoed so loudly through her mind that she feared she would not be able to recite the pledge over it. Then, just as quickly, it darted out, leaving her a little shaken but ready to speak when Gwyneth finished her pledge.

"I, Marion Carryer, accept your invitation to become a Willow Woman, from the bottom of my heart." Her words, cautious at first, grew stronger. "I have sat at the knees of my teachers. I have listened closely to what you have shared with me tonight. On my honor, I will be faithful to the Wise Ways and to our roots that go back to the Tree of Life. I give myself, heart, body, mind, and Spirit, to Nature, from whence they came."

Even though Suzanne and Elinor had worked with Marion and Gwyneth every week since Solstice on understanding the words of the pledge, each word Marion spoke tonight seemed to reverberate through the room. The words were bigger, wider, deeper than she had realized before.

Next came the part of the night that both Marion and Gwyneth had been secretly dreading. While Suzanne and Elinor could not reveal everything to them, they had let them know that one of the things they would be asked to do would require courage. Here it was.

Rosemary took from her waist a knife with a sharp blade that gleamed in the candlelight. She held it to her wrist and drew it swiftly across her skin. Instantly a little blood appeared at the cut; she handed the knife to the woman next to her and covered the gash with her other hand. The knife traveled quickly around the circle, each woman doing the same as Rosemary.

Much too soon, Basuba was handing the reddened blade to Marion. With no time to think or worry, Marion made a nick in her wrist and gave the knife to Gwyneth. When Gwyneth finished, all the women cheered. One by one, each woman walked up to the maidens and touched her open wrist to the young women's wounds, pressing the wrists together tightly for a moment as though to mix the blood. As she did this, each older woman said, "Welcome, Sister," or "Welcome, Willow Woman." By the end, almost everyone had tears in her eyes that sprang not from the pain in her wrist but from the joy in her heart.

All the women seated themselves around the altar in a loose circle, some settling down on blankets, others on a bench or chair. As everyone watched, Mary pulled a packet from her bodice and carefully unwrapped it. She held out her First Blood pouch for all to see. She pointed out the backside which had come from the hem of the oldest Willow Woman she'd known. The front side of the bag was a very faded red, for the local roots she used for a dye that long ago had little staying power. Too fragile to be worn at her waist any longer, but intact enough to be passed from hand to hand, it made the round. When the pouch was placed gingerly in her hands, Marion turned it over slowly. It was drawn tightly closed at the top, and she could feel a few small bumps and lumps in it that made her curious. She hated to let it go out of her palm to the next woman.

Marion and Gwyneth untied their pouches, and Marion had an odd feeling, as if she were almost naked, as she told Gwyneth later. They passed their pouches to the left to Rosemary. She held them high in her palms and prayed to St. Bridget to guide and protect her two newest daughters. Some of the others added their prayers.

Then Rosemary took two small seashells from her pocket and placed one in each pouch, saying, "May you always find comfort in knowing that you come from the Great Mother and Father and that you will return to them someday, like a drop of rain flowing to the ocean."

The pouches traveled on, and each woman added a gift to them—things like shiny stones, a root, a piece of dried umbilical cord, a tiny feather, a piece of jewelry.

Mary was last. Marion gasped as she watched the old woman untie her own pouch and reach her hand inside to feel for something.

Mary spoke in a voice that wavered slightly, for the night was growing old and it reminded her of her own age. "This may be my last initiation, so I want to pass on some of the treasures that have been part of my First Blood pouch."

She withdrew her hand from her pouch and opened her slightly trembling palm. There were two tiny hand-carved wooden figurines, a crescent moon with a woman's face in it and a woman standing with her arms reaching up above her in an arc.

"Choose whichever is right for you."

It was too confusing. How were Gwyneth and Marion to know which figurine was right for each of them? Marion wondered how she could be sure that she was worthy of such a special gift.

At last, Gwyneth spoke up, saying, "Thank you, Sister Mary. This gift is so special that I think we may have trouble making a choice now."

"Since Gwyneth and I are best friends, could we each take one tonight and then trade in a few weeks' time to learn what feels right?"

Mary beamed. "That's a wonderful idea. Yes, you may as long as you come for tea when you have chosen and tell me the story of how you decided." She closed her eyes and placed one figurine into each of the maidens' pouches, saying, "Mother Nature, you choose how the story shall begin."

# Chapter 5

# Stirrings

*East brings in Day at dawn.*
*South ripens Him by noon.*
*West harvests Him by sunset.*
*North knows His Teachings by midnight.*

Fiona wandered through the aisles of the big city market, picking up first this item, next that one, then putting each thing down just as quickly. Nothing was holding her attention. She was making her way to the aisle where fabric was sold. Going to buy the prettiest ribbon she could find, no matter the cost. To think that both Father and Matthew were solidly united against her was infuriating.

"How could Father go against what his own mother believes so strongly?" she fumed. "He thinks she'll see it his way when she hears his story. Hah! He's never taken the time to talk to her about reading like I...Ouch!" Fiona stepped back from the sharp edge of the cart she had just bumped into. "Now look at me. I'm all out of sorts over this. And they don't care, or they wouldn't be meeting with that scribe in a few hours' time. Where am I?"

Instead of cottons and wools and tins of colorful dyes, she was surrounded by eighty or so shades of green, bundles of sage, mint, comfrey, and the like, as well as bunches of roots like yellow dock. Fiona pulled herself out of the steady traffic of shoppers searching for cures among the herbalists and healers dispensing them. She spotted an available bale of hay and headed for it.

There, in a quiet corner, she sat and collected her thoughts. She remembered the time she first realized that only the boys in her village were learning to read, and not all the boys at that, only those from the bigger homes. She must have been about nine. What a shock. And the fight with her cousin Jack.

"If they won't school me because I am a girl, I'll learn from the wisest people around. Granny is one of them."

"Wise people, sure. You truly think that old Granny's any match for Pastor Copley? You're a fool. I'll soon read well enough to know more about the world than you'll ever begin to understand, Cousin."

Fiona had taken her questions to Alyona. "The books the lads read, that's not your wisdom written down, is it, Alyona? Are there other books that tell of what you know?"

"Nay, Lassie. The Old People, we do not freeze our talk like a pond in the Long Night's Moon. Talk changes as we change. What I can tell you of Life today, I did not know in the same way at yesterday's dawn. And if you were making a book, how would you choose my words over your grandpa's, or your own?

"I'd take your words over Pastor Copley's any day, Alyona."

"Fiona, whoever's words are taken, that person gains a hold over others. That goes against the current of the Wise Ways."

"But Granny, Pastor Copley can't hear the trees talk!"

Shaking her head, Alyona said in a tired voice, "We see that, Fire Child. Those who read books seem no longer able to read the lands and life around them. It does not bode well for any of us."

By the time Alyona finished talking that day, Fiona had made up her mind about reading. It was a loathsome power, used by the lords of England to destroy the wisdom of her people.

Now here were her trusted companions, Father and Matthew, behaving as though nothing were wrong with reading and writing. They were willing to spend money to have a document made up. They actually believed that having people sign their name on a piece of paper would carry more weight than their spoken word. What were they thinking about? People had always given their word with a handshake; that had been good enough. Most people she knew couldn't sign their names anyway; they would have to make an X for their signature. What use was a silent paper, easily crumpled up and thrown away, with a herd of X's running down it?

And to think that only a few days ago she had believed that she might be sweet on Matthew. How silly! She had felt her heart beating faster when he was around. She had caught herself worrying about how she looked. Even more foolish, she had convinced herself that he was sweet on her. Hadn't he said as much that night they walked under the full moon while her father enjoyed some ale in the tavern? Hadn't it been there in his kiss that night? Well, poppycock! If he could go against her like this, she was through daydreaming about him.

Fiona stood up quickly and scanned the aisle. Even if they were through, she still must have that prettiest of ribbons. Even more so now. Yes, she'd wear it to catch someone else's eye.

She went to the closest stall to get directions to the fabric aisle. Basuba looked up at her question and smiled. "I'll tell you in a moment and you'll be there in a flash. But won't you have a dish of hot chamomile first? Here, have it on me. It's a calming brew, and you look like you could use some of that." Fiona accepted the offering and, oddly enough, found herself in no hurry to leave. She stayed and talked for quite a while.

That same morning, Marion and Gwyneth, free from the customary shopping that kept their arms laden down with breads and produce, went poking around the market. Here was a chance to explore the alleys and side streets they had only peered down when they were hurrying back to their kitchens. They wandered through the aisle of smithies, ducking the horses that whinnied and snorted and swished their tails as they passed by. Next they walked by the carpenters and barrel makers and the exchange where folks brought used items to trade. The street opened onto a green where pockets of people gathered here and there to listen to someone speaking about one thing or another.

"You choose which one we should listen to," giggled Gwyneth. She was excited to think she might hear something that would be news to her mother, the know-it-all.

Marion looked around briefly and made a beeline for a group about halfway down the green. Standing on an overturned washtub that elevated him above the gathering crowd, a preacher of some sort gestured broadly to his listeners. His emphatic arm movements seemed to turn his words into pictures.

In a rich, rhythmic voice he told the crowd, "The New World is an expanse of virgin lands waiting for us, God's children, to tame it for Him. God has blessed that land with plenty of food, a sure sign that He calls us to the New World. Yes, and He calls us with the chance of Salvation. For, miserable sinners that we are, if we but do His work and clear away what is left of the devil-worshipping savages there, do not our chances of being with Him after the Final Judgment improve?

"Let me tell you a few things about the savages there to let you know how fortunate you are to be called to this work. First, these savages have no Scripture. No Scripture because they worship many gods. They worship terrible animal gods who give them the power of turning from savage to animal so they may hunt and kill with the fierceness of a lion. And when they pray to these animal gods, they wear no clothes and they speak in animal tongues. They have no House of the Lord but worship outside in their nakedness. And these savages, they take unto them more than one woman whom they call Wife. Now many a sinner amongst us may secretly, in his craven heart, want to do that. But he knows such a thing would be a terrible sin against God.

"My brethren, we cannot tell if these savages be human or animal. If human, they have fallen away from God and we, God's loyal servants, must punish them. If animal, they are to be hunted like the deer, like the bear. Whichever it be, the Great Hand of God favored us from the start, for with his Great Hand he hath swept away their multitudes with smallpox. Yes, for three hundred miles around Boston, He hath cleared our title to the land. And we gather now to finish His Good Work...."

Marion felt the blood leaving her cheeks. "This man is so hateful," she whispered to Gwyneth. "I can feel the poison of his words coming right into me. Look at the others—they appear to be swallowing all that he's saying."

She started to reel, close to fainting, the ground swimming beneath her feet. Gwyneth squeezed her hand hard enough to hurt and said, "Let's get out of here. Now." She grabbed Marion's arm and tugged at her.

"No, we must stay a bit longer. To try to understand more about these savages."

"Tell me now if the poor New England folk that some of the nobles here like to laugh at, tell me if they be not the forerunners of Christ's Army? Had our parents, in ancient times, refused to leave their chimney corner for God, the Gospel would have stayed pinfolded up in a few cities, and we would not be here as Christians today. Nay, this very land, the England that bore us, would be overridden with just the same savages we find in the New World today. And do you not think that God looks with favor on those who spread his Gospel? If you have eyes to see the Light, brethren, return with me and God to the New World..."

"Time to go, Marion," insisted Gwyneth, tugging hard at her elbow. This time Marion let herself be led away. She was silent for a long time.

"What are you thinking?" asked Gwyneth.

"Two very different things at once. First, how horrid and vile and hateful that preacher is. And second, how much the savages of the New World sound like us. Did you notice that? The preacher said as much. That strikes me as marvelous."

"But we don't go naked. Nor do we speak in animal tongues. Nor do our men take many wives. I don't see what you're getting at."

"I don't mean that we're exactly the same as the people who live there. But, use your imagination, Gwyn. And remember the stories. Like about the Bleeding

Time huts where the women sat naked. And Peter Mann, how he moves around
the circle at Fall Equinox, calling out to all the animals he plans to hunt. You've
heard him caw and growl before. And, most of all, worshipping outside."


Working at Nick's that afternoon, Marion's mind was abuzz with the preacher
and all that she had learned. She simply could not concentrate on the letter she
was copying. Just as a huge bubble of black ink oozed out of her pen and onto the
page she had nearly completed, two country men came into Nick's quarters. They
requested his services in composing a petition for the common folk to sign that
just might be taken to the King in the end.

Marion was all ears. Quickly, she shoved her splotched page under a stack of
papers, hoping that the two visitors would not notice. "Oh, to help draft something
that the King himself might read!"

Her usually steady hand quivered even more as she rewrote the page she had
spoiled a moment ago. The men seemed to be so new to reading. They asked Nick
a hundred questions, which made her guess that neither one of them could read a
word nor sign his name. In fact, teaching them to sign their names became Marion's first task; it gave the men and her something useful to do while Nick figured
out the best way to address the King.

"So, you hope to take this to the King?" Nick brimmed with curiosity.

"That's more a pipe dream of my young friend here, sir. What we want now
is a piece of paper that has the same thing a fellow would say to another man when
he was giving his word on something. We want you to write that and then teach
us what the paper says so we can tell others and get them to sign on."

"What would a fellow be giving his word to?"

"He'd be saying that the will of his village is to join with us to protect the
Commons," replied John Carter.

"Then we go up the road to the next village and show them that their neighbors are with us and they'll be more likely to sign," added Matthew. "Then, one
day, if the Spirits be with us, we'll stick this paper, full to bursting with names,
under the King's nose."

"You can see which one of us is the dreamer," said John with a grin as he
slapped Matthew on the back.

By the time John and Matthew left that afternoon, each man had copied his
name at least a dozen times. It was slow going since neither of them had studied
the shapes of letters before. Marion kept her tongue when she saw their first few

tries; the letters looked more like chicken scratches than members of the alphabet. By the tenth or twelfth attempt, everyone could see some progress.

As they were getting ready to leave, Matthew asked Marion to spell out one more name on a slip of paper that he could take with him: Fiona Rose Carter.

"See you tomorrow around noon," said the two cottagers.

When they were out of earshot, John turned to Matthew as he untied his hound from a fence post. "You truly have your head in the clouds, Son, if you think that Fiona will even glance at her name there on the paper. Or perhaps you have not known her long enough to see how stubborn she can be."

"Or maybe I'm smitten with your daughter. To tell you the truth, this paper is for me, not her. I just wanted to see how her name would look. I will teach myself how to form it."

"Go easy. Fiona's like a mare that hasn't been broke yet. And mind the color of her hair. It's not a brilliant red for nothing."


Nick listened to John and Matthew's footsteps fade away. He looked at Marion with a smile. "How lucky for you to have a document like this to work on while you're still in training. As you know, we scribes may get to change a phrase or two in a letter to make the message clearer. Or we may get to think out how to word a contract. But to fashion a paper that will go from village to village and maybe even to the King—that's rare. First time for me. How lucky for you! But the news these men bring us, my dear…Why are you crying?"

Marion stood facing Nick, her arms full of papers, pens and inkwells to put away. Tears rolled down her face.

She put down the supplies she held and buried her face in her hands. "Nick, how can you call me lucky when every other day you give me another reason for leaving England. You were starting into one right now, weren't you?"

"Well, yes, I was. Marion, it is because I see no other way. Here, everything is falling apart. There, it's all new. A time of beginning, building. New possibilities. You know I'd go with you if I could. There, there, now, don't cry anymore. I can't bear to see anyone cry."

Marion pulled herself together. She needed a good long cry; the intense aching in her throat told her that. But she must be off by herself, not in front of someone who couldn't understand. She wiped her last tears on her apron and picked up the mess she'd made setting things down so fast. After fixing the table for Nick's dinner, she put on her cloak and scarf.

Nick looked up from his work. "Marion, here's the address of the lodging where Carter is staying. I'd like you to go by there first thing on the morrow. Ask Carter to come here early. I've two more questions for him before I can put the final wording together. That's a good girl. And how about a smile to show we're still friends? Thanks. Now I'll sleep all right tonight."

Up at dawn, Marion headed for the address Nick had given her. It wasn't far away, someplace near the river, but she had to ask directions of a number of folks to find it. That's always how it was getting around the city. Only the big streets had formal names that everyone knew, and a body still had to ask someone what the name was for there were no signs.

"I've never been so confused in my life," mused Marion as she followed one lane and then another. First there was Nick. She could hardly bear working with him anymore. It was as though he had a mental list of all he meant to teach her. As each item was ticked off, he pushed her another step closer to the door. She felt like a baby bird being shoved to the edge of its nest by an uncaring parent. And she, the little one, couldn't even tell where her wings were, let alone flap them. But Nick cared for her; there was no doubt about that.

She shrugged. "What difference does his affection make if he wants me to leave?"

So Nick was like the caring big bird, and it was her mother who was the uncaring one who couldn't be bothered bringing her baby worms anymore. Marion had started counting four days ago; only once in all that time had her mother said anything to her that wasn't about a chore or something to do with one of her other children. Just last week that holy Mr. Edwards who went to church every Sunday had called her over to the table where he sat counting his coins. He said she must start paying to sleep there; it wasn't enough that she put money in the cup for every meal she ate at his table. His table! It was her father's table, ensconced in the house long before Edwards came along.

Then there was Basuba. All week long while Marion had been helping her sell the poultices and salves that she brought into the city this week, Basuba could not stop talking about the New Land. It wasn't that she had a plan to leave yet; it was more in the way her thoughts ran that Marion picked it up. Basuba had held up a certain favorite plant of hers and wondered aloud if it grew "over there." And she said that next time Marion came to visit her they'd best make a list of everything in her garden so they could take along samples if ever they were to move.

Marion was careful to hold her tongue to these comments. Maybe if she did not say anything, her aunt would forget about it, too. Just maybe. Despite Gwyneth's badgering, Marion had decided not to tell Basuba about her problems at home. That could be the piece to tip the scale towards leaving once and for all.

The last straw was the preacher. She shuddered when she thought of him. Christians! Never in her life had she heard someone speak with so much venom towards other folks. The confusing part was that now she was curious about the New World, half-frightened and half-eager to meet its inhabitants. How she hated all this bother! Tears tightened her throat into a narrow tube that ached down into her chest.

Marion pulled herself together when she saw the lodge. After all, she was on an important mission for Nick. This was business.

When she asked after John Carter, she was told that he was at market, but his daughter would be easy to find with her washing down by the river. "She's the big woman with fire for hair," said the lodgekeeper.

This being Thursday, the day after the local women gathered to do their washing and their visiting, the stretch of the Ouse River closest to the lodge was almost deserted except for youngsters playing along its banks with dogs and sticks. Marion spotted Fiona Carter as she neared the fast-moving water that was flanked on both sides by grassy banks. There, squatting at current's edge on a good rubbing rock with her back to the path, was the young woman she needed to find.

Before speaking to Mistress Carter, Marion scanned the banks of the Ouse. "This is a good place for a cry after I deliver my message," she decided. "There's even a willow down the bank whose skirts I could hide behind."

As she approached the washing rock, Marion could hear Mistress Carter singing. "I know that chant," she thought with surprise. "Not the tune that we use, but the words are the same." It was the Equinox chant that she and Gwyneth sang yesterday while they carded wool. She liked Fiona Carter already.

"Maiden, Mother, Crone in Me. Three Faces of Destiny. Maiden, Mother, Crone in Me. Three Graces in Harmony. Maiden, Mother, Crone in Me. Three..."

Marion stopped where she was and listened while Fiona repeated the chant again and again, sometimes singing, sometimes falling into a hum. Yes, Gwyneth had been right; the chant did sound different to her ears now that she was a Maiden.

When it seemed to her that Fiona might go on chanting until she had washed every stitch of clothing she had with her, Marion called out, "Are you Fiona Rose Carter?"

Fiona spun around quickly and stood up. She took her time to look the tall, thin, brunette over thoroughly. Guessing her to be somewhere between eleven and fourteen years old, Fiona was surprised that she could not tell the girl's age more precisely. As for Marion, she was surmising that Mistress Carter was probably eighteen or twenty years old. She surely had gorgeous red hair.

"If I am Fiona Carter, what kind of business would you have with me? And how is it that you know my full name?"

"I'm looking for your father. My employer, Nick Adams, must meet with him before he can finish his work. And your name, why, I learned it when Mr. Fields asked me to write it out for him. And, Mistress, I know the song that you sing, too. We sing it at Equinox."

"Since you know my name, I suppose I may know yours."

"Excuse me, Mistress Carter, my name is Marion Carryer."

"Marion Carryer, you consternate me. Your first words about my father make me angry; I don't want to help you find him. Your second words about Mr. Fields annoy me greatly; I want no one to be putting my name into writing. And your last words cheer me. Equinox comes tomorrow and I am far from home. Do you let strangers celebrate with you?"

"Sometimes there are strangers. I could check with my aunt Basuba about your coming. It's tonight that we gather to prepare our part of the ceremony. If she's back from the healing they called her to, that is."

"Basuba, the herbalist? We met yesterday. Right before I bought this beautiful yellow ribbon." She pointed proudly to her head. "I'd enjoy celebrating with her and her friends. As for John Carter, I was going to say you could search the market for him, but that would only be hard on you with no punishment in it for him. I heard him tell Matthew Fields to meet him back at the inn midmorning. You could leave your message with the innkeeper; I'll be out by then."

"Thank you. My friend and I were chanting the same as you yesterday. Do you sing to ready yourself for Equinox?"

"Yes, indeed. I have rarely felt so out of balance as I do now. I could chant from now 'til tomorrow eve without stopping and still be full of anger. Is that why you were chanting?" asked Fiona.

"Yes, ma'am. I think so. My friend and I, we just got initiated. We want to be sure that we know the chants full well for the ceremony."

"So, New Maiden, what is it you need to balance this year?" asked Fiona with a touch of sarcasm in her voice. What could a girl so young as this one have to stew about?

"I don't know." Marion's eyes moved out to the river. "Wait—I guess I do. There are signs that speak of my leaving England for the New World. I don't want to part from everyone." Her eyes clouded with tears.

Fiona shrugged and said, "Well, Marion Carryer, if you must have a cry, do it around here and I'll watch over you. Keep the boys and dogs away. I still have some wash to mind."

Leaning her back against the willow with its thick skirts to camouflage her, Marion felt the scorching ache take over her throat. She prayed to the river, asking it to pull the tears out of her as it coursed by. The fast moving current was a strong yes to her sobs, and soon she was face down in the grass, crying her heart out, safe to abandon herself to the tears, knowing that Fiona was keeping an eye on things.

She lay there until it felt like the storm had passed out of her and she was filled with a kind of peace even though nothing in her life had changed. "It's the same way a rainstorm passes over the Earth," she realized, amazed.

She thought of the heavy storms she had watched and how fresh the air was when the heavens had emptied themselves. And the water in the river that ran to throw itself into the arms of the ocean. Holy Water, that. So, her tears were holy healing water, too. She couldn't wait to tell Gwyneth. She was sure that she wouldn't have understood all these connections before their initiation.

Marion helped Fiona carry the clean clothes, heavy from being wet, back to the lodge. There sitting on the front step was Matthew Fields. Marion watched Fiona brush past him without speaking.

Matthew threw the young scribe an embarrassed look and rose to his feet. "Fiona," he pleaded. "You haven't given me a chance to explain. Hear me out."

But in she went without a glance. Now it was Marion's turn to be embarrassed. She greeted Matthew shyly and followed Fiona inside.

As though Matthew did not exist, Fiona looked sharply at Marion and said briskly, "Will you come for me for Equinox, or do you still want to talk with Mistress Basuba first?"

"I'll be at your lodgings a bit before sunset."

## Chapter 6

# Spring Equinox,
# March 21

*Maiden, Mother, Crone in Me.*
*Three Faces of Destiny.*
*Maiden, Mother, Crone in Me.*
*Three Graces of Harmony.*

Gwyneth and Marion met that night with Basuba to make final preparations for the Ceremony of Balance. This was one of two times in the year when day and night were exactly the same length. Spring Equinox heralded the end of winter, cold and darkness and the beginning of growth, blossoming and moderate temperatures; it was a time of celebration and expectation. It was also a time of personal reckoning.

As initiates, Marion and Gwyneth had an important role in the ritual for the first time. The three began their planning time by sitting and chanting.

"Maiden, Mother, Crone in Me. Three Faces of Destiny. Maiden, Mother, Crone in Me. Three Graces of Harmony," they repeated until it became a drone.They chanted long enough for Marion to grow bored and restless. Still, they kept on; over and over the same words, the same simple tune.

Then Marion's resistance fell away, like a cloak dropping from her shoulders to the ground, and it seemed that her mind had moved to another place. A place hard to describe in words, a place that felt close to wherever it is that dreams come from.

Basuba seemed to recognize when both Gwyneth and Marion had made that shift in their mind. Soon after, she brought the chant down to a whisper and let it die out, saying, "Tomorrow night we will gather to balance the Maiden, Mother and Crone in us. We meet separately from the Willow Men, who gather to balance the three faces of the Male in their own way. It is you two who will lead us in honoring Maiden energy. Your part comes early in the ceremony and opens the path for all that follows."

Gwyneth and Marion looked at each other. Marion felt her shyness creep forward as though it would strangle her. She tried to push it back. She must take comfort in the fact that many wise Willow Women had decided that she was ready to join them. And so she would be.

"What do you know about the Maiden?" asked Basuba.

"She stands for Beginnings, for all that is new. That's what I've learned," replied Gwyneth.

"Good. What else, Marion?"

"I don't know. I guess she is brave because she must make something out of nothing. Oh, yes, and she has fun. She dances and is playful."

"She gives her heart to no one," added Gwyneth, whispering as though she were sharing a secret.

"Good. That is an important understanding about the Maiden for you to keep in mind. She has no mate, no children yet, so it is her time to know herself, to find her own way. She is free in a way that the Mother and Crone are not. All these things you must hold in the front of your mind when you stand for the Maiden at Equinox."

Then Basuba showed Marion and Gwyneth the pose they would take as Maiden. She gave each of them a beautifully decorated bow and arrow to use in the ceremony and taught them to stand as though they were just about to shoot an arrow off into the distance.

"Hold this stance and tell me how this is the Maiden," she directed.

Marion steadied herself and raised her arrow to the sky. She listened inside to what her body could tell her. "Oh, I see. It's easy. All my mind and body are set on sending that arrow out. Like starting something new. Not thinking about anything or anyone except how far the arrow will go and where it will land," said Marion.

"You have it," beamed Basuba. She continued to rehearse the young women until they knew exactly how to lead the other women into the world of the Maiden.

Then she smiled and teased, "The teachings of the Mother and the Crone shall wait as secrets until tomorrow."


Meanwhile, Fiona was having an awful evening. For the second night in a row she had persisted all the way through the evening meal in silence. Her father and Matthew tried at first to engage her in conversation. She would have none of it. Shortly, they fell into an awkward silence themselves.

Tonight was harder than last night because they had a meeting to address. Recent immigrants from the farm to the city were gathering at a granary to listen to them. All these folks had family back on the farm and understood the importance of the Commons.

John and Matthew had the document from Nick. The ink on it barely dry, it was ready to be presented tonight. But that was not going to happen, for the document was at the base of Fiona's stormy silence, and the two men quickly agreed that until things were settled between the three of them, there would be no mention of the paper.

John Carter groaned aloud in the middle of drinking his soup from thinking about it all. He was a man of action; what frustration to have a new tool in his hand and to be prevented from using it.

He was edgy, too, wondering how they would divide up the speaking role this time. He didn't care much about speaking himself, and he was satisfied that both Fiona and Matthew could handle it well. Fiona was the stronger speaker; she blended facts, passion, and good stories. Matthew was straightforward and concise. The problem lay in Fiona's attitude. She wanted to open the meeting every time. And well she might, everything else being equal; the original idea had come through her, as she reminded them often, and her vision of the future was as strong and as clear as Matthew's.

But everything else was not equal. All the villages they had visited were accustomed to having community gatherings run by local men. Not only was it a break with tradition to have strangers leading a meeting, but having a woman speak at all, let alone first, was almost guaranteed to set folks off. In the worst cases, some of the men in the front rows would turn around and walk out. At other times, two or three men gathered around a council fire might start up a conversation of their own, talking loud enough to drown Fiona out. Of course, she would become outraged, and in the End confusion would reign with little being accomplished.

The three of them had argued about the problem often as they walked between villages. No doubt about it, Fiona was a powerful speaker. When folks were willing to listen to her, she could certainly move them. In fact, in the last month the word was out that they had aroused enough folks to have Sheriff Worthington on their trail. But it was also clear that having Fiona speak worked against them. Too often.

John was in favor of expediency. Wrong as it may be, if men were not able to give Fiona their ear, then for the sake of the cause Matthew should go first and, in extreme cases, do all the speaking.

Matthew thought it made sense for him to begin every meeting and, when the crowd was warmed up, turn it over to Fiona. Or stand right next to her as she spoke so that he might answer questions that came from hostile men. Once when Fiona pinned him down, he admitted reluctantly that if that tactic did not work he thought that Fiona should put aside her interest in equality between women and men until the Commons had been saved.

Fiona could not settle on a position. She was torn apart by the dilemma. As she saw it, either way she was betraying something important to her: the cause of uniting people to save the Commons, or her belief that women were as important as men. To her, the least painful compromise was that she start out every other meeting and take the consequences of losing some supporters. But, many times she felt that position was not a strong enough one to take for women. So, she made the decision afresh each time.

John groaned aloud again and set his spoon down on the inn table. His head was beginning to ache. How would they ever jump from total silence into talking about this thorniest of subjects?

Matthew caught his eye and said in a low voice, "It's possible that men who've been living in the city are more used to women speaking up. If she's intent on running the meeting, I say, let her."

Another groan from John. There was a chance that Matthew was right, and his suggestion would certainly make things easier between the three of them. But the memory of the meeting at the last village which had disintegrated into little more than bad feelings was still strong in his mind.

When John brought the subject up as they walked to the granary, both men were surprised to hear Fiona announce that she was not interested in taking the floor at this meeting. John was immediately relieved, but Matthew felt concerned. He was used to Fiona being right out in front, fighting hard for everything she wanted. Here she was backing away instead. Why? But she would not say, and he could not budge her to address the meeting.

On the surface, the evening was a success. Matthew presented the information clearly and vigorously. People listened closely, a handful of men and one woman asked questions, and many volunteered to help get their friends and neighbors involved.

John sat on the sidelines, the document burning a hole in his back pocket. He was sure many of these folks would have signed on, especially being city folk more familiar with written documents than their country peers.

Fiona remained on the sidelines, too, but she sat at a distance from her father. She absent-mindedly kicked her left heel repeatedly against the bench she perched on. It was only when two men in the row in front of her turned to stare that she realized what she was doing and stopped. She refused to be embarrassed. Why should she care about their opinion when it would never be formed fairly anyway?

As the meeting progressed, Fiona could not help but notice how positive the response to Matthew was. Here was a group of people with their full attention on the cause of protecting the Commons. For the first time in her adult life she felt close to crying. She searched inside for her anger, but it seemed truly to have given way to sadness, at least for the moment.

When the scraping of chairs and benches along the floor marked the end of the event, Fiona watched John go over to Matthew with a big grin, shake his hand and slap him on the back. The three started back to their lodgings in silence.

After they had walked for about five minutes, Fiona spoke calmly, "The meeting went well, Matthew. You had people with you."

Matthew sputtered, "Fiona, thanks. It did go well. We have more folks on our side. I missed having you up there with me…I'm glad you're talking to us again."

John could see it coming when Fiona said, "Now don't go falling all over yourself, Matthew Fields. I said something about the meeting, that's all."

John stopped and bent down to loosen a stone from his boot to let the other two go on ahead.

Matthew pleaded, "Fiona, we must talk about all that has come between us."

Rage and sadness battled over Fiona's innards. It was all she could do to say, "Not tonight. I need to clear my mind first…but we will soon."

She slowed her pace until John caught up with them. The older man shook his head at how little patience young ones had for sorting things out these days.

"How different this site looks at Spring Equinox. And only three months have passed since we were here," exclaimed Gwyneth, peering quickly all around. "Remember how stark the bare branches were then? Winter Solstice is surely the Time of No Secrets. Now, every branch and twig is clothed in green. Look at those tiny leaves."

"Yes. A celebration of the Maiden in their newness, they are," replied Elinor.

The ceremony began when a woman blew a conch shell, sending an ageless hollowed sound out to draw everyone into a circle. When the time arrived for them to string their bows and raise their arrows in front of the others, Marion felt that she and Gwyneth had grown bigger than life. It seemed as though they towered over the others and that the arrow each of them aimed was not a single arrow, but the very Beginning of every feeling, thought and action that any of them present at this ceremony would ever make in the Future. "Without our arrows of the Maiden to honor Beginnings, is it possible that nothing new would ever come into this world?" mused Marion.

Soon the older women were joining them in making the gesture of priming a bow. Everyone held that posture long enough to teach her something she had not known before about the start of things, some lesson particular to her own life.

As the honorary Maidens, Marion and Gywneth had to hold their bows in place until the last woman had finished her work and let her arms drop. Maintaining the position was one of the hardest and most wonderful things that Marion had ever done.

Basuba had not told her students that they would be showered with lilac blossoms by the others to bring on Maidensight. The friends laughed as they looked at each other covered in delicate bits of lavender and pink. They were giddy with receiving the gift of seeing more clearly all that was Beginning in every situation.

A few moments later, directly across from them in the circle, two women stepped forward to shift the ceremony to Mother Time. The pair moved slowly in studied unison to the circle's center. There they turned around until they stood back to back. They each raised their arms in a broad, strong curve and looked up to the sky.

Marion nudged Gwyneth, "The sign of the Mother."

All the women raised their arms majestically to the sky. One of the women in the center called out "Mother" and the circle echoed her.

Her partner called out "Mother Creatrix," and the circle responded in kind.

Next, "Creatrix Ripening," then "Ripening Merging" followed by "Merging Giving" becoming "Giving Birthing," then "Birthing Nourishing" to "Nourishing Fullness," and on and on until Marion's arms moved beyond aching into numbness. Finally the words returned full circle to "Creatrix Mother."

"May you find all that is Mother Creatrix in you tonight. May you call Mother Creatrix to you whenever you want to stay with something, to let its life come to full ripeness in you. May you release Mother Creatrix from you when you are holding on to something for too long." The two women delivered the blessing together.

All those women in their Maiden or Crone Time lowered their arms. Those whose arms remained raised began a slow dance, turning around and around.

"How can they bear to keep their arms up so long?" whispered Gwyneth into Marion's ear.

"How could I know? But they must do it if they want the Mothersight to enter them."

Fiona was not amongst those women who danced on with their arms raised to call in the Mothersight. She stood at the side of the circle and seemed to gaze right past them. She was thinking, "I'd much rather be aiming the Maiden's arrow at something I want than doing nothing, like the Mother does. She just stands there and takes in whatever the Moon sends to her."

Her thoughts turned to her grandmother. Alyona would be disappointed to see the child she had guided to womanhood refusing to move on from Maiden to Woman Time. Fiona knew that; Alyona had told her as much at the Spring Equinox last year in Blue Fens.

"Granddaughter," the old woman had said then, pulling on Fiona's arm, "listen to me. Your years, your body, your knowledge all say it is time for you to join the Mothers. I have passed on to you all that was handed to me when I moved on from Maiden. Why do you hang back?"

"It cannot yet be my time to change. My body still moves swift and free as the deer. My heart lingers for no man. My mind rides the fiercest wind. I will not give that up." Those words still rang true in her heart this spring. "Maybe it is that I prefer Sun and do not desire to raise my arms to draw down Moon's power," she mused.

The shift from Mother Time to Crone Time was announced by a thick silence that wrapped around Marion so tightly that she tasted what it would be like to never speak again. She sucked in her breath. Crone Time was the last phase of womanhood, the scary one that led to death. She took a step backward as though she could keep herself from being touched by knowledge of it.

Now the women molded their circle into a gauntlet with about four feet between the two facing rows. When they were all in place, they turned to the East where their eyes locked onto three hooded figures robed in black, standing at the far end of the gauntlet.

Starting down the aisle, their hoods shrouding their faces, the Crones walked even more slowly than the two Mothers had. They moved in single file, separately, as though unaware of their companions.

Marion could not take her eyes off them; the gait of each one was etched so uncompromisingly by Life. One woman was bent over with age, supporting her large frame on a cane that rocked forward at a steady pace with each step she took. The second Crone moved her body along ever so cautiously as though her balance could be overthrown by the slightest dip in the path. The third walked lightly with a spring in her stride and a quick glance here and there that made Marion think of a seasoned cat on the prowl. Suddenly her heart was swimming with tenderness for Basuba.

"How will it be for me when I am old?" she wondered. But Crone Time seemed so far away she could not hold on to the question for very long.

The silence that surrounded the women in that sacred grove grew deeper with every step a Crone took. It expanded into a silence greater than what Marion had ever known, into a silence that made Fiona restless and impatient. She fancied stomping her feet wildly or snapping a dry branch—anything to break the pervasive power of quiet that seemed so empty to her.

When the Crones reached the midpoint of the gauntlet, they stopped walking and turned counterclockwise three full circles ever so slowly. Marion gasped; in all the ritual work she had done, the instructions were always to move in a clockwise direction. It was dangerous to do otherwise.

The bent woman called out in a long, low voice, "The Crone has the courage to make an Ending. To turn things around. To say 'Enough!'"

The second woman trembled as she spoke, a current of shakiness rippling through from her head to her toes. "The Crone sees every fork in the road. She knows she must choose between two paths in order to go forward. Must leave something behind."

The cat-like woman called out, "Life. Death. Rebirth. One season dies so the next can be born in the Cycle of Life."

More silence. Then the Crones made their sign for all to see and copy.

Fiona spread her legs and bent her knees, expecting to slice the air with an imaginary scythe as she had always done at Spring Equinox in Blue Fens. But no. Instead, the Crones crossed their arms at the elbows to make a shears. With a sharp cutting motion, they brought their hands swiftly together.

Together in one voice they commanded the others, "Find what it is in your life that must be released tonight. What it is that needs to die. The End that must come. Surrender it now to the Crone who lives in you. She is calling to you. Hear Her. Follow us."

Assuming their earlier pace, the old women made their way to the western end of the gauntlet, slashing into the air that suddenly held unseen obstacles with their shears that closed, then opened, only to close again. Severing invisible ties and bonds as they went. Women from the eastern end of the gauntlet were the first to fall in line behind them; then came the rest of the participants.

Marion's arms shook with resistance when the end of the procession passed her. She burned with a desire to turn and run, run far away. But her Year of Initiation had barely begun; if she left now, some would surely say it had been a mistake to bring her into the Willow Women.

Forcing one foot to follow the other, she joined the line. "Is this how it feels to take that last walk to the gallows?" her mind asked, reeling crazily.

When she did close her shears, it was very slowly and only slightly. She could not bear to make that last move that would finish the cut. There was nothing Marion wanted to offer up to the Crone. She longed to have everything in her life go on as it always had. No endings. No changes. She held her arms still for a long time so that she would need to make very few slashes during this slow march.

About five places behind her came Fiona, relieved to be moving, to be active again. She snapped her shears closed with relish, not waiting to ask inside what it was that needed to be gone. Whatever might leave her, she could handle it. She was strong and fast and ready for any challenge.

When the Crones at last led their followers into a circle, Maidens and Mothers released their shears. Eyes darted here and there to mark who was joining the Crones this year, who still held the shears, whose Sacred Bleeding Time had ended.

The three Crones who had spoken before crooked their index fingers and beckoned to those who would join them to come to the center of the circle.

"Welcome, Sisters," cried the first one to the four women who came towards them, their arms still shears. "The blood that flowed out from your body all these years now stays within you."

"The Gift of Life that you gave out now stays with you to become your Wisdom," called the second.

"May you always know what it is that must end. Blessed Be," said the third.

As Basuba moved in the line of Crones who cut with their shears, something was different for her from the other times before. Tonight her shears cut thin air in a symbolic gesture, and yet she knew that tonight was an important preparation. Soon she would be called to cut away something enormous. She could sense it there—its density, its great proportion—between the blades of the shears she was imagining. Tonight she must practice finding her courage, keeping her balance, releasing her resistance to letting go of something she loved. Tonight she must let into her heart the knowing that a huge change was coming. She took a deep breath and focused all her attention on closing the shears, on the Walk of the Crone.

There arose a chant new to Marion's ears: "We all come from the Mother and to Her we shall return. Like a drop of Rain. Flowing to the Ocean." It seemed to repeat itself until she relaxed into a warm wave of comfort that swelled through her body.

Then, in that very moment, the chant changed to "Birth, Death, Rebirth. Round and round in the Circle of Life. Here we are. There we go. Here we come again. Round and round in the Circle of Life." There was a lilt to this chant that made people reach out for each other's hands and swing their arms back and forth as they had done when they circled the Maypole as tiny children.

The chants continued, the pace quickened, the volume grew. Out came drums and pipes to replace voices as the younger women picked up their skirts and began to dance, turning and twisting as fast as they could. Marion and Gwyneth watched for a few moments from the sidelines as the music swirled on and on.

Marion blushed with shyness when Gwyneth grabbed her hands and tugged at her. "Let's dance with them," she cried.

"But we don't know how," moaned Marion.

"No one will even notice us. They're all moving too fast. Once our feet get used to it, we'll be just fine." Gwyneth spiced her words with three little tugs and drew Marion a short way into the circle with her.

A few minutes later both girls were at ease. Gwyneth had been right; the music spoke to their feet and they seemed to know just what to do.

Basuba and her friends grinned and clucked and shook their heads as they made their way to a grassy knoll. There they spread their skirts and sat to look down on the bodies of younger women that swayed the way theirs used to do.

Fiona danced wildly, on and on, long after most others had stopped. A circle of younger women formed around her, clapping loudly to keep her going. At last, laughing, she dropped to the ground in exhaustion, oblivious to the chill in the Earth beneath her. Stretched out on her back, she watched the stars spin in the sky until she regained her senses.

As Basuba walked home by her side in the late hours of the night, she asked, "What did you glean from tonight, Fiona? If you are willing to say, that is."

Pride rushed through Fiona. She would prove to this crone that she had enough wisdom to know what was happening to her.

"When I met with the Maiden, I saw that I am willing to turn my back on others to set my own arrow free." She swallowed. It was no fun to admit her weaknesses, but the words had popped out before she saw them coming. She shrugged off her discomfort. After all, Basuba was safe—a stranger, someone she would most likely never see again.

Fiona continued. "My quiver was so heavy. It holds many arrows. Maybe too many arrows. The Mother spoke so softly, I could barely hear her. She always seems that way to me. I know very little of her for I hurry from the Maiden to the Crone."

Fiona paused and then said, "Interesting. I hadn't seen that before. That Crone, she speaks loudly. I pull her shears out fast and cut the cords if someone or something is stopping me from getting what I want."

"Fiona, the Spirits spoke clearly to you tonight. They must sense that you are ready to make some changes to give you so many messages."

"Oh, but I am not ready to change," the young woman said sharply. No one had the right to give her advice about changing anything about herself. "I am me, I am Fiona. I'll change only when I want to."

"I see," said Basuba.

They reached Ely's outskirts as the egg and milk ladies were coming into town with their goods. The Willow Women said their good nights softly, parting in ways that let them mingle with the vendors as they passed by. So much more comfortable this was than when they returned earlier in the night from a secret ceremony with no one else about on the city streets. On those occasions, the women wrapped their shawls to hide their faces so they would not be recognized by anyone watching for misfits.

Marion and another woman escorted Fiona to her quarters. They slowed their pace as they neared their destination. Who could say when and if they'd meet again?

"You know how to find us when your travels bring you back to Ely. And you know all the holidays. You're welcome any time," said Marion, reaching for Fiona's hand.

Fiona smiled broadly, "You're my first home-away-from-home. I'll be back someday. Blessings on you."

When Fiona turned to go inside the lodgings, her carefree mood was shattered. She caught sight of Matthew dashing up the stairs from the front step of the inn where he had been sitting, waiting no doubt.

"Oh, bother," she said to herself. "He's my shadow. After all he's seen me do, he still doesn't believe I can take care of myself. He's got a lesson coming."

The next morning, Fiona announced to Matthew that she was ready to talk.

"Good. Let's go now. We can walk along the river. There's plenty of time before we leave for Sutton." His voice was full of anticipation.

When they were out of anyone's earshot, Fiona said with metal in her voice, "We don't need much time for this."

Matthew's chest tightened. "Fiona, when I explain about the docu…"

She burst in, "Matthew, I don't want you dogging me anymore. I can't stand it. When we first started this trip, we agreed to make a decision in Ely. We're here, we've walked by the Cathedral, and I've made up my mind: it is time for us to go our own ways. You and your glorious document off in one direction, me and my father in the other. You can choose first. Which way will you head?"

"But, but, you can't mean that. What about the Commons? What about having so many folks with us that we scare off the sheriffs? What about us?"

"I've made up my mind. Besides, you explain things very well. You don't need Father or me. We'll divide up the villages and talk to twice as many people that way." Fiona spoke in a no-nonsense tone that Matthew had never heard her use before.

"Fiona, wait! A lot of good has come from us working together. For the cause. And for you and me. How can you throw it all away? You can't!" Matthew regretted the challenge the second he made it.

"Oh, yes I can, and I am. As for what was between you and me, that was only some silliness I can barely recall now." She would not look at him.

Matthew swallowed hard. What should he say? She had given him her hand so readily that night they walked together. Then, the kiss. The passion in both their bodies that cried out for more touch. For the last two weeks, he had caught himself dreaming about the life they could make together when the Commons fight was over. He had imagined being in the fields under the Beltane Full Moon with her to make the Fertility Blessing. Now, she wanted to break off from him completely. He felt his heart cracking.

"Listen to me," he begged. "I know it's reading and writing that's got you so angry. But the document's partly for you. John and I figure that if we showed folks right at the start of a meeting that other villages had signed on, they'd be more likely to hear you out. And it's *you* who should be speaking. You're better than I am. Your words light fires under folks. That's what we need."

Fiona's face turned bright red; Matthew had no idea if that was good or bad. She cupped her hands over her ears to block out any other words.

From inside her, she heard the soft voice of the Mother from last night in the ceremony saying, "Daughter, everything on this Earth needs time to ripen. You move too fast from the Beginning to the End." She did not want to listen to that voice either. She ran back up the hill to the lodging.

In two hours' time, Fiona was packed and ready for the road. Only John showed up to meet her in the front room. When he inquired of the lodgekeeper about Matthew, he was told that the young man had paid his bill, called his hound, and left without a word as to his destination.

## Chapter 7

# Dangerous Days
# and Nights

*Freedom is a steady yearning.*
*Oh, Freedom is a steady yearning.*
*We've been yearning so long, we must be Free.*

*Freedom takes a constant calling,*
*Oh, Freedom takes a constant calling.*
*We've been calling so long, we must be Free.*

For Basuba, Equinox was the calm before the storm. Later, when she looked
back on the terrifying events that unfolded so quickly afterwards, she was grateful for every ounce of fortitude she had garnered from the ceremony that night.
And grateful at last for those painful dreams; she could see now that they had prepared her to recognize danger at once and to respond swiftly.

Basuba rested the day after the Equinox ceremony by relaxing, chatting with
friends, swapping stories of healings with other herbalists. The following morning she wakened Marion before dawn, and they prepared to head for the market.
Borrowing one of Elinor's wooden carts, they carefully filled it with a variety of
salves, teas, dried herbs, and tinctures, a healing liquid made from plant roots,
stems, leaves and flowers. Off they went, steering the slightly lopsided carrier
down the dirt lanes and cobbled streets.

They rounded the corner to Basuba's stall—and a terrible shock. Instead of
finding the familiar wooden framework and awning, the table for the wares and
the two stools they expected, their eyes fell upon a pile of broken boards and torn
curtains. They stopped dead in their tracks.

Their arrival roused a burly middle-aged man who had been sleeping in a nearby rubbish heap. He strode over to them, arms crossed, and declared to Basuba, "I'm here to see that you keep moving on, you old biddy."

Marion noticed out of the corner of her eyes a few other herbalists who were just opening their stalls. She watched them drawing close enough to listen in on the conversation.

"You are responsible for this destruction then," said Basuba sharply, filling her lungs and standing so that her body took up as much space as possible.

"Yes, I hurried this shack along on its way to becoming rubble," replied the man, kicking at one of the boards so hard that it shattered.

"And it is Percival the Apothecarist who hires you," said Basuba.

"The very one. He said to tell you that he will crush every stall you set up in this market." The thug kicked at the pile of debris again, sending a board scuttling over the ground.

"You tell him he will not silence Basuba the Herbalist, or any of the rest of us, so easily," said a bewhiskered young man who had edged close enough to hear the exchange. "Now, get out of here while you can," he said, stepping up to come face to face with the apothecarist's man.

After they had collected the remains of her stall, Basuba and Marion sat with her neighbors a while.

"Percival himself was here yesterday. Ranting mad, he was. Said he'd ruin you because you cause trouble for him whenever you come to town," offered a middle-aged woman in a brown shawl with whom Basuba had shared remedies over the years.

"Seems that Lord Bayfield's agent complained loudly yesterday morn at King's Crown Tavern that he could buy herbs from you at a quarter the price Percival charges. And get them much fresher, too," added the herbalist who had shooed Percival's man away.

"And that you said there was no such thing as ground unicorn's horn," chimed in a man who specialized in home-grown remedies for arthritis and other joint problems.

An older woman shook her finger in Basuba's face and cried, "If you add that to what Percival's said about you before, it's no wonder he destroyed your stall."

"Now, Auntie, you know that we all think it foolish to make a cure out of anything that does not grow near the land where a person takes ill," chided the woman in the brown shawl. But she went on to peer closely at Basuba and say in a frosty voice, "You cannot be surprised by this when you have always been so outspoken. You brought it on yourself, though I am sorry for you."

"Here, here, Millie," cried one of the others, "you've said before that Basuba speaks the truth. She has not said anything to the public that we herbalists do not grumble about every week to each other. And her prices, why they speak for themselves. Who in his right mind would pay four times more for a limp herb or a dried one that's gone moldy?"

"Well, if she'd kept her mouth shut, she'd still have a stall," replied the woman, sticking her nose up in the air.

"Ah, Basuba, you've done well," said the young bearded man. He smiled and thumped her on the back. "Hard to tell if it's the apothecarists or the physicians who you upset the most, old friend."

Things went from bad to worse.

Marion and Basuba sold goods from their cart for most of the day. Working in such a limited space was inconvenient, but they were determined to carry on. Just as vendors were closing down their stalls for the day, and even the fishmongers were starting to agree that their wares smelled too ripe to attract another customer, a lady's maid rounded the corner at top speed, flushed and out of breath. She stopped short when she saw the empty space that used to house Basuba's stall. Basuba called to her from close by.

"Diane, Diane. Over here."

Diane wiped her sweaty face with her apron and tried to smooth away her worried look. She came close enough to whisper her message to Basuba, as if the fewer folks who heard it the less damage it could cause.

"Lady Jane sent me. You must hide! Dr. Egleton, the Baron's physician who said Little William would die, is claiming that you are a witch. He says that when William was born you raised him up to the sky and then touched him to the Earth and so gave him to the devil before the parson could bless him for god. He says that's why he couldn't cure the boy two days ago and you could."

"Basuba, what happened?" asked Marion.

"Oh, that pompous man. He was giving that five-year-old child enough mercury to kill a grown man. Purged him six times for worms. Emptied the poor child's insides out, he did. William nearly died from weakness. Egleton could see that and he was scared enough to call the parson in for final prayers. Lady Jane dismissed him on the spot and called for me. I dosed the boy with herbs and laid my hands on his belly for a healing. William was resting comfortably by the time the Baron returned," said Basuba.

"Egleton was let go of entirely," explained Diane. "He's never gotten along with My Lady. Blames his dismissal on her and you. He's gone to the parson with his dreadful story about you working for the devil. Told the parson you cursed him when you came into the sickroom and now he's ailing badly."

"So, I'm to lay low until the trouble blows over. Is that Lady Jane's message?" asked Basuba.

"That, and more. She thinks you should leave the region, maybe even the country. Egleton is physician to the Bishop, mind you."

"I see. That proud man has powerful friends, then."

"Yes. And he knows that you have spoken out against chemical medicines before."

"But who am I to him? I serve the poor who cannot afford the likes of a physician."

The bearded herbalist had followed his curious ear once again and had stood close enough to hear most of what had transpired between Diane and Basuba. "Ah, but there's enough of the wealthy who seek you out instead of him these days. And since you, an old, plump, uneducated woman who limps—worthless in his eyes— have now cost him his position with the Baron, Dr. Egleton will do all he can to stop you."

The woman in the brown shawl stuck her nose in, too. "You have no husband, no family name. But a big reputation. If they do hunt you, there's many could find out who you are and gladly turn you in to collect a reward. Be on guard, my friend."

Late in the night, sleep surrendered Basuba to another dream. This time she could see the forest floor far below her. Something, someone held her. Gripping her flesh. She could not move. She knew she was about to be dropped and that she would break into pieces when she hit the ground. She began to feel the crack lines opening in her body and awoke to Rosemary's gentle tapping on her shoulder. Time to rise. Her friends were gathering early, before dawn, at the candle shop to help her figure out what to do.

Just as Basuba's freedom was being threatened, Fiona fell into danger of losing hers. She and her father had continued on the route they had mapped out with Matthew, John hoping that the young man would be waiting for them somewhere ahead. But there was no word of him.

Instead, they learned on the second day out from Ely that someone else had been looking for them. A village Elder told them that Sheriff Worthington's man had been through his village two days before asking if "the three rabble-rousers from Blue Fens had bothered them yet?"

John took his daughter aside and said, "Fiona, we should go home. Without Matthew the men are not accepting you. Any fool can see that. I'm not a speaker; I can't fill his boots. And since we must always be looking over our shoulders for the sheriff, people have a good, easy reason for not wanting to talk to us." He looked worn and older than before.

Fiona shook her head. "You're just tired, Father. We've come many miles these last two days. We'll be fine without Matthew, you'll see. You start the meeting tonight; tell people why we are here and who we stand for, and I'll light the fire under them. I promise I can."

"And the sheriff, Girl?"

"We'll talk to the young men this afternoon. Get them to make an escape plan for us. Then, they'll already be on our side for tonight."

John shrugged and twisted his hat around in his hand. "You're as hard to argue with as Alyona. You win for tonight. But, I'll agree to nothing after this until we talk more."

That night Fiona and her father were meeting with folks at a country parsonage about fifteen miles from Ely. John opened the meeting briefly and turned it over to Fiona.

She stood near the pulpit of the church, a bright green ribbon in her hair, saying, "Anyone who travels more than a few miles from home sees the results of enclosure. Empty houses without any roofs mark the spot where a village stood just a few years ago. The fallen-in church—that is now a sheep pen.

"The squires and sheriffs act today as if the land belongs to them. We know that it does not. It never has and it never will. The land gives life to all of us—we folk who till it, the crops that grow on it, the trees, the birds. The wealthy take too much from us as it is. We must not let them take more. Already they push us to put aside growing the food our babies need to raise sheep instead. The wool we sell to them they sell at ten times the price to sea merchants…"

The sheriff's private militia entered the village.

The boys who were guarding the paths into the settlement got their whistle relay system going quickly enough to give a warning. Fiona slipped into the crowd as the village parson rushed to the pulpit and commenced with a sermon.

As the doors to the parsonage burst open and the sheriff entered with a dozen or so men, an old woman in the congregation, frightened by the confusion, pointed at Fiona, calling out, "There she is! The redhead with the ribbon in her hair. Take her and leave the rest of us alone."

A youth threw a grain bag over Fiona's head, and two villagers hustled their guests out the back door and over a small hill to a shepherd's hut where they could hide.

When a young man from the village arrived an hour before dawn to guide the Carters over the hills to another road, he had bad news. Posters that offered an award for the arrest of Matthew Fields and John and Fiona Carter, the Red Rebel, had been nailed to the parsonage door.

The sheriff and his first officer were asking questions about where the roads out of town led; the sheriff's men were scouring the land in twos and threes. The youth who led them to the road suggested that they'd best go in opposite directions, but John refused. He would not have Fiona traveling the byways alone.

They reached the road as the sun was just beginning its climb to the top of the sky. Three shepherdesses walked by, guiding a flock of sheep in the direction of Ely. Fiona ran over to speak with them and learned that they planned to arrive at the city market in two days' time. While they looked startled by her request to join them, they seemed not to have an opinion against it.

"Go with them to the city," urged their guide. "The sheriff's officers have horses; those posters will be in every village square by tonight. You'll not be welcomed anywhere in these parts for a while. Folks have enough trouble with the authorities as it is. You're safer in the city."

Fiona looked at John. He held his hands up and stared at them. "My hands long for the soil. There's still a bit of the first planting to be done, if I hurry. I miss your mother and my kin. I'm not a city man, Daughter." He looked up the road at the shepherdesses. "Looks like Fortune provides you a way to Ely, if that's what you want."

Fiona nodded yes. John went on, "The sheriff'll have a harder time spotting you there. When this blows over, we'll find each other again. I'll send messages to you through Nick Adams...Any messages for Matthew when I see him next?"

She felt her heart tug a little. "Only that we'll meet again someday. Greet Mother and Grandmother and the others for me."

"They won't be happy that I've come home alone."

"It's safer for us to part, Father."

"Hurry now, will you! Day's breaking. Those soldiers could be anywhere," said their guide impatiently.

"All right then, Daughter. Mother Nature and Our Ancestors be with you. Hurry now, catch up with your cover."


After lots of talking with her friends and praying, Basuba laid her plans. She would leave for the New World.

The first step was a hasty trip to her cottage to collect some herbs to take along, to say good-bye to the cats, and to pick up something she had carefully hidden away in case she should ever face a crisis like this one.

As the herbalist made her last walk through the heaths and marshes, memories poured through her: walking among the purple heather and observing the skylarks who careened from plant to plant, trilling ceaselessly; hours squatting by the edges of marshy broads, creeping through reed beds, following streams so as to watch ruffs, black terns, bitterns, avocets, godwits, too many cormorants and snipes breed and nest, swim, fish, learn to fly, and gather in great groups to migrate. And then to await their return in the spring.

But here it was spring, and it was she who was leaving with no season to be calling her back. Time to bid farewell to her long-time home and all the animals she'd been feeding—the deer, the rabbits, the one-eyed bear. Parting with the cats would be like leaving a part of herself behind. They were wild enough; they would have no trouble surviving without her, yet how she would miss sharing her days with them.

Elinor accompanied Basuba to assist her in gathering and packing up samples of all her herbs.

At moonrise after the long day of bundling and sorting, Elinor asked, "How much of the Willow Women's herbal lore is leaving England with you, Basuba?" She asked the question in a teasing way as her eyes surveyed the heavy load they had to carry back to Ely.

Basuba sat down on a large rock and looked around her. Her answer was anything but funny. "That question pours salt in an open wound, Friend. I always thought I'd spend my last years right here in this herb garden, teaching what I know to Marion and others who'd follow after her. That's all changed." She stirred the earth idly with a stick for a moment and went on. "I am the only Willow Woman left who is charged with passing on the herbal lore; Sarah and I, the only two in midwifery."

Throwing the stick down, she looked up at Elinor in pain. "Sister, am I going against the teaching of those Dreams I've been having by leaving? Turning my back on the fragments, instead of collecting them?"

"Basuba, are you asking now for my insights?"

"Yes. I'd like to hear what you sense about the Dreams."

Elinor grew thoughtful. "When you tell about your Dreams, it seems that collecting the fragments hurts you. Makes your fingers bleed in one of them. Makes you frantic in the others. That is what I hear. When I ask you if the Dreams could be saying, 'it's time to let go of the fragments,' do you feel any response in your body?"

"Let's see," said Basuba. She went quiet for a minute and listened to her body. "Why, how surprising. Yes, yes, I do. The thought of letting go makes me feel very calm deep in my belly." She was quiet again. She looked up at Elinor and said, "But, I cannot understand why that would be the right thing to do."

Elinor put her hands on her friend's tight shoulders and rubbed them gently. "Could trusting the calm feeling be enough for now?" she asked.

"But what will become of our lore if I let go?" asked Basuba in almost a cry.

"Thank Mother Nature that there are so many other small circles like ours. Perhaps we can trust that the herbal lore known by them is much like ours. So that whatever you take with you also has roots that remain here."

"Ah, yes. That image is a comfort, " said Basuba. "But, Sister," she added in a rush as tears trickled down her cheeks, "how will I find my way without you and the others there to talk with? You've helped me so much over the years."

Elinor pointed up at the Moon above them. Basuba's eyes traveled with her. "Follow the Moon, Basuba. Follow the Moon West. Follow the Moon through her Changes. As She grows from a crescent sliver to fullness, as She shrinks from fullness to darkness, and then starts over as a crescent again. She will remind you how to sense and follow the Holy Wisdom that is always there inside you."


The Willow Women hastily drew together plans for a farewell ceremony for Basuba. Since Rosemary and Elinor's shop was no longer a safe gathering place, the simple ceremony was planned for the grove.

"As it must be," said Basuba to Rosemary. "Bittersweet is the flavor that tempers our lives in this time. This ceremony will give us another meal of it."

Basuba dispatched Marion and Gwyneth to knock on the doors of all the Willow Women and other healers they knew and bid them come to the gathering. As they left her steps, Basuba took the maidens by the hand for a moment.

"Look each woman directly in the face and tell her, 'The mistletoe blossoms out of season,'" she ordered.

"What does that mean, Aunt?"

"It's a message that warns we are not safe. It lets women know that this gathering is urgent for their own protection and for the well-being of all of us."

"Why mistletoe? It does not bloom now."

"The saying comes from a story about one of the gods of the north, Balder. All living things agreed never to harm him, except the mistletoe. So it was with the mistletoe that his life was taken. Only people who follow the Old Ways remember this story, so the message means nothing to anyone else who might hear it. Hurry on now."

Basuba watched the two maidens leave and frowned at the anxiety that lined their eyes and mouths.

"The first time I've seen fear for our kind grip their hearts, crease their sweet faces. It hurts to see it happen," she confided to Rosemary. "But there's nothing to be done about it. It's part of being a Willow Woman in these days. Oh, Friend, will it ever be different?"

But she did not expect Rosemary to answer; hers was a question meant for the skies, for the stars, for the Creator.

As she spoke, Basuba felt a wave of guilt wash over her. In truth, she was not entirely sorry that Marion was frightened. Basuba had been playing with the possibility of the New World for some time now. She wanted Marion to go with her, but she would never demand it of her. She had seen Marion pull back whenever she brought the subject up. She guessed that the young woman had not let even a single daydream of life there float through her head. But time was no longer on their side. If Marion was to come with her, the choice had to be made at once.

Basuba shook her head ruefully. Perhaps the sour taste of fear was necessary.

When Marion returned, Basuba asked her to go on a walk. They stopped to rest on a stone bench under a spreading maple tree in a park. Basuba took the bottom of her overskirt in her hand, turned it over, searched along the hemline for a small lump and, when she found it, stuck her finger into the hem right at that place. Marion watched her odd behavior. Her surprise tripled in size when Basuba pulled out a small diamond. She placed it in her palm and held it close for Marion to look at.

"I will tell the story of this diamond on my last night in Ely when the Willows gather. But there is a part of it that I would have you know now," said Basuba in a low voice.

Marion's stomach tightened. "The diamond has to do with our fourth pumpkin on Hallows' Eve, does it not?"

"Yes. Did I tell you that?"

"No, we've never talked about the Spirit you called 'Little Sister.' I was full up that night with Father, Grandmother and Grandfather and wanted to know of nothing more. But now I remember that the tears I felt inside that did not belong to me were shaped like diamonds," said Marion as if she were recalling a dream.

"Ah, so it is. Well, the time for her story approaches. The beginning I'll save for the gathering. It's the very end of it that I want you to hear now." She spread her skirts out a bit and went on. "This diamond will buy my fare to the New World." She paused for what seemed a long time. "There is money enough for two more fares. One of them is yours if you will come with me."

Marion was silent, staring hard at her hands in her lap. She saw her world splitting in two. And she saw herself falling down the huge, bottomless gap between the halves.

Basuba put her hand over Marion's and patted them gently. "I don't expect you to answer me now. I want to say just one more thing about this. You are in your Maiden Time. My Maiden Time was one of beginnings, of spinning dreams, of adventures, of casting my fate to the winds. I want the same for you. It will be next to impossible for you to find that here in England; the byways are narrowing for our kind, not opening."

Marion still had not looked at her.

Basuba continued with great gentleness. "Please find a place in your heart to let my words steep for the coming day. I would not force you to do anything, my dear First Crocus. You have 'til the moment I must purchase the fare to choose what seems best."

Marion leaned her head against her aunt's shoulder as she had done as a small child when she sought comfort. Basuba put her arms around her and rocked her ever so slightly. Whatever Marion decided, Basuba knew she would always love her as deeply as she did in this moment.


Fiona parted ways with the shepherdesses on the outskirts of Ely. How strange to feel safer in a city than on a country byway. Through asking directions of a number of folks, she made her way to Rosemary and Elinor's shop to find Basuba. As she hurried through the streets, she thanked the Great Mother for having met the Willow Women. If anyone would be willing to take her in, it would be them.

When Basuba looked over to see Fiona walking through the door of the candle shop, she realized that she had half-expected the young woman's return. Even though her thoughts had not been on Fiona, it was somehow fitting that she be coming back into their lives now.

After their greeting, the two women sat on a bench to exchange their tales.

Rosemary left them alone to talk, but hovered in the back of her store, rearranging some of the candle stock, moving a basket from here to there. Suddenly, she put a block of creamy beeswax down with a thud in the middle of the floor, walked over to them, and interrupted their conversation.

She said,"Young woman, we will certainly help you, but it may be dangerous for all of us to have you stay here tonight. How close behind you are the sheriff's men? Did you see any sign of them?"

"Yesterday mid-morning, at a crossroads west of here, two men approached us, asking if we'd seen three travelers with a yellow hound. I carried a crook and had my hair tucked in a cap. I did not speak, but let the others answer for us. There's been nothing else."

Rosemary let out her breath and her body relaxed all over. "Let's pay attention to any intuitions that may come to us on this. I feel shaky about it." She could not help herself; she stood just inside the doorway and wrung her hands. "What irritates me most is that I cannot tell if it's my fear or my Wise Woman Knowing that rides me so hard," she said.

Next day, Fiona set off with Basuba at dawn's first light for the marketplace. The streets were just coming to life as they passed through with early hawkers calling out their wares, dogs sniffing for any new territorial challenges since their last check, horses stamping and whinnying as they were put in harness in front of carts being loaded with wooden chairs, or milk jugs, perhaps.

The two friends parted near the center of the market where the grain merchants congregated, agreeing to meet back there when the bells tolled eight. Basuba was headed for the shipping lanes to inquire about fares.

"It seems the better part of Wisdom to show your locks only when you get to the Ribbon Lady, Fiona," Basuba warned as she turned to leave. Those auburn curls had been on her mind since they set out from Rosemary's. Bright enough to catch one's eye, they were, even in early morning light.

The younger woman grimaced. "Surely I am safe in the busy marketplace of such a big city," she replied.

"The sheriff's men have their dragnets, just as we have our webs, Sister. If anything, they can draw them tighter in the city than in the country."

Fiona shrugged and tucked her hair carefully back into her cap.

Two hours later, Fiona started the journey home with something better than a ribbon—a new sky-blue scarf—in her pocket. The women stopped at the produce stands. It was nearly impossible for anyone to come to the market without picking up some fresh food, and Fiona and Basuba, both country women at heart, were no exception. Only the earliest greens, tender watercresses and clovers, were available. While they were paying for their purchases, Marion ran up to them, breathless and panting.

"At last I've found you," she cried out. She pulled them aside and started to whisper rapidly.

"Calm yourself, Willow. Act as though your Mistress just remembered something she needed at market and sent you along to tell us. We don't want to set the stage for other suspicions," counseled Basuba in a quiet, artificially light voice.

"Right," said Marion, relaxing her body and making a show of peering into Basuba's basket as she talked. "Two soldiers came by Rosemary's right after you left. Said they'd gotten word that a redhead they were searching for had been seen approaching the shop. They questioned her hard."

"Rosemary—how did she answer them? She was so nervous last night." Fear etched Fiona's query.

Marion smiled a real smile for the first time. "The way Elinor tells it, she shone. She grinned and joked. 'Oh, yes, all of my fourteen nieces have a shock of red hair,' she said. 'If mine weren't so grey, you'd see where they got it from.' She offered them tea and spun a good story about a family reunion with lots of laughs at the expense of the country bumpkins. One of the officers chuckled with her, which made the other one huffy, so she hoped she had driven a bit of a plank between them. But when they left, the huffy one, who'd recently come from the country himself, said they'd be back if need be."

"What do you suppose will happen to me if I'm caught?" Fiona's words came so slowly that Basuba wondered if this could be the first time she had actually considered that possibility.

Basuba answered confidently, "I've been keeping an eye on that very matter. You wouldn't be hanged or tortured like those brought in for witchcraft. You'd be treated like a political prisoner, same as what happens to them who speak for a different kind of Christianity than what's popular with the King. Probably five to ten years in a prison cell with whatever food and drink your family and friends could supply."

If Basuba expected her words to bring comfort, she was wrong. Fiona looked like a wild horse ready to bolt for freedom. Her eyes darted from side to side, her body tensed, and she started to breathe fast and shallowly.

Basuba said evenly, "Start walking out of here. At a stroll. We've given these produce folks enough to gawk at." She gave her basket to Marion and linked an arm with each woman. "Marion, we need to find another place for Fiona to stay."

Basuba led them past the hosiers and the steady "tink, tink, tink" of the cobblers on out of the market.

Marion thought for a moment. "Nick's. Strangers come and go from his place all the time. There's the back room that no one goes into."

"Good. He's the next person I need to see anyway. Though I think that Fiona and I, each on somebody's WANTED list, had best separate. I'll drop behind you two a few paces. That way I'll see if there's any trouble brewing for you. Fiona, keep talking to Marion about what you want to do. Plans must be made quickly."

It was all Fiona could do to follow what Basuba was saying. She walked beside Marion in silence. Her head swam with images of cold, dark prison cells. No rustling of the wind through the trees, no scent of cut hay, no bird songs, no soil to dig in, no sky. No room to move. Thinking about it made her chest tighten so much she could barely breathe. She'd lose her mind in prison in four months, let alone five years. No, she'd rather die.

Suddenly every man they passed on the lane was a potential enemy. Fiona veered so far to the right to avoid one courier that she had to jump over a huge puddle at the last minute. She looked back over her shoulder repeatedly to prevent anyone from sneaking up on her. She picked up her pace. The bottoms of her skirts quickly browned with spatters of mud.

"Fiona, you'd give a mere child reason to think that you're running away from something," Marion said, hoping to tease her friend into another humor.

Instead, Fiona threw her a panicky look and leapt ahead, walking even faster.

"Fiona, wait for me. Wait. Listen," Marion said in her most commanding voice.

Fiona stopped, but kept looking quickly from right to left over her shoulders.

"I know many of the shops and folks along here," said Marion, casting her gaze over the two bakeries, the butchery, the hardware store that lined the street. "If anyone approached us, we'd have help. You'd be surprised to see how quickly a simple barrel stave can become a weapon. We'll be all right. It's not far now to Nick's. What are you thinking of doing?"

"I don't know. I want to hide wherever I have to, for as long as it takes. Cut all my hair off. I won't go to prison! It'd kill me." Fiona turned quickly to face Marion and took her by the arm. "Has anyone spoken for the other two fares Basuba's diamond will buy?" she asked.

"I haven't heard," Marion said and started walking again.

"That could be my way out," Fiona said excitedly. "Look, I'm strong. I'll make a good traveling companion for Basuba. There's land, land that never ends, they say. Woodlands that have never known a fence. Folks just starting to farm. Good rich soil. Yes! I think it'll work. I'm saved."

"Well, I may be going, too. Haven't made up my mind yet," Marion said in a strained voice. She was startled by the words that flew out from her own mouth and hurried on to change the subject. "What about your father, and Master Fields, and that hound that follows you everywhere? Wouldn't you miss them too much to leave?"

"Father, yes. Mother. And Grandmother most of all. But she'll understand. She's the one who gave me my wandering blood. Matthew Fields, no. His dog, yes. But I can find a dog there."

"And the trees, the Commons?"

"I'll miss leading the fight to save them. But there are plenty of folks who know about that danger now. And not much they'll let a woman do. I was the best speaker, but too many men just walked out on me. In the New World, there'll be room for us all. Besides, if I stay here, I'd have to be on the run for a while. There, I'll be free."

"You'd give up Master Fields?"

"Didn't you hear me say just now that I wouldn't miss him, Girl? Yes, I'd give him up. I have already. He makes me feel like a mare on a lead rope. Always reining me in. Always wanting to know what I think. Always wanting me to be nice to him. When I have a man, I want him to be someone I had to fight for. Someone who won't give his heart easily. Someone hard to tame. That's not Matthew."

But Marion wasn't really listening anymore. She was imagining Basuba and Fiona stepping off a big ship on a bright sunny day somewhere in the Massachusetts Bay Colony. She fancied them grinning at each other and looking around to choose a home. She saw them in a grand cottage in a huge woods—Basuba teaching students to collect herbs and make poultices, Fiona helping her with classes. Basuba known to all as a respected healer. No need to hide. No reason to feel fear.

Suddenly, she wanted to be there, too. She wanted to be in this story with Basuba, learning all she could about the herbs. If Fiona were there or not, it didn't matter. But Marion knew she had to be with Basuba.

The two young women were quiet the rest of the way to Nick's, each following her own thoughts. When they arrived in the courtyard of Nick's lodgings, Fiona waited outside for Basuba. She watched the cool morning breeze lift the branches of the lone tree whose buds were beginning to unfurl.

Marion called out to Nick and then went in ahead to explain Fiona's situation to him. By the time Basuba and Fiona entered Nick's rooms, Marion had a pot of water cooking over what was left of last night's fire and was putting another log in place.

Nick combined various piles of papers into one and invited his guests to gather around his worktable. He greeted Basuba warmly, saying, "It's been too long." He extended his hand to Fiona, which pleased her.

The four put their heads together. Nick agreed to handle the diamond. His scribing had brought him business acquaintances in every sector of the city, and he was confident he could secure a good exchange for it. Basuba agreed to arrange for three fares, but she said that the final decision on who would use them would depend on whether another Willow Woman was also interested in going.

Even Basuba, who was used to having people take her words seriously, was startled to find that both Fiona and Marion had made the big decision about their futures on that short walk to Nick's quarters. To Fiona, she gave encouragement, for she could immediately see the merits in her choice.

To Marion, she said, "Niece, I am glad to hear you say you will come to the New World. But I must know your reasons, for the last time we talked you spoke strongly against it."

"Since Equinox, every morning I've been holding out my hands, cupped like scales, and placing all the reasons to stay in one and all the reasons to go in the other. Each time I've prayed for guidance, but until today my hands remained in perfect balance. It was imagining you there, Aunt, freely passing on the Willow Women's healing to students—with me beside you—that finally tipped the scales."

She looked over at Nick. Tears welled up in their eyes.

"I'm ready to go."

## *Chapter 8*

# Leave-taking

*Wherever I go, you are with me.*
*Where you stay, I'm at your side.*
*The cords of Love that reach between us*
*No New World can ever hide.*

Things moved quickly after the great decision had been made. Fiona kept out of sight at Nick's and took over the cooking that Marion had been doing. Marion and Gwyneth, inseparable now that the die was cast, made various excursions to the diamond sector, carrying messages back and forth. They scouted out information about the ships leaving soon from London.

Gwyneth and Marion never really talked about their parting during the first two days of preparations for the trip. Marion, feeling responsible for making such a huge change in the future of their friendship, brought the subject up three or four times. The first few times Gwyneth interrupted her and started talking about something else; the next time, Gwyneth flashed Marion a look of such anger that Marion lost her nerve.

By the afternoon of the third day, none of the other Willow Women had contacted Basuba about going to the New World, so passage for Basuba, Marion and Fiona was secured on the ship *North Star*.

One of Nick's male couriers accompanied Marion and Gwyneth to the shipping office lest any thief, watching them enter the establishment to negotiate fares, thought they might be leaving with a large bulge still in their purse.

It was when the clerk handed the three tickets to Marion that Gwyneth's resistance broke. She barely made it out the door of the office before bursting into tears. Her sobs called up all of Marion's grief about leaving, and soon she was crying just as hard. The two young women leaned against the office wall and wailed.

Soon they had their arms around each other, which reminded them even more of how much they would miss each other and made their crying fiercer.

"We were initiated together. I thought we would always be together," said Gwyneth between sobs. "Always be best friends. And you'd live next door when we marry and have babies."

"That's what I wanted, too, Gwyn."

"You wanted it, but you're leaving. I'll probably never see you after this."

"We will too see each other again! You'll always be my best friend. Once you see how good it is in the New World, you'll want to come over. We'll have a big home by then, with plenty of room for you."

They cried more. The courier, looking very uncomfortable, put his hands in his pockets and kicked at pebbles while humming loudly to block out the sounds of distress. He decided he'd ask Master Adams for double pay for having to endure such a scene in public.

Good-byes were made as best they could be.

Fiona hoped that a message would come back to her from Blue Fens, but she waited in vain for a knock on the door. At least this way of leaving was easier than what she would have faced if she could have gone back home and done it in person. Alyona and her mother crying. Her brothers asking her how she could go like this. Those last looks at the fields, the homeplace. No, it was definitely much better like this.

More than once she found herself picturing Matthew and Yellow, the hound, walking away from her down a well-worn cow path, off into the distance. Suddenly he looked so vulnerable in her mind's eye, the young man with the dog that all the sheriff's men seemed to know about. What if he had been picked up and now faced the fate that she was leaving England to avoid? Could he bear prison any more easily than she? Would she ever know what had happened to him? She pulled herself up short as those thoughts churned through her and turned her attention to checking the strength of the straps on her bag one more time.

Marion dreaded her farewells. She knew that each one would stir up different regrets she had about going. It wasn't fair: being the Maiden at Equinox meant she should have only Beginnings to face. She prayed that she would not lose her nerve in the end.

The good-bye at her mother's home she expected to be perfunctory. She hardened herself so that she would not feel too much sadness about all the disappointments she'd had under her mother's roof. The children said good-bye to her as though she were going off to Basuba's for a few months, the greatest separation their little minds could conceive. Mr. Edwards, seated at the wooden table, began to talk about accounts. To Marion's surprise, her mother shook her fist at her husband and asked him to hold his tongue and say a proper farewell. She looked at him severely until he mumbled something, then she escorted Marion outside so they could be alone.

She said, "It's never been easy between us, Daughter. I see why you want to go away from here. I don't hold it against you."

She put her hands to the back of her neck and unlatched a silver locket. It was a simple chain that held a little heart. She beckoned Marion to come closer, and she fastened the clasp around her neck. "This locket was your father's first gift to me. It belongs to you now. I wish you well."

Marion could barely find her voice. She clutched the locket and said, "Thank you, Ma'am. Much beholden. I wish you well."

"Since Nick Adams has made you a scribe, you must write to us now and then, Marion."

"I will. Farewell now." She swallowed hard, turned, and briskly walked away, wondering if she would ever see that face again.

On to Nick's. With Gwyneth, there was the possibility that she would come to the New World someday. With Nick, there really was not. If Marion were to see him again, it would have to be in England. With all the scrambling to leave today, it was hard to imagine coming back in the future. But Marion promised herself she would return as she walked over to Nick's. She knew that without that promise, however flimsy its grounds, she would not be able to leave him behind. She pictured Nick to get his face set in her mind only to find that all her memories of her father rushed right into the mix.

Confused, she stopped walking until a comforting voice from inside reassured her, "It's all right. Nick has been like a father. This mixing of memories serves only to let you know how much he means to you. Later on, they'll sort themselves out, and you'll be able to recall each man on his own." Calmer, she continued on her way.

When Marion entered his quarters, Nick opened his arms wide and she flew into them. They hadn't hugged like this since she was a small girl sitting in his lap. Marion felt a glow inside knowing that her love for Nick was a lot like what she would have known with her own father. How blessed they both had been in this friendship! Nick got her laughing with some of his latest gossip. They promised to write often.

When he saw Marion straightening her cloak, getting ready to leave, Nick fished inside his breast pocket for something. Holding a small object in his hand, he hesitated, searching for words. Could he be embarrassed about something, she wondered?

"Here. This is for you to take. To protect you." He reached his hand out to her. In it lay a small stone cross. Now it was Marion who hesitated a moment.

"Carved this when I was a stonemason. The stone came from my great-grand-father; he saved it from the last cathedral built in England. It's been my talisman and served me well. I'd like to know it's watching over you now."

"But, Nick, you know I…"

"The Christ I follow always knows a pure heart. That's what counts. Please," he said with a catch in his throat. He pressed the cross into her palm. "Take it for me. Keep it close by. It's the only way I can bear to have you go."

"All right. It will make you seem closer."

He found his way back to a smile. "And it never hurts to have double protection these days!"

They both grinned. Then, suddenly, Marion had to leave—and quickly—or she never would.

"I'll be back to see you before too long, Nick," she called out.

He mustered a gay wave from his chair. "That's a grand dream, Daughter. If we're lucky, it may be more than a pipe dream. The door's always open for you."


Soon after dusk of their last evening in Ely, guests began to arrive in small clusters at the ancient grove. After everyone was present and the circle called, Mary led the women in some chants of thanksgiving for the sisterhood of the Willow Women. Basuba, Marion and Fiona were guided to the places of honor at the Western side of the circle, the direction in which they would be traveling.

"My dear Willow Women, there is something of great urgency that must be told tonight. It begins with a story and ends with our bidding farewell to three beloved women," announced Mary, who stood in the East. Those who listened closely could hear the tears in her voice, even though she held them back from her eyes.

Basuba sat down on the soft grass, and the others followed, settling in for a long story. She opened her palm to show the tiny diamond she held. She tilted her hand so that the jewel dazzled.

"My story comes to us from long ago. This tiny diamond, along with a ruby and an emerald, equally as delicate, was intended for an infant's pendant. It was a gift from the Pope sent to honor the birth of the royal heir of a country across the English channel from us. But a few days after the honoring ceremony, one of the Queen's courtesans, her best friend, had a baby boy of her own who sickened. Unable to keep down any food, he was. The Court Doctors gave up on him, saying that he was doomed to die for having been born on Christ's birthday. An insult from the babe's mother to Virgin Mary, they declared.

"But his young mother refused to accept their curse. At great risk to herself, she dressed as a poor woman and slipped into the city to make inquiries about healers. She found her way to a small band of healers who worked in secret since the city had a bad reputation for Burnings, and these were Burning Times. It was a Willow Woman, the youngest in the band, who urged her companions to take the babe in despite the risk.

"The courtesan brought the babe four times, and on the morning of the last visit the healers pronounced him cured. This was very fortunate because word of the babe's recovery was traveling through the Court, and the Bishop was asking many questions so the healers knew they must leave the city at once. As the cocks crowed and they mounted their horses to go, the courtesan pressed the beautiful jewels, a gift of gratitude from the Queen, into the hands of the youngest healer.

"A few months later, the little band of healers was separated from each other by a fierce storm. Everyone was caught by the Bishop's men except our sister. The maiden got a message to the others saying that she would ransom them with the jewels. But their message back to her forbade her to do so because the gems would be identified with the Queen. The healers had pledged never to put anyone else in danger as a result of their own choice to break the law. They would honor that pledge.

"The young woman was heartbroken. They say she stood in the crowd at the Burning, weeping openly. Very dangerous for her. After that she vowed that the jewels would be used when they could no longer be traced back to a living Queen. They would be used only to buy the freedom of Willow Women in dangerous times. Two stones have been sold—with the first, a sister and brother of ours were smuggled out of jail; with the other, two midwives were saved from the gallows.

"My friends, with a heavy heart, I tell you that this diamond goes at dawn to pay our passage for me, for Marion and for Fiona to the New World. Thanks to the expert bargaining of our good friend, Nick, there will be money to leave here with you to use as needed."

Basuba looked around the circle and found all eyes on her. Would one or two brand her a coward for leaving?

She went on. "I have been named directly by a powerful doctor as one who works healing through the teachings of the devil. My limp gives me away—they say a sure sign of their devil's hand. My face gives me away, for I have spoken out against the dangers of chemical medicines and the tricks of the apothecarists. I am no longer safe here, nor is anyone who would associate with me were I to stay. I have prayed about it and I am ready to go from here. I long to carry our healing wisdom to the New World and help it take seed there."

When Basuba's story was finished, the women sat in silence for a few minutes. Her leaving was fresh news to some of them. She needed the silence, too, for speaking about her decision to all her friends at once brought it home to her on a new level.

After the questions that followed, the women broke into a kind of dance that Marion had never seen before. If she half-closed her eyes, it seemed that the women moved as though they were flames of fire, not people. Loud whistles and shrieks of anger shot through the night. The pounding of their enraged bare feet made the ground under her tremble.

The anger gave way to a wordless, high shrill sound that came from deep in the bellies of the women. Two of them started the keening, and the others picked it up from them. It reminded Fiona of the way the dogs howled when one of their pack had died. Marion could tell that it was a special way of mourning that people had used since the beginning of time.

Mary and Elinor brought a large clay pot and placed it in front of the three who were leaving. Rosemary laid a plate of herbs next to it. Then Suzanne poured a bucket of warm water into the pot. Elinor sprinkled some red and white rose petals on the water to season it with love and friendship. Suzanne tossed in a handful of green nettles from the herb plate, asking for protection for both those who were leaving and those staying behind. Delicate rosy-violet buds of heather were added next to bring relaxation and to sweeten the visions of the future. Last came the purple flowerets of lavender to bring purification. Elinor slowly stirred the herbs into the water.

As the three travelers gathered around the pot and held their hands out over it, one woman after another came forward and gently ladled the perfumed water over them. A body prayer to Nature for letting go, safe journeying, and renewal.

Basuba then rose to her feet and said, "Sisters, when I walked the Walk of the Crone at Equinox, I knew that I would soon have to sever the cords of something very important to me. This is it. Leaving you is the greatest loss of my life. Please witness for me as I do my best to cut this cord that contains so much of my joy and learning and Life itself." She looked out at the heavens, "Oh Mother Nature, receive this act as my prayer that I can cut the ties I need in order to move on."

Her sorrow too deep for tears, Basuba slowly and painfully made the gesture of cutting a huge cord with her shears.

Elinor stood to address her friends at the closing of the ceremony. "My companions, remember as you leave here that the stars tell us that the long span of the Burning Times has spent itself. There will be small outbreaks here and there as the star patterns that hovered over that era dissemble, but the worst has surely passed. We are entering a new age. Hopefully, this will be the last time any of us need to flee."

"Blessed Be, Sisters."

"May the Great Mother be with you."

"And, you, too, Sisters."

Women wrapped their shawls around their heads, partially covering their faces for the midnight walk through Ely's streets. A few more women departed whenever those just ahead of them had disappeared from sight.

It was done.

The next day dawned beautifully, as if to mock Marion for leaving such a fine homeland. She looked long at the great expanse of tall grasses that lined the wide cow path they followed. The greens were just beginning to free themselves from the extra weight of the early morning rain, straightening their slender bodies to reclaim their true height. Here and there bursts of yellow and orange heralded the arrival of the first wild roses.

Gwyneth and Marion walked together as the little group left Ely. They fell in the middle of the procession with Fiona taking the lead and Basuba and Elinor bringing up the end. Gwyneth had begged for days to accompany the three travelers for the first leg of their trip to London, saying that Elinor could come with her so she wouldn't have to make the return journey on her own. Basuba thought it best that they cut their ties all at once, but Marion persisted in pleading for the idea.

Basuba knew the young women must make their own choices, but she shook her head, saying wryly to Rosemary, "Of course, the Maiden who loves the beginning of things does not know much about clean endings."

It was hard. When Gwyneth talked about all the things they'd done together since they were small girls, Marion's throat hurt and she brushed wetness from her cheeks. When Marion talked about the future, Gwyneth fell silent and fought the tears that welled up in her eyes. It seemed like the day would last forever, and it felt like it flew by faster than any other they'd known.

"What shall we do about Mary's wood carvings?" asked Gwyneth when they stopped for a rest under some trees on the bank of a merry stream. She was holding the one she had kept, the woman with raised arms, in her palm. She loved stroking its smoothness with her fingers.

"I don't know. How about finding a way to leave it up to the Fates?"

"Like me holding each in one of my hands, and you choosing a palm?"

"Yes. I like that. Can you mix them up so that you don't know which one is which?"

"Sure. Give me yours. And let's each think of a prayer to guide the choosing."

When they were ready, Marion put one of her hands on each of Gwyneth's outstretched palms and looked up at the skies.

"Dear Lady," she prayed to Nature, picturing a beautiful serene woman with arms wide open to receive her, "please help me to choose the carving that will teach me what I need to know next about being a Willow Woman. Help me to leave for Gwyneth the one that is to be her teacher…'til we meet again."

Gwyneth prayed, "You Who Protects Travelers, guide Marion's choice now so that we both journey well 'til we meet again."

Marion looked into her friend's eyes and listened to her own heart for a moment. Then she opened Gwyneth's left palm. There, waiting for her, was the standing woman. She opened Gwyneth's right palm and then pressed that hand and the crescent moon it held against her friend's heart. "So it is. Blessed be!" they said together, smiling wide.

That night the travelers bedded down in a fresh haystack they found near the roadside. From the pockets of matted straw they found they knew that others had slept there before them and guessed that the farmer did not mind. The two Maidens tucked themselves in on the far side of the great hay pile. Despite Basuba's reminder that the morrow would bring a long dusty road for each of them, they could not bear to sleep.

Each moment was a precious jewel. Sometime during that night, they promised they would stay in touch by looking into the night sky at New Moon and Full Moon each month for the rest of their lives or until they met again. The rising dawn met their steady, calm gazes, and when they parted, they did so with dry eyes.

Gwyneth and Elinor returned on foot to Ely, freed of the bags they had carried for their friends the day before. Marion, Fiona and Basuba walked into the next village and found the inn. There they waited for the next wagon going to London that had room for them and their gear.

As the sun rose on the third day of their travels, the byway that Basuba, Marion and Fiona traveled was changing. All the miles between Ely and London had led them through countryside and small villages. Now these cottages, many of them both home and shop to their occupants, that cropped up first singly, and then in twos and threes, were signs of a big settlement of people. The packed dirt of the byway was cobbled over here and there to smooth out the worst wheel ruts. The noises and smells of the city rushed in on them.

"We've made it! If we've gotten this far without being stopped, we're safe," crowed Fiona.

Marion was not convinced. After all, they'd had a scare the first morning which they handled by stepping off the cow path quickly and hiding behind a deserted barn for an hour, letting two officers on horseback get far ahead of them. Then yesterday afternoon, they had noticed two men talking earnestly to their wagoner when he stopped to water his horses. Fiona was sure that the men had glanced in their direction more than a few times. Thank Nature, the men, who had climbed on their own wagon and fallen in line right behind theirs, turned off the byway right at dusk. Last night, they spotted the WANTED! poster nailed to the Church in the village square they passed just at dusk. No one said anything to them about it at the farm where they paid to sleep in a haystack. Marion decided secretly that she would declare herself safe when their ship, the *North Star*, cast anchor.

"Get out of the way, you commoners," yelled a coachman who barreled down the cobblestones and dirt lane upon them, whipping his horses as he went, not caring who he splashed with the morning's muddy puddles.

At a large crossroads near London's marketplace, they left the wagon and turned right, towards the docks.

"Elinor was right. I am taking practically a whole field of herbs with me," thought Basuba as she hoisted a makeshift pack onto her back. "Where is my faith that I'll learn the remedies of the New World?" she worried to herself.

"I've never been to the docks before," crowed Fiona, excitement pouring through her voice. How was she to know that if they had taken a left turn and gone no more than two streets she would have come across Yellow Hound pacing anxiously in front of the Lone Sailor Tavern?

Matthew and Yellow Hound had entered London by the same byway almost exactly twenty-four hours before Fiona and the others. When Matthew, back safely in Plainfield, learned from John that Fiona planned to leave England, he did not consider for even a moment sending a message to her through anyone else. He knew at once that his only chance, and a slim chance at that, of warming her heart to him lay in his finding her again. He knew, too, that he must find her in London. Perhaps if they talked at the edge of that huge ocean she would grasp the enormity of the decision she was making. So, despite the warnings from John that a WANTED! poster with his name hung in every village square between Blue Fens and Ely, if not all the way to London, Matthew set out with his dog, moving along mostly at night, avoiding the bigger roads.

In London, Matthew headed directly for the dockside street that held the shipping offices. He went from one to the next until he learned that one *North Star* was pulling anchor for the New World the next afternoon. He scanned the passenger list, looking for the name that he had memorized as surely as his own, but he could not find it.

"The passenger, Fiona Rose Carter," he said to the clerk. "Is she leaving on this ship?"

"You think I have time to know each passenger by name? If the name's not on the list, she's not signed with us, Simpleton," sneered the man who had moved in from the country only three years before.

Matthew hesitated for a minute and then left the office.

On his heels followed a heavyset man whom Matthew had not noticed before. "Curses on those shipping clerks. Always the same. Can't be bothered with the likes of us," growled the man.

He matched his pace with the youth's. "Not to worry, the day's young. Your wench will be signed in when we come back this afternoon," he said in an accent Matthew could not place. The stranger threw an arm across Matthew's shoulder and continued, "Come up the street with me to my tavern. I'll buy you an ale."

"No, thanks." Matthew shrugged off the arm. "I'll just wait here for Fiona."

"Ah, man, it's your first time in London. You've never seen the ships. I'll take you by and show you our gunners." The man fastened his arm around Matthew's elbow and tugged.

Matthew gave in. Probably a better way to pass the time than standing in the hot sun outside the Maritime Shipping Office, he thought as his new acquaintance hurried him along.

Douglas Grant proved to be a long-winded fellow. He swamped Matthew with more details about the Men of War ships than the lad would care to know in a lifetime. When Grant finally turned his back on the waterfront and insisted they slip into a tavern and drink a toast to these great ships that protected their homeland, Matthew was relieved to have a change of scene.

They stopped outside an aging wooden building larger than any commercial hall Matthew had ever set foot in.

"You can tie your dog up at this post," said Grant, gesturing to his left. He watched Matthew secure Yellow Hound, thinking the whole time how he could use a dog just like this one to chase the neighborhood brats off his property.

Matthew looked up at the faded sign that hung by the tavern door and tried to work out the name of the place. A sailor with a rope in one hand and a mug in the other, some words underneath the pictures that were of no use to him. Maybe something like "The Sailor's Ale"? But he didn't feel like inquiring about his guess the way he would have back home. For some reason, he didn't want to take a chance on being wrong in front of this sailor.

Grant was at his elbow again, pinching tight and steering him through the door. "You're a lucky man to be seeing The Lone Sailor on your first visit to London. Not every country boy finds his way here so soon." He laughed as though his words were truly hilarious, slapped his thigh, and pushed his knuckles into Matthew's back so he'd move along faster.

"And another mug for the men who sail them," Grant ordered the waiter as he thumped Matthew on the back. The tavern was dark inside, its walls painted over long ago with pitch. Long, curved whaling spears and enormous mastheads, a motley congregation of mermaids and toothy dragons, served as decoration. The place bustled with business, and the two men had to speak up to hear each other. Matthew learned quickly to keep his elbows tucked in as burly, unwashed sailors strode up to the bar to quench their thirst, never minding whom they jostled on the way.

Matthew had eaten only a bowl of gruel in two days, and the ale, a stronger brew than what they made from dandelions at home, went right to his head, colluding with the dark interior of the building to make him feel very groggy. Grant quickly downed the second mug of ale, challenging Matthew to keep up with him.

Then, the sailor struck his empty mug on the counter in front of Matthew and said, "Well, Countryman, it's your turn."

Matthew flinched and looked away. His pockets held little coin and his head far too much drink as it was.

"No, Grant. I've had my share. Thanks for the drink. I'll be on my way. Got my hound waiting outside." He turned to go.

Instantly Grant had a tight grip on Matthew's arm. "You're going nowhere. You're a man, even if you are fresh in from the country. You owe me drink," he growled. Then he relaxed his grip and exchanged his scowl for a grin. "All right, all right. The first mug was on me, a welcome to our fair city. But, the second—you must go tit for tat on that one."

Matthew moved his weight uneasily from foot to foot, trying to measure just how tightly Grant still held him.

Grant spoke again, "Look, man. You've got money in your pockets for sea fare. You've surely got enough for a pint for me." He paused, reading Matthew's face."Oh, it's your woman who's got the fare. No wonder you're so anxious to find her. That's all right. We'll go collect from her." He threw his arm around Matthew again and started to leave the bar.

Matthew's head reeled; he could not think straight. But he did know that he would not appear with a thirsty Douglas Grant on his arm when he met Fiona. He stood his ground, weaving a bit. Maybe buying Grant a mug now was the easiest way to be finished with him. Matthew pulled some coins from his pocket and turned back to the bar.

Grant grinned and nudged him happily, "That's more like it. That's the Matthew Fields I know."

"One ale," called Matthew to the waiter in his steadiest voice.

"Make that two!" Grant overrode him in a louder voice. "Haven't you heard, Countryman, that it's very bad luck to let a man drink alone the day before you cross the ocean? So how does this wench of yours come by all her money anyway? Enough for two fares. Only one way I know of that a woman can bring in that much." Grant jabbed Matthew in the ribs and chortled, flashing a gaping grin at him.

Matthew pulled back a fist and swung at Grant, missing him but causing the men around him to stand back.

"Not to bother," said Grant to the others. "My friend is fine. Only that he just learned that his woman has signed up to be someone's bride in the Americas." There were sounds of laughter and guffaws as the other drinkers turned back to their own affairs.

"What are you talking about, Grant?" cried Matthew. He was close to throwing up, head pounding, body swaying; he could not get his words out clearly, and now he was totally confused. This man knew nothing about Fiona. How could he?

Grant leered down at him. "Fiona Rose Carter. That's her name, isn't it? Yes, I signed her up early this morning as a bride for the Newcastle settlement. She sails tonight on the King Henry. She had no money for her fare. Didn't mention you. She moaned and carried on about a fellow named Thomas." The trader took a large swig of ale and forced the other mug to Matthew's lips. "Poor fool, she's forgotten all about you. I sent her right out to the ship with the others soon as she'd made her mark."

Now Grant became all condolence. Arm around Matthew, he pushed the mug to the youth's face after every endearing comment he made. At first Matthew protested. Then as Grant described in great detail the man or probably, men, who would likely be waiting to paw Fiona over when she stepped off the ship in Boston, Matthew saw the scene so clearly in his mind that he grabbed the mug with both hands and chugged it down just to wash away the images. Grant was talking to someone else and never noticed Matthew slump to the wooden floor until the young man's head struck his left thigh on the way down.

The smell of tar assaulted the women's nostrils when they approached the docks. They stopped to look out over docks lined with barrels of grains and cereals, hogsheads of beef, vinegar, and aqua vitae, and bushel baskets of peas, mustard seeds and the like, to the dark-planked hulls of the sailing vessels moored in the harbor.

"Where's the *North Star*?" she called out to an errand boy.

"That smaller one, out there, anchored on the far side of the bay, Mistress," he answered, pointing. "They're just taking some cargo out to her now."

Amongst the crates and barrels was a hemp bag that covered something about the length and width of a person's body. A keen observer standing a bit closer than they were might have detected some movement from inside the bag and probably would have wondered what on Earth it held.

"And why is our ship stationed out there instead of in here with the others?"

"She only carries passengers and cargo to the New World. These here, they're Men of War," he said, standing up straighter and puffing out his chest as he spoke.

"Where do we register, then, lad?"

"See that red banner across the lane and down a ways. That's the Maritime Shipping Office."

The women registered, Basuba and Fiona each using the name of a grandmother to give themselves a little protection. "Ah, Mari, one way we can pass the time on the ship is for you to teach Fiona and me how to sign our names properly. I'm eager to have more than an 'X' to put down," said Basuba as they left the office. "I want to know how to write 'Willow Women,' too."

"An 'X' suits me just fine." Fiona said sharply. Then she asked disdainfully, "Why did you ever take the name Willow? Willows are thin, reedy, blown about by the slightest wind. Oaks, elms, they stand tall and mighty, while willows bow over, their leaves sweeping the ground. I want a name that says who I am: strong, brave, proud to hold my head up high." She stopped in her tracks and faced the others, arms crossed over her chest.

"I can tell you why we chose Willow, but if it will satisfy you, I cannot guess. You stand so fierce and stern there, you don't look anything like one, I must say." Much as she treasured the name herself, Basuba could hardly keep a chuckle down. No, Willow and Fiona did not seem to have much in common. Well, she would tell the story and they'd see what would come of it.

Basuba told a shortened version of what Marion had learned at Candlemas. Fiona's stance relaxed as she listened. She nodded at one or two points. When Basuba was finished, Fiona thought a moment, shook her head and said, "I have never been drawn to Willow. It'll always be Oak and Elm for me."

Their final day on English soil was quickly coming to a close as the three friends made their way towards the dinghy that would deliver them to the *North Star*. Approaching the dock, they saw that a sizeable crowd was gathered around a man who stood on a seaman's trunk. Even from a distance, they could see his wild gesticulations. Although they did not wish to go any closer, they had to pass by him in order to reach the gate to the dinghy. Standing in line at the gate, they could not avoid the crowd which was growing quickly.

Marion gasped when she recognized the features of the long-limbed, brown-haired man who addressed the crowd in loud and impassioned tones, crying, "All that is in this world is the lust of the flesh, the lust of the eyes and the pride of earthly life…"

"Oh, no! That's Preacher Denton. Gwyneth and I heard him at Ely Green. He is a horrid man. It chills me to hear his voice again."

"Worms will not spare your flesh, nor will the dust that was once your bones bear the emblem of your gentility…"

Shuddering, Marion turned away and covered her ears. She stopped herself from wondering if meeting up with him was a bad omen for the trip.

When the crowd cried out "Greatcoat!" in unison, she swung around quickly to look. She exclaimed, "What's going on? People piling up their belongings: great coats, books, mirrors, and…What's that? A noblewoman taking off a necklace and laying it on the pile?"

The three women could no longer keep their eyes off the eerie scene. People began to chant the name of each item laid on the pile. Then, in between each cry from the crowd came the preacher's shout of "Vanity! Pride! Lust!" Soon there was a rhythm moving back and forth between preacher and crowd forceful enough to cause the dock to sway slightly.

"If he's building this much force this fast, something big is sure to happen soon."

But Fiona was wrong. Perhaps the preacher wanted the event to last longer, for he was suddenly slowing the chanting, then halting it and preaching once more, using vanity, pride and lust as the touchstones for his sermon.

Night was heavy on the land, bringing in a strong cool wind, when the women lowered themselves into the dinghy, and still Preacher Denton waxed strong. The crowd grew, the mystifying scene drawing in passersby. No one left, fixed there until they learned what would become of the pile of beautiful, discarded treasures.

The dinghy ferried its passengers quietly across the long stretch of open water to the ship while most of its occupants kept their eyes on the strange event at the dock. The *North Star* awaited them hungrily, the wind sending her leaping against the leash of her anchors.

Looking out at London's profile from the ship's railing once they had climbed the swaying rope ladders to board the *North Star*, the women were shocked to see flames rising from the dock they had left. The voices of excited passengers soon brought the captain out.

He called for the first mate, exclaiming, "The fool, the fool. Is he trying to ruin me?"

Then one of the last dinghies pulled up with the first arrival exclaiming excitedly, "He started the fire to save us all from the sin of covetousness."

The captain shook his head and said, "This is the last time."

"Why is Captain Billard going on so about the preacher?" wondered Marion.

"I hate to be thinking what I'm thinking," replied Fiona.

They stood at the rails, drinking in what the night sky could reveal to them of the port city. When Basuba looked back at the dock again, she noted that the flames had died down considerably. One last dinghy, visible like the others because of the torch it carried, had left the dock and was almost upon them. All at once, three more torches set out from the dock, following quickly after each other.

Soon the captain was back, hovering near a ladder. "How many are there in that boat, Peters?" he asked. With Peters' answer, the captain commanded, "Well, if there's only him and the crew, pull up all the ladders now, save one. The anchors are on their way up. The wind is with us. Williams better be as tight with his timing as he claims he is. Prepare to leave harbor."

The three women tucked themselves back into the shadows, finding a good spot from which to watch what would happen next. Marion was the first to see the passenger from the last dinghy scramble up the rope ladder onto the deck. Her heart sank when she recognized Preacher Denton.

Even with all the evidence mounting, she had continued to hope that he would not be joining them. The idea of spending seven or eight weeks confined on this small ship with him made her feel crazy. Fear swept through her, filling her with the desperation of a caged animal.

"Ah, ha!" Fiona said. "Those other torches, then, must be from boats coming after him. The captain's going to get us out of here before they make it. Up comes the last ladder now."

One sailor growled to another, "That preacher's daft. He burned those fools' clothes and jewelry and destroyed part of the dock. Now the Harbor Authorities are after him. They won't catch us, by Jove. I've sailed with this captain before; he can cover water fast when he wants to."

Already they were skimming out to sea.

Suddenly Fiona burst out laughing. Basuba and Marion looked at her in surprise and at each other, and then began to laugh so hard they cried. Relief raced through their bodies as they threw overboard the feverish question that had been darting, unspoken, through each of their minds: "Are the torches coming for us?"

## *Chapter 9*

# God's Soldier

*God walks with me*
*And He talks with me.*
*I'll name you Sinner*
*If ever you be.*

Rising with dawn, as they were accustomed, the women explored the ship quickly. As they had expected, their personal space on the lower deck was confined to their pallets and to a spot for stowing the bags they would use at sea. Luckily, their pallets were fairly close to a porthole, not so near as to be able to look out, but close enough to watch the sunlight filter in on a clear day and, more importantly, to get some fresh air in rough weather when they would be confined below. Above deck there was a walk they could take around the circumference of the ship. They would spend as much time as they could outside, but they knew that the intense heat of the sun over a full day, its potency magnified by the sea's reflection, was more than they could bear for long stretches of time.

Fiona scanned the passengers. "There must be some handsome, strong men in this crowd," she said loudly. What fun it would be to flirt with some of them, to see how many would turn their heads when she walked by.

Marion stood at the stern, looking back at her homeland. "In just a few days, it will be Full Moon and I'll know exactly what Gwyneth is doing!" She looked at her hands and counted something out that turned her smile into a frown. "I figure we'll be on this ship well past Beltane, Basuba," she said dourly as she turned to her aunt.

"That seems about right, niece."

"So England is as far away from the New Land as Beltane is from Equinox."

"Yes, and to your thirteen years that must seem like a mighty long time."

"It does."

"Maybe it helps you to know that to my forty-six it seems like not much more than a blink and a nod. Come and find me before you let yourself get too lonely for what we're leaving. Promise?" Basuba continued on her way around the ship.

A cry from a sea gull close at hand brought Marion back from Ely to the present. She turned to her right to follow the sound and saw Preacher Denton standing at the railing a short ways from her. She startled and then frowned deeply. The *North Star* suddenly seemed much too small to endure for six or seven weeks. She left the stern immediately.

George Denton flexed his muscles by gripping the railing tightly in his hands and then releasing it. He sighed. He would be happy enough once he set foot in the New World again, but how he dreaded the long sea journey ahead. Yes, it was his duty to follow God's commandment to bring new recruits to conquer the wilderness for Christ, but he fervently hoped that this would be his last trip. He turned his ruddy face up to the vast sky.

"God, is this truly the work you have appointed me to do?"

Small spaces like this one made him feel so restless. Why, in two hundred paces he would be all the way around the deck; he might as well have one foot nailed to the floor for all the good that did him. His body, always rippling with energy, threatened to explode when it could not move. The agitation that tensed his limbs made him irritable, almost frightened. His breathing began to quicken and perspiration beaded his brow. He wiped the sweat off with the back of his hand. Oh, how he hated his father for giving him this terrible fear of enclosed places.

Denton wrinkled his nostrils to take in the sea scent, heavy with salt. He squinted his blue-green eyes hard to push his focus out as far as possible to the horizon, as if stretching his vision ahead of the ship could somehow hasten the journey. His thin dark hair, cropped short as per Puritan custom, offered no protection against the cold northwestern breeze that assaulted his face. He glanced up to the rigging, at his salvation. Yes, both Jesus, his spiritual savior, and the rigging he could climb, his physical savior while imprisoned on this ship, inhabited that realm. Thank the Lord he was young and quick.

A smile lit George's face as his thoughts moved back to last night. What a spectacle that had been! He'd first learned of ordering people to destroy their earthly goods from the stories of the exploits of a charismatic Puritan preacher two counties away. Daring to suggest that the wealthy gentry, most often from the rival Anglican church, burn their furniture and fancy baubles under his nose appealed to him at once. He couldn't believe that people would part with their treasures, any one of which could have financed him for more than two years. And yet, the possibility that he, unschooled, uncouth, and poorly dressed, could convince a person of means to do just that hung in front of his eyes like a gold nugget before a miner.

He could really move a crowd, of that there was no doubt. Even in his worst moments of self-condemnation, he knew that to be true. He was no longer amazed to learn the great distances from which his listeners came to hear him. And the hats passed at the close of each preaching session brought in more cash every month. Watching the faces of his audience, George knew that it took him less time than ever to capture their concentration. Why not try for the pyre, find out if he could speak well enough to outshine his worn clothes, his laborer's accent?

Once word was out about the Offering Up of Goods Unto The Lord, it spread fast. True, the vast majority of the crowd that had collected were poor people who had to see for themselves the rich giving up their goods. George had chosen the eve of the ship's embarkation, just in case the event was a failure. He had waited with mounting apprehension that last day, wondering what he would do to keep his audience with him if none of the wealthy appeared to take advantage of this opportunity to gain salvation.

In fact, there had been seven, widows and elderly merchants mostly, who responded. George had explained to the crowd, "When The Lord works through a servant like me to call His People away from sin, there will always be a few who hear His Voice. Sometimes, it is the most worthy who can hear Him; sometimes, the greatest sinner."

George had loved almost every minute of the spectacle: the excitement in the crowd fed by the age-old animosity between classes, the tension about the event that he could work the same way a master chef stirred a simmering pot, the thrill of wealthy folk submitting to his word, the pageantry of the fire itself, and the adventure of escaping the port authorities whom he had not asked for a permit. Everything had gone according to plan, though truly, there was not much of one because part of George's gift was his ability to craft so well in the moment.

It was only when he had stood with a flaming torch in his right hand and had prepared to gesture hugely with his left one that he had been thrown off course. Suddenly, looking down at the fine oak table, the silver tea set, the ruby-red necklace, the bearskin greatcoat and the rest that would soon be reduced to ashes moments after his sweeping right arm brought the fire to them, he had longed to stop it all. He, conceived from poverty and hard liquor, had never touched, never been so close to, even one of the treasures that now lay at his feet.

He barely kept himself from crying out. What he had wanted so badly was to bend down and swoop these valuables up in his arms, to hold close to him the security that wealth brought, a safety always denied him.

He had pulled his thoughts back to the waiting crowd, scanned their faces for a moment, and then, with great aplomb, poured thick, oily kerosene over the lavender silk gown that graced the top of the pile and plunged the torch into the pyre.

His shoulders twitched violently as he recalled that moment. In the clear light of day, he could see that it had been Satan once again, tempting him to disobey the Lord. Nothing else. And, after last night, surely God would never more doubt his loyalty? Never have to subject him to such an excruciating test again? George looked up at the sky, but saw nothing that he could take as a sign. He scanned the horizon for something he could count on.

Time passed and Denton's mind, used to darting here and there, was lulled by the relentless span of the waves before him. Before he realized it, the preacher's thoughts had made way for memories, and he saw in his mind's eye the narrow, lined face of Letticia, the barmaid who had taken him in when his mother left, drunk and distant, on the arm of a sailor. George's father, lost to liquor himself and furious with his son for looking so much like his traitorous mother, had locked the boy inside a shed. The lad had cowered in the farthest corner while his father cursed him roundly for "having the devil in you, just like your ma does." It was Letticia who had heard the child crying and wheedled the key out of the raging man by pouring him an extra glass of liquor.

Letticia had six children of her own and not much time or attention for George. But she had given him a place in the loft with a grain sack for a mattress and, when she saw that the little boy was willing to fetch and carry for her in the tavern, she was content to feed him at her table. She had become the constant in his life, a dull steady beacon. He could always stay with her, and she could rely on him to help out.

George suddenly realized that Letticia's image floated across his mind whenever he began a sea voyage. Yes, now that he focused on it, he could recall standing like this at the beginning of each ocean crossing, staring out to sea and finding her there in his mind.

Sharp as a knife, he caught himself, "But this is no good! I shall not indulge myself in memories of the old woman."

When he found God and took up His Way, he had had to leave behind everything that smacked of sin. Letticia knew only tavern life, and the one time George had broached the subject of her leaving her home to save her soul, he had found himself silenced by the bewilderment on her old face that quickly turned into stony recalcitrance. She could not hear him. For a brief moment, he had pictured himself on his knees, begging her to change her life so that he could still be a part of it. But the chance of rejection had kept him still and silent. He had left with the next dawn, knowing that he would never return. Nowadays, when thoughts of her arose, he assumed that Satan was back, playing with his mind again.

George fought the devil off by bringing his thoughts to the days to come. Turning his back to the rail, he scrutinized the deck. Just where would he stand to address the passengers, he wondered, looking for a natural pulpit amongst the bulwarks and the dinghies. And how many recruits would he make for Chapman settlement? Would there be any dissenters, Quakers or Seekers, perhaps, to roust out? What would the Lord call on him to speak about? Would he know any of the crew from earlier trips?

Suddenly, Denton found himself praying, "Lord, let this be my last sea crossing! Moses led his people through the desert of Sinai once. Crossing this huge ocean in this tiny wooden box is similar, God, to that desert. The smells, the vomit, the dysentery, the wretched water— it is more than I can stand. I have crossed this watery Sinai five times now. I am not Moses. Why do you ask so much of me?"

He stopped himself the instant he saw that his fist was in the sky. He quickly opened it into an imploring palm. Had God seen that fist? It hadn't really been a fist, just a hand he held in close from the cold, he told himself a few times.

Glancing furtively around, Denton wondered if he had been heard. There had been a roaring in his head, to be sure, but maybe he had not spoken aloud. No one close by, just a woman along the railing to his left, and the strong breeze blowing hard. His spoken words, if any, had most likely been broken apart by the wind.

What would he do once he reached New England? Recruitment had rescued him from previous work that he could not bear, but now it was time for something else. No more sea crossings. Some way to preach; he had to have that.

He eyed the rigging again. Soon as he'd found his sea legs, he'd be up there, crawling through those ropes, as far away from this little wooden matchbox as he could get. Bracing himself against the railing, he pumped his stomach and thigh muscles rhythmically, release and tighten, release and tighten.

The daily routine of life at sea established itself quickly, there being little opportunity for choices. Once arisen and out of their canvas-covered straw pallets for the day, the passengers lined up for a simple cooked grain or broth to break their fast. Then they could return to the hold, walk the deck, or sit on a bench outside. When evening came, another meal was served. Supper was usually a meally gruel and sometimes bread, cheese, peas, porridge, or biscuits. The sailors fished throughout the sea journey and sometimes set off for part of the day in a dinghy. They caught a variety of fish: whitings, gurnards, swordfish, dolphins, cod, haddock, and occasionally, shark, though that meat was too tough to be favored. On a lucky day, when the catch was sufficiently large, the steerage gruel was flavored with fish.

Of the eighty or so passengers on the *North Star*, about sixty belonged to a family as a parent, a child or a servant. Some families traveled singly, but most were parts of larger groups joined together by locale, kinship or religion. Some folks were landless peasants leaving the same village together in search of land in the New World; others, second sons of farming families whose plots had grown too small to subdivide once more. Of those leaving for spiritual reasons, Congregationalists wanted relief from the religious restrictions of Anglican rule; some were religious pilgrims who followed Denton to a life purer, more godly, than what they left in England; others were Anglicans who feared that the monarchy would soon fall; a few, Separatists and Seekers, wanted a place where they would be free to determine their own course of worship. And then some were rolling stones, constantly on the lookout for another opportunity. There were about ten men who were single or traveled without their families, intending to send for them later when they had earned the fare. These men had signed on as laborers, planters usually, with a land development company that financed settlements in the countryside. Most were poor men, others were adventurers; a few, debtors or outlaws. There were a small number of gentlemen who crossed the Atlantic for business reasons and a handful of traders who traveled for the same reason. Aside from Marion and her companions, there was only one other woman who traveled without a male companion.

People formed themselves into groups in only a few days' time. Many religious sect members stuck tightly together, placing their pallets side by side in the hold, eating, talking and walking only with each other. The laborers tended to be either solitaries or men who formed little clusters of two or three of their own kind, having little social means for interacting with families and no money for socializing with the traders who set themselves off from the others with their card-playing and drinking. The wealthy bunked separately and supped with the captain in a small dining room where they were served their meals. The remaining passengers, some from one village, a couple from a more northern village, one or two of the laborers, some of the Seekers, and Basuba, Marion and Fiona, let their curiosity guide them to speak with each other, eager for the opportunity to exchange information, stories, ideas and opinions.

Preacher Denton was also assessing the passengers, alert to potential converts and sensitive to obvious sinners that he could point out to his followers. Positioned in the prow of the ship where he could get a good look at the passengers as they emerged from the hold after a night's sleep, he rubbed his hands together in anticipation. This part of the sea crossings he did enjoy after all. God was bound to give him something to work with—a storm, a sweeping illness, some deaths, a surprise—something with which he could rally the onlookers to his side. It was always fun to pick out the players early and start building the suspense. It did not take him long to notice the women traveling without men, without a community to protect them.

The moon grew quickly into a fat, cool, white globe. On Full Moon night Marion led Fiona to her favorite spot in the stern, the place from which she had first looked back at England. It gave her everything she needed. She was facing East, looking back towards Gwyneth. The night was excellent; the sky, cloudless. The Moon blazed a path of sparkling moon beams that danced along the glassy surface of the ocean directly to her.

Fiona stood with her young friend for a while, entranced by the incredible beauty of the scene. She said, "Full Moon, back home, about half of the women will enter their Bleeding Time today or tonight. The others bleed on the New Moon. My bleeding started this afternoon."

"Mine too," said Marion shyly. "It would be grand if all the women on this ship had their Bleeding Time now. But I remember Rosemary saying that it doesn't happen so much for city women. It's only women who live close together who bleed at the same time."

Fiona wished Marion luck, gave her a hug, turned her back, and moved away a bit to provide better guard. It would not do for just anyone to know what Marion was up to.

Trembling with excitement, Marion sang her beloved lullaby. The fondest greeting she knew for the Moon.

"I see the Moon, the Moon sees me. The Moon sees the One I long to see. Nature bless the Moon and Nature bless me. Nature bless the One whom I long to see."

Ah, how well the words fit this night! She laughed when she realized it. Just where might Gwyneth be standing to gaze at her through the Full Moon? Maybe the grove where they had danced with the Sun King on Winter Solstice. The trees would be fully leafed by now; the nights, warm and languid.

Marion pulled out her First Blood pouch and fingered it gently. Yes, she could feel Nick's stone cross, the necklace that linked her to both her parents, and next to it the wooden figure from Mary. She sighed and held the pocket close to her heart for a moment. Then she stretched her arms up to the sky and sang all the songs she could recall that had "moon" and "night" in them. The whole while she sang, she held her arms up in an arc. After about ten minutes, her shoulder muscles screamed for relief. Marion responded by singing more loudly. She sang right through the pain in her arms, and when it lifted she saw that the moon beams had danced themselves into a staircase that led right up to the Moon. She knew she must imagine that she could climb it.

Making her assent with her heart full of prayers, Marion was soon aware of a soft, gentle voice wafting down to her from above. She looked up quickly and there was Gwyneth seated at the top of the staircase with her arms around her knees. Marion rushed up the steps to her. Soon, they were laughing and hugging. They did not talk; instead, they just were together.

The clanging of the ship's bell, signaling a change in shifts for the crew, bellowed its way into Marion's consciousness. She felt her attention shift in spite of her desire to keep the link with Gwyneth. Suddenly the moonscape disintegrated, and she was standing firmly on the ship. She herded her mind back to the trance-like state from which she had first drawn down the Moon and strained to imagine the staircase again. It was harder this time, the light beams more ephemeral. She did her best to sense the steps beneath her, tried to hasten up the stairway, but, alas, she felt heavy and elongated, and most of her remained solidly on the deck.

She looked up to the top of the golden radiance. Gwyneth was still there, but ghostly and distant. Fie! The bell had bothered Marion's concentration more than she would have guessed. Marion reached out her arms as far as she could, hoping she and Gwyneth could somehow infuse each other with more substance.

Fiona's voice cut sharply into her daydream. "Marion, stop singing! Someone's coming. Drop your arms!"

Marion quickly said goodbye to Gwyneth and released the vague image of the staircase so that she could put her arms down. It was grating to rush so. She worried that she had better not thank the golden orb out loud. She rubbed her arms hard; how they ached from being held aloft for so long. She stood gazing at the Moon, silently separating from It and collecting her thoughts.

Fiona came to stand beside her. When she saw how upset Marion was, she decided not to mention that the passerby was the preacher and that he had most certainly caught sight of what she was up to.

## Chapter 10

# Days at Sea

*Dear little ship on these high seas,*
*Our cradle be.*
*May the Mother rock us gently*
*'Til we're home free.*

By the third day at sea, most passengers who had a craft were occupied with it. Some carved and whittled wood or bone or sharks' vertebrae, others spun wool with a hand spindle or knitted, some tinkered and puttered, others stitched and sewed, a few read or wrote. Children either worked alongside an adult or played together if their parents permitted.

Marion busied herself with writing. Two forces drove her to it. First, she was curious, and a little fearful, about how she would do on her own. What would it be like without Nick's guidance, without him to check over each page for spelling and grammar? Would anyone choose to be her customer? Would she have thoughts of her own worthy enough to set down on the precious paper? Second, she wanted to forget about how the Moon was making her feel. With Full Moon over, every night meant that another piece of the globe was gone. Somehow she could not help thinking that she was losing a part of her past with each piece that disappeared.

Her spirits perked up when one of the friendlier passengers stopped as she was strolling the deck and asked, "Mistress Carryer, I see you here now with your papers and your inkwell as I did yesterday. Are you a scribe, then? Would you take a letter to my sister in Norwich? I promised I'd send her my first impressions of the trip."

"Yes, certainly, Mistress Lock." And with that, Marion put her pen immediately to the paper as though she had never known a moment's doubt. She glanced at the sky and thought "Take that, you Fading Moon. In spite of You, here is a Beginning!"

Accustomed to long days of physical labor in the fields at home, Fiona could not find patience for fine craft work. She walked the deck around and around. Sometimes she pulled out her drop spindle, twining wool into yarn as she went, but neither that nor her beading held her attention for long. She wandered the ship looking for something to occupy her time.

Basuba's intention was to organize and then record the remedies that had proved most useful over the years for tending the sick. She would hold an herb in her hands, gaze at it while she recalled the occasions on which she had used it, and select what Marion was to record.

"...And inflammations of the eye and dimness of sight you can always treat with clary sage. Looks like other clary but lesser, with many stalks about a foot and a half high. Stalks are square and hairy. Flowers a blush color. Make a distilled water of clary for redness, wateriness and heat. One seed, placed directly in the eye until it drops out, will cure dimness. Coats the eye and cleanses it of all filth and purified matter."

The healer marveled at how the odd lines and circles inscribed on the paper enabled Marion to repeat word for word a remedy that she had given her three days earlier.

Marion was not the only reader on the *North Star* who worked for a fee. The woman who traveled by herself soon set up a makeshift shop near the stern with a pot of tea and some cups for her tools. Madame Dora read tea leaves. By far the most colorful figure on board, she was easy to spot, and Fiona had quickly guessed her trade.

"She is a woman you cannot take your eyes off. I fancy that she's revealed many folks' futures to them. And to think of all the secrets she must know," Fiona exclaimed to Marion. "Perhaps she'd teach me how to do that, too."

Soon the Maiden followed her curiosity close enough to the tea table to be beckoned over by Dora's curling index finger. "Yes, yes. You are right if you are wondering whether I can tell your fortune, my dear. Mistress Carryer, is it not? The friend of that comely Irish woman. I'm Irish too, with a bit of Gypsy blood. Come right over. Don't be shy," she called out in a voice that had boomed many times across a crowded marketplace to attract a customer, even though it sounded far too large for her petite size.

Marion drew nearer and looked into a face that had been painted as carefully as any gold-edged plate that ever graced King Charles I's dining table. Two piercing blue eyes covered with heavy hoods were fixed on her. The Madame motioned rapidly for Marion to sit down, but she was not ready to become a client yet, so she remained standing.

Catching her eye, Dora deftly swirled a green mixture around in the bottom of a waiting teacup and then quickly turned the cup on its side to let the water drain out, "There, my sweet, now we'll see some figures."

They both peered into the cup, and Dora pointed to various patches of leaves, saying, "Ah, ha! Something here about wishes. Very big wishes. Over here, a person, a man possibly." She studied Marion's face briefly for any reaction. "These leaves that point to the cup's handle speak to me about money."

She turned the cup upside down and looked up at Marion. "If that had been your cup, your leaves, young lady, what a future I could have told you. For a mere tuppence, I will look into yours now. Sit." She finished her statement forcefully and made a sweeping gesture with her hand that was almost enough in itself to draw Marion down into the seat.

"Much obliged, Ma'am. But no, thank you. I'm just passing by."

"Pass by then this morning, dear. But you will find yourself thinking about me and the tea leaves. I'll see you back here before long. Mark my words. I am never wrong." As Marion smiled and left, Madame Dora added, "Tell your friends about me. Perhaps one of them will be brave enough to come first and then you will follow after."

"I am not afraid, Mistress. I am just not ready today."

"That's fine, dear. You'll be back soon enough."

Marion completed her stroll around the deck and sat down beside Basuba again. For some reason she didn't understand, she decided not to mention her encounter with Dora. Instead, she took out of her pocket the coins she had collected from writing two letters for the Locks and counted them one more time.

Fiona looked forward to each dawn. There was something about that sun, so proud and glorious, that drew her to it. She loved to watch it cut its great path across the sky; she admired how it vanquished every shadow.

Early one morning, just after her prayers, she was studying the sky. How much of what she knew about predicting weather conditions back in Blue Fens would hold true in the midst of this vast ocean?

"High clouds at dawn. That'll bring us high winds today, Mistress," said a voice in a style of English she had never heard before.

She turned to face the speaker, the first foreigner she had met. He stood the same height as she, his hair black and tightly curled, his face a wide oval with a thick scar line running from his right ear down across his jaw, his skin a warm brown as though he were especially beloved by the sun. His linen shirt checked blue and white marked him as a sailor.

"Could be rough seas, then?" Fiona asked with interest.

"Yes, these two or three days after the moon's full, they're days a sailor must watch. Rough seas or, if we're blessed, swift passage. We've been making good time."

"It's been such an easy sail so far, I guess I'm ready for some excitement," said Fiona gaily.

"You are, Mistress? Now a sailor doesn't often hear a fair maid like yourself say that. A young man who's got a lot of buck in him, yes. But not many women. Still, I've seen you out here each dawn. Easy to tell you like weather."

"I do. I'm a field worker. Weather is my second mother."

"Then you have a mother with a temper. You should see how angry this ocean gets some days."

Fiona laughed with the sailor whose name was Jean-Paul.

She met each dawn, and he always came by, a rope or a bucket in his hand, and stopped to chat. He told her many things about the *North Star* and the voyages she had made. One morning he brought his small hand accordion to show her.

"The captain doesn't like us sailors to mix with the passengers much, so we usually keep our music to ourselves," he explained. Then he looked into her eyes for a time. "Some night, I'd like to play this for you."

"I'll be there," she said with a grin as Jean-Paul returned to his task of tightening a rope.

As soon as he had gone, her head swam with thoughts of Matthew. Fiona shook them away and turned her attention to the sails.

She eyed the giant canvas wings, wondering about joining in on the repair of them—anything that would give her something new to do with her hands. Both the gentle, repetitive rhythm of working the spindle and the tiny movements required for beading were so tedious. Wrapping her hands around some heavy canvas and pushing hard to get a needle through to mend a hole so that a sail was fit again— that sounded like a wedding of work and pleasure.

Alone once more, the country maid scanned the skies for any sign of the high winds that Jean-Paul expected. These skies were so distinct from her own; she was only beginning to recognize patterns. As her eyes moved through the rigging, she was startled to see the creature way above her head who was dressed in black instead of the usual wide red baggy breeches of the crew. Gawky, with limbs splayed, he clung to the spiderweb of ropes that ran from mast to mast. "A spider! That's just what he looks like, perched there, waiting to spring. The preacher, that's who it is. Why he has no more right to be crawling through that rigging than I do. And I could move faster," she thought scornfully.

In the same way that Fiona was attracted to the dawn, Marion found herself called to mark the Moon's journey through the night sky. Never had she seen such a vast expanse of sky; thus, never had she appreciated the crossing that awaited the Moon each evening. It was enormous. But for her, the time was one of sorrow. While Fiona's prayers were full of thanksgiving for the beginning of another day, Marion's were pleas that she not break apart over missing Gwyneth and Nick and all that was familiar.

During the day, Marion did her best to keep her spirits up, both for her sake and Basuba's, and because she feared that Fiona might pounce on any weakness she perceived in her. But the nights, they were hard. Another part of her heart wore away each night from missing Gwyneth and Nick and all the rest. The Waning Moon seemed to shout out that leaving England was a huge mistake. Some nights she tried not to go out to look for the moonrise, thinking that she would be happier if she ignored it. But something in her demanded that she witness it.

Each night the Moon rose later, and eventually Marion was having to wake from her pallet after a few hours' sleep to slip out to the deck to watch it. Grateful for her grandfather's teachings of not fearing the dark, she moved carefully, not wanting to speak with anyone. Often, she saw the silhouettes of the sailors who worked the night shift. Sometimes she heard them call to each other.

Fiona joined Marion and Basuba on a bench in the stern one hot morning. They had tucked themselves into a shadow, desperate for protection from the sun. Fiona sat down abruptly, knocking against Marion's elbow. A big blob of ink oozed out from the scribe's nib.

"Fiona, careful when you sit down, please. I'll have to start over now and the price of paper's so steep."

"Sorry. I'm not used to being near such dainty work," she replied with a trace of heat in her voice. "And I suppose you're saving your pennies for one of Madame Dora's tea leaf readings, eh?"

Marion blushed and fumbled with getting a new piece of paper from her packet. Basuba brought her gaze in from the ocean and looked closely at her two companions. "Have either of you had a reading?"

Silence.

Then Fiona said quickly, "Yes, I have. She knew everything about me—that I come from a small village, that I have four brothers, that my grandmother is very dear to me. She told me a bundle of things about my future. Said there was a man on board this ship for me, and I met him the very next morning. A French sailor, he is. And other important things, too."

"Did she say, perhaps, that you'll be coming into some money before long?" asked Basuba, trying to make her voice sound casual.

"So what if she did?" Fiona's voice grew defensive. "It does happen, you know."

"Yes, indeed it does. The saying of it also brings many customers hurrying back soon for another reading. Does Madame Dora ask you what something might mean in your life, or does she tell you what she sees?"

"She tells me precisely what is in my future, of course. Why shouldn't she since I am paying her?"

"But who knows how to read the signs of what is coming into your life better than you?"

"She does, of course. She has special powers that let her see things that I could not see. She told me stories about what has come to pass for other people she's read for. She is very talented."

"I see," said Basuba simply. "And you, Mari?"

"I may have a reading. It's just hard to spend my first earnings so fast," she replied cautiously. Then her voice picked up some momentum. "But, perhaps, she'll be able to tell us where we'll be living, Basuba. That would be so helpful. We wouldn't need to waste time looking around. We could just go there immediately."

Basuba coughed and said, "I'd much prefer to read the signs around me and make my own choices. Doing that keeps me sharp and alive to my life. It makes my life my own."

"Maybe you're jealous, Basuba. I've never heard you read people the way the Madame can. That means she knows more than you, that she's more powerful," Fiona needled.

"Jealous? I was jealous of such a gift when I was twenty. I believed then that to have it signaled that a person was favored by the Spirits. Now I understand that we each have different gifts. Gifts that cannot be stacked one against the other and weighed. Gifts that most likely match the lessons we each have come to this life to learn." She looked at Fiona and continued, "It is not the gift that matters, but how it is used. Our Willow Sister, Elinor, has the same gift of Sight as Madame. She does not use it to build a throne for herself."

"You mean you would be willing to go without knowing what Madame Dora can tell about your future? Why throw away a chance like that?" asked Fiona fiercely.

"It's simple for me. I believe that we help each other with advice and love. We can offer our reading of the signs for someone else. But to give our opinion as the absolute truth? No. We are each different—each another dream of Mother Nature. Only the Wise One inside each of us, who works in unity with our Creator, can truly guide us through this life."

"Well, just think of where you might be now if you had listened to someone like Madame Dora." Fiona felt hot all over.

"I do think about it," said Basuba as she reached for another bundle of herbs. "Did you find this plant around Blue Fens, Fiona? Maybe you've never seen it dried?" She gingerly unfolded some desiccated leaves to resurrect the herb's original look, and then handed it to the field worker.


Basuba had seen the dark circles growing under Marion's eyes and had noticed how her sadness was increasing with them. That night Basuba sat up when Marion awoke to go out to the Moon. Without a word, she reached for her young companion and pulled her down to sit next to her. Then Basuba pointed to the Moon through the small porthole that was near them. Arms around Marion, Basuba rocked her like she was a small child until, comforted and exhausted, the Maiden fell asleep.

The next morning as they supped their barley gruel, Basuba said only this to her niece: "Water is the element of the emotions. Here on this ship, we are surrounded by days and nights of water, miles and miles of water. No wonder that emotions should run high. The Moon pulls the tides in and out. Just as water responds to the Moon, so do emotions. They ride high, then low."

The three women chatted with other travelers, exchanging stories of what moved folks to leave England and gathering hearsay about the communities in the Boston area. One couple whom they all liked was Barbara and Peter Turner. The Turners were Seekers. Marion had learned something of Seeker practices during her apprenticeship with Nick Adams. These folk were often in one kind of trouble or another, and missals condemning and applauding their actions flew back and forth furiously. Barbara and Peter Turner were the first Seekers that Fiona had met.

When people asked Peter why he was going to the New Land, he would reply, "Got tired of doffing my hat to the nobility, and tired of going to the stocks for not doffing it. So, we're off." His story would usually bring a chuckle, folks bobbing their heads in agreement.

Marion began to notice a certain pattern in Fiona's strolling of the deck. It seemed that her restless friend never stopped to chat when any kind of book or writing material was in sight.

"If I ever want to get rid of her, I only have to reach for my pen," thought the scribe wryly, but it hurt her. Reading and writing were her ticket to independence; tools she had worked hard to get. And now she was learning something that Nick had never spoken to her about—recording her own thoughts. Noticing how they changed from day to day—deepening here, turning there, questioning now, flights into fantasy and the future, plunges into fear and worry—was teaching her who she was with an intensity she had not guessed possible. How odd that the very thing that was bringing her home to herself should be building a wall between her and Fiona.

Once when the two of them were talking, Marion dove into the hornet's nest and asked, "Do you expect that you will wish to let your family know where you've settled once we find a home?"

"I suppose. They would like to know that I am safe and happy."

"And won't you want to know how they are?"

"Yes," replied Fiona in a guarded tone. She had wind of where this conversation was taking her.

"And you liked Matthew Fields well enough to want to know that he is married, with lots of children and making a good living…"

"I hate this, Marion. What are you trying to lead me into?"

"All right. I'll just say it. I know you care about your family; you talk about them almost every day. Why won't you send them letters? I don't understand it. You know that I could write them for you."

Fiona's reply came quick and hard.

"I'll not have any part of something that the rulers—the kings, the judges, the church—use to shape people's stories to fit their own needs. Don't you see that whatever is written down is believed over what other folks say? It forces the broad cloth of stories and ballads and lore into the eye of a needle through which only one thread is drawn out. Their thread."

Fiona looked out to sea, her face as hard as the glassy waves she watched. She turned back to face Marion directly. "Are you blind? Or maybe you're just too young to understand? There is a book that tells witch hunters how to clear a village of all its women. There is a book that says that only those who follow Christ are Holy. That is what your wonderful writing and reading does for the likes of us."

Marion, her mouth hanging open, looked at Fiona in shock, got to her feet, and ran to the other side of the ship. She had never left her precious writing supplies behind before, but this time she could not bear to take them with her.

"Thank Nature, I'm not missing Matthew Fields enough to ever be even tempted to send him a letter," thought Fiona to herself. She looked up at the sails and imagined herself darting up the rigging to adjust them here and there.

By this, the middle of the second week of the voyage, the two Willow Women and Fiona, the Turners and a few others had fallen into the habit of gathering on deck to watch the sun set. Knowing it could be hard to find the time for this treat once they were again on dry land, they savored sitting long enough to watch the entire western sky move from day to evening.

As they sat together, they talked sometimes and were silent other times. Often the beauty of the scene before them was so intense that their words fell away without anyone noticing. Other times, a conversation might be picked up after a few moments, then dropped again. One enduring conversation was the state of the food they were served.

"Fie on this horrid food we are fed. My stomach does not take to it well."

"Most of it's too old and overly salted. Especially the meat," observed Basuba. "I give one person a remedy for constipation and his neighbor, something for dysentery. I'm treating headaches, bleeding gums, and boils because of the food and the water. In an odd way, I'm grateful that many people on this ship will not come to me for help, for I would not have enough to meet all their needs."

Another subject they dug into often was religion. Perhaps it was knowing that they were all free thinkers of one sort or another in this small group, or perhaps it was the realization that their paths would most likely separate once they docked, that allowed them to be as bold as they were.

Fiona was one of the most brazen. One evening she said with passion, "I must know about the Christian god. All Christians speak as though he were one god, but to my mind, he takes on a different character with each sect. There is the god who has people killed for not following him only. Then, the god of the people I met who wanted to stop enclosures seems a strict one with lots of rules and little laughter, but he didn't smell of blood. And then there is your god, Barbara and Peter, who fills your eyes with love when you talk about him. But you don't give your allegiance to his son, Christ. And yet, this god stays with you and is not angry, or so it seems."

Peter Turner put his head back and laughed. "Fiona, you amaze me. I've sat through many an endless discussion over theology during my Oxford days, but never have I ever heard it put like this. Your words pull the scales from my eyes. But, how to answer you?"

Barbara asked, "And did you not grow up a Christian yourself?"

"No," responded Fiona. "I am a Pagan. We see Spirits in everything. My granny calls on St. Bridget and Jesus and the Great Mother. She calls on other Holy Ones, too, when she wants a favor or needs help. She called on Jesus whenever a child was in trouble, so I always thought of him as a child." Fiona looked away, caught by surprise in the clutches of an unexpected memory. "How I cried the first time I saw that twisted body hanging from a cross and someone told me 'There is Jesus.' I'd always fancied Jesus as a happy boy playing in the woods like we did."

"Fiona, I have never attempted to answer the question you put to us before, but I will do my best. Peter, add on as I go, if you like," said Barbara Turner. "All Christian churches understand God to be a personal god who reigns in Heaven. He is all-powerful. There are no other gods. Our one God speaks to people through the Bible, through His son, through the Pope, or through ministers, or through us all. This is where the separation of the different churches comes in. Some believe that He has said all He will say in the Bible. Others say that He still speaks today, but only the learned and the powerful may address Him directly. Others believe that He still talks to us through the most ordinary of hearts and will always do so.

"Some people see Him as a fierce warrior who demands strict obedience, others as a kind teacher who lets us, His children, make our own choices. Some believe that He has laid out a plan for each of us before we are born. Some believe that only certain people will be saved; the rest of us are sure that we will all be with Him in Paradise. There, that's as big an answer as I can give right now."

"And why do some Christians hate us Pagans so?" asked Marion wistfully.

Barbara Turner looked at the young woman and bit her lip for a minute.

Then she said, "I think those who hate you must be the ones who believe that God and Christ are harsh, jealous masters who hold all that is holy in their own hands. When you Pagans insist that you find holiness, not evil, inside yourselves, those Christians believe that you blaspheme the only God there is."

"So that is what it is," said Marion slowly, as though she were sorting through her thoughts carefully.

Just as the last rays of the sun receded from the sky, Peter Turner told of his own belief that God's Light shines within each person.

"Good place to end," said Basuba. "It brings us back full circle to where we all have the most in common, I dare say."

*Chapter 11*

# Labor
# and Birthing

*Baby's coming from Spiritland*
*Into my waiting arms.*
*Her ears hear angels' voices,*
*Her eyes still see their charms.*

Biddy Jacobs, a very pregnant woman from one of the groups that Preacher Denton had recruited, walked slowly, heavily, on the arm of a young man past Basuba. He was stiff and awkward, not knowing how to hold her in a way that was helpful.

The herbalist found her eyes following the mother-to-be, naturally deciphering the roll of Biddy Jacobs' body, sensing the readiness of the child within to be born.

"No. Mind, you must return to me," muttered Basuba to herself. "This is no business of mine. My work is to concentrate instead on the remedies I'm ready to record."

Then, when her mind refused to obey, she spoke against it again. "Help me, Mother. Here I am already thinking of it as 'my problem.' That woman was with child long before she boarded this ship. She must have someone ready to help her with the birth."

Still, Basuba could not keep the situation out of her thoughts. "The baby's dropped. That's clear. Who will be there with her to bring it in? Surely not the oldest woman in that group. She's the one most likely to have seen many babes come in. But her stiff body, the scowl firmly lined into her face, the balled-up hands that never move from her sides—no, the touch, the sight of her could be enough to send a little one clambering back into the womb. Perhaps Biddy Allen? She'd be able to keep her wits about her anyway, and talk straight to Biddy Jacobs, but would her hands know the route? Could she stay on her knees for a long stretch? Aren't her clothes too fine?"

Basuba tried to ignore the urge in her hands to move across that wide belly, to learn the map of just how that baby lay, to then relax or to begin to imagine what course, what turns, they would need to make to guide the child out. She forced her eyes not to slip into a soft focus when Biddy Jacobs walked by, the soft focus that would let her glimpse the colors in the woman's aura, to read how fearful or how serene she was.

In spite of herself, Basuba began to sort through her satchel of herbs and set aside certain bundles. Marion watched her and then said, "Hollyhocks, betony, mugwort, marjoram. Let me see if I can remember…If you add chamomile, I'd say you're making up a bath for a woman who's ready to go into labor. Am I right? But I'm forgetting one or two more ingredients."

"Here they are—mint and parsley. Good memory, for we must have recorded that one at least two weeks ago. No spiderweb in here for stanching blood, though. That was too hard to bring along." She pulled her eyes away from the satchel and said briskly, "Don't know that I'll need them, Mari, but keep your eyes open for webs. Fresh ones that still hold their stick."

Marion teased, "There must be a baby on the way."

A few hours later, Biddy Allen hurried over to speak to Basuba.

The women knew each other by name because Biddy Allen and Biddy Jacobs were the two members of their group who were willing to chat with the other passengers. Once when a breathless Biddy Jacobs had walked by on her friend's arm a few days' past, Basuba had invited them to join her on the bench and rest a spell.

With Basuba's goods spread out around her that day, the talk had naturally turned to herbs, poultices, ointments, and other remedies.

As they were rising to leave, Biddy Allen had asked quickly in a hushed voice, "Do you have remedies for childbirth, Biddy Hutchinson?"

Her pregnant friend had blushed scarlet, looking off to the side.

"I do indeed," Basuba had replied.

This time Biddy Allen's voice was full of urgency. "Biddy Jacobs' time has come. As the women talk, I hear no one who is well prepared to help her. The woman who has the most experience with birthing is frightened. Her hands move so roughly over Biddy Allen's belly I can see that she does not like to touch people. I know it is God's Will that rules these matters, but I'd prefer it if one of us was ready to help on this side." She paused. "My folk, our preacher, would not approve of my saying this, Biddy Hutchinson, but I wish you could help us. I guess that you have helped many babes into this world."

Basuba looked at her hands for a moment. They had started to hum, as she called it, the moment Biddy Allen began speaking. Yes, her hands were clearly ready to jump in. But, they did not have permission from her mind.

Then she looked at Biddy Allen. "Yes, I am a midwife." She went on gently, "Many babes don't need much help coming in—just loving arms to receive them. We can pray that be the case for Biddy Jacobs."

"Yes, we can pray for that," said Biddy Allen impatiently, almost bitterly. "And that is all my folk are willing to do. But, if it is not an easy birth…What then?" She paused and then spoke again forcefully. "If I were to step in for this birth, is there a way you could guide me? Help me prepare now. And then, if I send little Anne with messages later, would you tell me what you think is best?"

"I must tell you that I am not Christian, Biddy Allen," said Basuba evenly.

Biddy Allen paled and took a step backwards. Her eyes fell to the ground. Silence. Then, "But-but you said you'd pray for her." She twisted her hands together into a knot. "To whom do you pray?"

"For births, I call on Mother Mary and Nature Herself."

"I see," said Biddy Allen slowly. More silence. Then she straightened her shoulders, looked Basuba right in the face, and stepped forward again. "I don't think who we pray to is the most important matter right now. Your experience as a midwife is what counts in my mind."

"Your companions may disagree. The consequences for you could be harsh," Basuba pointed out. She looked out at the sky and collected her thoughts.

When she faced Biddy Allen again, the woman was still standing there, as steadfast as before. Basuba shrugged and said, smiling, "Seeing as how we ride this ship together, I will never be far away from you. Let's talk a while now. I'll tell you the story of how the birth is likely to go so you'll know what to expect. And yes, send little Anne out to me if need be. Meanwhile, my friends and I will ask for the Lady's help with this one."

Biddy Allen glanced quickly around to see who might have their eyes on her and then sat down next to Basuba.

"You must get your friend a pallet by the wall and then cordon off the space as best you can with some sheets and rope so she'll have a bit of privacy. You'll make her a bath out of these as soon as I blend them," Basuba said, indicating the herbs she had put aside. "Then, when her contractions are close and regular, send someone to the cook for hot water."

"You'll help us then. Thank the Lord! Tell me everything I need to know."

In this odd fashion, Basuba guided the birthing of a child that she did not witness in person. Never before had she worked this way, nor was it something she would willingly do again.

When the contractions began, the midwife stationed herself on a bench just outside the entrance to the hold that was closest to Biddy Jacobs' pallet. She sent Marion to fetch Fiona so the three could pray together to ask for blessings on the birth. When her friends were settled in beside her, Basuba brought out from her Healing Pocket the amulet she always wore when she attended a birth. It was a soft purse of lamb's wool that held a lock of hair from each babe she had brought in. As she did every time, Basuba now opened the purse and slid in some dried cinquefoil leaves. Cinquefoil, the five-fingered grass, was ever a friend to a woman's uterus. And, with its five fingers cupped like a hand that could turn a babe caught in a bind with the birth cord wrapped 'round its neck, a true friend to the midwife.

She held up to the heavens the purse and a sprig of cinquefoil she would send in with little Anne to tuck under Biddy Jacobs' pillow and prayed, "Blessed Cinquefoil, may your five fingers serve as the five fingers of my old healer's hands. May this baby swim out to us easily with your help."

Marion added, "Nature, may Women's Wisdom of the centuries be visited upon Biddies Jacobs and Allen." And Fiona asked, "Cinquefoil, Gift from Nature for us today, protect the two women and baby from the fears and doubts of others attending the birth, others riding this ship."

During the next couple of hours, Biddy Jacobs' husband—the nervous young man Basuba had spotted the day before—paced the deck in front of them. As the sounds of his wife's labor intensified, he covered his ears with his hands. A few minutes later, he moved as far away from the hold as possible.

"I'm glad he's gone," muttered Basuba. "We need to send something to ease her pain, and I sense that he does not want to know that we are involved." She reached into her satchel for a particular herb bundle, untied it, and gingerly handed a few sprigs to Marion, saying, "Take this vervain in."

A frightened Anne appeared in front of her. "Oh, Mistress, it's horrible. Biddy Jacobs is screaming like she's fit to die. Only Biddy Allen and I are left in there to help her."

Basuba handed the girl the vervain sprigs and gently wrapped her hand around them. "Anne, it's going to be all right. Make a tea of these leaves and flowers for Biddy Jacobs. It'll ease her spasms."

Anne nodded and dashed back inside. In the twenty minutes it took for the plant to ease her, four or five women who had been helping with the birth came out of the hold. Two held their hands over their ears.

The oldest woman stopped in front of Basuba and frowned. "This pain is God's Curse on Eve. You'd better not be interfering with anything, you country scold, or you'll surely feel His Wrath on you." She turned on her heel and left.

Marion shivered and looked at Basuba, fear shriveling her face.

Basuba nodded in response. "Yes, Precious One, some folks believe that a woman must bear all the pain of childbirth without any soothing from our plant friends."

"Why, Basuba? Why would anyone want that?"

"It has to do with their ancient story of Eve eating an apple that god had forbidden her."

Biddy Jacobs' pain subsided, and after a while her cries were replaced by the squalling of a newborn. Anne rushed out at once, crying, "Mistress, the babe is gray, not pink."

Basuba calmed her and sent her back to watch for a rosy hue to creep across the girl-child. A triumphant Anne returned before long.

"Oh, if only you could see her. She's so beautiful."

Basuba smiled at the maiden's jubilation. "I'll catch a glimpse of her before long. Soon as her mother brings her out on the deck. Remind Biddy Allen she's not to rest yet. There's still the afterbirth to bring through."

And there was work indeed remaining for Biddy Allen. The afterbirth came out in a gush of blood that seemed to have no end.

Anne ran again to Basuba, who asked, "The blood, is it red and coming fast, or darker, more sluggish?" She had both yarrow and shepherd's purse ready at her side. At Anne's answer, Basuba reached for the yarrow.

"Here, Child, take these stalks and webs in to staunch the bleeding. Biddy Allen can pack these firmly into Biddy Jacobs' uterus. Keep the babe at her mother's breast so the heartbeat'll steady her."

Anne hastened to leave. Basuba, noticing her frightened body, added, "And, Child, calm yourself. You are proving yourself a friend, indeed, today. You're part of a miracle."

Turning to Marion, Basuba ordered, "More spiderwebs. Get Fiona, and both of you scour the decks for them. Come back when you have two big handfuls."

Alone on the bench, Basuba closed her eyes and leaned her head back against the hold. To the passerby, she looked like she was napping. But behind her eyelids everything was action. She pictured her hands first feeling for the ruptures in Biddy Jacobs' womb, next placing the yarrow gently over them, then packing the leaves in place with the sticky webs. Emanating a beam of love from her heart, she sent her deep knowing into the hold, praying that it guide Biddy Allen's thoughts and hands. Turning her attention to Biddy Jacobs, she offered this prayer: "Dear Woman, I send you yarrow, spider's weavings, and love for the Wounded Warrior. May they assist you in this time of bleeding. Blessed be!"

Two days passed before Biddy Allen came, empty handed, to Basuba. She blushed bright red and said shamefully, "I daren't bring the baby for you to see, Biddy Hutchinson. Many folks are angry with me. The preacher says the bleeding was God's rage that we'd consorted with someone who's not a Christian and that we eased Mary's pain. Some folk listen to him. A few whisper to me that Biddy Jacobs' is still with us because you sent in the yarrow and told me what to do."

The hard part of her story told, the young woman finally relaxed. "You can keep a secret, Biddy Hutchinson? Mary Jacobs and I have given the babe the middle name of Basuba. For your help. What a sadness that we can't tell the others about it."

"I'm honored," said Basuba, smiling to think how many little girls bore her name as part of theirs. "The father, does he share in this secret?"

Biddy Allen looked troubled. "No, not yet. He was so scared when Mary was gushing blood he would have agreed to anything then. But he's confused now."

"It's hard for you and Mary, then."

"There are some not speaking to me. I think that until Mary is strong again she'll not feel the heat of their anger."

Basuba said quietly, "I'll continue to pray for your protection. But it is better for you that you not be seen talking to me again. Farewell, Biddy."

The third week on the *North Star* began with the rough seas that Fiona had been half-waiting for. All afternoon the velocity of the winds mounted, and the little vessel heaved back and forth like a pig on sotted hops.

The passengers stayed below for fear of the pounding winds that brought heavy biting rain with them. Before long, many people were sick to their stomachs, and the stench in the battened-down hold brought others to their knees to retch. Basuba was dispensing rolls of peppermint and sugar and a pinch of conserve of wormwood to the nauseous. The miserable, long day was matched by an equally miserable and long night.

Fiona had thrilled to the furor of the storm, but her stomach was grateful for the return to calm that came with daybreak. The sun was rising, giving birth to a day of blue skies, when she came out on the deck, grateful for the crisp air.

There, in his preacher's attire, straightening his collar, was Denton. Fiona turned her back and moved away. A short while later, the minister started preaching, and the curious woman looked around to see a trail of pasty-faced people stumbling and half-crawling out of the hold to get some fresh air and to find a way to clean themselves up a bit. In spite of herself, she listened in.

Making the most of their weakness, Preacher Denton poised himself near the hatch and pounced. As he surveyed the group, he was very pleased to spot Fiona standing off to the side. Perfect! God was delivering her right up to him.

"Every day, I go up into the skies, climbing my way up into those riggings, to be closer to Him, to talk to the Lord. I ask him how His people on the *North Star* are doing, and He tells me. He tells me, 'George, a few of my people are doing all right, some of them are just barely making it, and most of them are walking the road to hell. Yes, even as they ride this ship straight across the ocean, they are, most of these people, actually descending to hell.' And I said, 'Lord, Lord, how can we warn these people so they can save themselves before it's too late? What can we do, Lord?'

"Yes, I asked My Father this question, for I have seen troubling signs on our fair ship. The painted harlot who earns her fortune in coins, pretending to read other people's fortunes, as though she could see what only God can know. That red-headed woman over there, that one with a yellow silk ribbon in her loose hair, reeking with vanity and lust." Denton pointed Fiona out to whoever was willing to look. "The men who drink ale and gamble, another. The wicked, lame midwife who interferes in God's birthing of babies, daring to quiet the pain of childbirth which is the Cross that You have given to women to bear…Godless heathens, all of them. Oh, yes, signs a-plenty of sin on this ship.

"That's what I was doing, asking God what He had in mind. And I told Him what I hear some of you say: 'What an easy journey we're having. God must be on our side.' And I said, 'God, your people take your name in vain. They sin. Oh, how they sin. And still they blind themselves to it. You better do something to set them right, Lord,' I said.

"'George, my son,' He answered, 'I will do something. I will send them some weather that will stop their blaspheming. I will send them some weather that will let them know I am familiar with their sins. Some weather that will remind them that I can and do look inside each one of their souls.' And, folks, you know what weather He sent. And you sinners, you know in your heart who you are, and you know that dreadful, dreadful storm was sent to our ship because of you. Yes, we all suffered because of you and your sins."

Here, Denton hesitated for the tiniest moment. On the one hand, he longed to make a point about the vomiting. Anyone who stuck his nose in the hold for a second was immediately informed that there had been a lot of it. "Vomiting up your sins" had such a punch to it. But, on the other hand, he himself had snuck out to the deck last night, desperate to be without an audience, and had thrown up his dinner, not even making it to the railing. What if a sailor or a passenger had seen him? No, he had to let that tidbit lie.

He focused his thoughts and went on, choosing his words carefully. "And you must cleanse yourself of the Evil inside you today, or the Lord will turn that old tiger of a storm right around and bring him growling back over here to tear up our ship. Maybe to tear it to pieces this time. Repent ye now! Repent ye now!" He raised his right arm to the sky.

Fiona waited for people to break out laughing, but no one did. A number of folks muttered something and walked away, turning their backs on the motley crowd that gathered around Denton. But there were quite a few who stood by the preacher, actually listening, actually looking up into his face as he spoke, actually appearing to believe him. And how had he dared to pull her into his talk? Was he blind to her power? Couldn't he see that she was not anyone to play with?

Then, behind her, at last there was laughter. Bellyfuls of it. She looked over her shoulder and saw Jean-Paul, her new acquaintance, and two other sailors guffawing and pointing at the preacher. She began to laugh, too. It felt so good, so freeing. Here was this ridiculous man, and she had no reason to be mollified by him; she could laugh as hard as anyone else. The sailors saw her and grinned.

Just as she was leaving to stroll, the preacher fixed her with a hard gaze. That man had to touch everyone with his spider's tentacles. She stopped laughing then and shrugged her shoulders.

"How can you be so calm?" asked Marion who had come up behind her a few minutes earlier. "The way he cut through you with his stare was frightening."

"He did not cut through me. I didn't let him. That's the difference between you and me. Besides, I know I am as strong as he is."

One hot day soon after, Basuba found her usual spot on the bench and pulled out a few bundles of herbs. On the top of the pile lay a handful of comfrey tied together with some dry hemp. The bundle looked so much smaller since she had separated some out to make boneknit tea for one of Jean-Paul's friends.

"What if there is no comfrey in the New World and this stock has to last me forever?" She cringed at the thought and pulled her satchels closer to her.

She turned her attention away from her worries to her task. It was a favorite chore of hers that called on one of her special gifts: the ability to sense the healing qualities of an herb. To get at the information, Basuba held an herb in her hand and studied the sensations it brought. Sometimes a plant would send a little charge into her hand, sometimes her palm would heat up or cool down, sometimes it might throb. Any of these signs, added to what she already knew about an herb, could help her guess at more of its healing potential.

Basuba focused her mind, relaxed her body, picked out some wood betony, laid it carefully in her palm, and closed her eyes to give the greens her full attention. She had used the herb often for stopping migraine headaches. Yet she had always felt that it contained untapped healing potential which she longed to decipher. She waited with all her attention on the greens in her hands. Nothing came.

Basuba sighed. Sometimes she could get knowledge through her hands this way; other times, like now, there were no sensations. Ah, the remedies! People used to know so much about the healing power of these herbs. But every time there was a witch hunt, healers were forced to flee their homes quickly, leaving potions and recipes behind, destroyed or hidden somewhere—and now long forgotten—in hopes of protecting the rest of their family.

Basuba tenderly placed the herbs on the bench beside her and let her eyes wander to the clouds above her. They flew across the sky like racing horses, their heads high in the wind. And so she, too, was racing to the New World.

She sighed once more, shook her head and smiled ruefully at herself. How naïve she had been to think she could leave her problems behind her by boarding a ship. Here she was, a few short weeks out of England, and she already had had to swallow far too much: pretending she was not helping with the birth, keeping silent in the face of Denton's public humiliation of herself and those she cared about.

She put her head in her hands. Had she cashed in that last jewel, left that herb garden and dear cottage, those blessed cats, her trusted friends, for so little?

The heavy, hot breath of her anger hung on her neck. Yes, this was where her anger lay. Why should Holy Work, rooted in knowledge gleaned from the centuries, have to be hidden as though it were shameful, hateful, evil?

Basuba looked at her hands that had lovingly escorted so many babes in. She helped people be born into this Lifetime, tended their bodies while they were here, and then helped them out of their bodies when it was time for them to travel on to the Next World. It was as simple as that.

And yet, not simple at all. How ironic that only men were allowed to train as doctors at the universities in Europe and England. Thanks to King Henry the VIII, herbalists' rights to prescribe remedies were protected by the law. A healer who called herself an herbalist and kept her head down, worked only with the poor, and attended church every Sunday, was pretty safe. Any powerful woman who openly defied physicians, laid her hands on folks for healing as well as giving out herbs to them, and recognized Nature as the Creator, walked a fine line.

One way for a healer like her to stay out of trouble was to get a midwife's license. Basuba had never done that. She refused to get a license because it meant she would have to say Christian prayers over anyone who died. Now, she was happy to say prayers for a dying person; that was not the issue. But to direct everyone— Pagan, Jew, and folk of other faiths—to the Christian heaven was asking too much.

Looking for a solution, Basuba had gone to the Bishop, with Lady Jane as her guardian, to explain her views and to recite the prayers she would use. No exemptions were granted her, and since, by such an appeal, she had made it clear that she had no license, anyone who used her services was liable to receive a fine. If she were caught at a delivery, she could be sent to prison.

Nonetheless, people called her to their beds, and she traveled to them discreetly, by night if possible. Healing was her life's work; she would find a way to do it.

"Our Father, Who art in Heaven, Hallowed be Thy Name..." The words of the Lord's Prayer popped into Basuba's head without her calling them up. She always felt funny reciting that prayer, as though she were peeking into someone else's celebration of the Mystery of Life. They were fine words for making a connection to the Creator, but they were not her words. She had memorized them and the words of the Apostles' Creed by heart only to protect herself. That made her uncomfortable, too—to use someone else's prayers as a coat of armor. But, without the safeguard of a midwife's license to keep her from arrest as a student of the devil, she must have these.

It was whispered everywhere that these two prayers were used as tests for witchcraft. Folks believed that the devil would not allow His followers to speak those words so hateful to Him, even for the purpose of tricking the witch judges. Therefore, being able to recite the lines from memory was a sign of innocence.

Basuba shivered, remembering the nightmare of a few years' past, as vivid in her memory today as it had been when it shook her from her sleep then. She had dreamt she was standing, unclothed, in front of a gallows, searching for the words to the Apostles' Creed, knowing that the judge had captured them and tied them up in the bag that he was sitting on. She stared at the bag that squirmed as the words tried to free themselves so that she could see them and speak them. That was when she had awoken in a cold sweat.

"How will it be in the New World?" she muttered under her breath. "Will I ever find a village where I will be able to say directly 'I am a healer'?" She glanced up at the sky. "The clouds still race by. How I wish I were going forward with the same ease."

That night Basuba felt in her bones that it was time to hold counsel with Waning Moon, the Moon that disappeared a little more each night.

She knew that something in her outlook had to die. Something that was holding her back—an attitude, a habit, maybe—had to change. Her Crone Sight told her this much, but it had not revealed to her what must go.

Standing at the stern of the *North Star*, her hands wrapped tight around the railing, Basuba called out to Waning Moon for help. She ran her mind over the possibilities again and again but came up empty.

The loudest voice she heard inside her stated flatly and cold as ice on a January pond, "What, pray tell, is left to die? Have I not lost the bulk of what I am already? Broken are many of the tools of the Old Ways; the Dreams testify to that. Gone or shrinking away are the groves of trees where we were free to worship Nature. Gone or shrinking away are the unfenced fields and moors where we were free to roam. Gone, the liberty to heal folks with our Wise Ways. And gone are my friends, the evenings around the fire, the ceremonies, the birthing times and the dying times when we were together.

"I am empty. My hair streaks with grey; my limp increases. What more is there to let go of?" She paused and felt the rage from deep inside. "And why do you ask more from me? Haven't you taken enough? Even the last baby I had to birth without seeing or touching. What other sign do you need that I am walking the road of Crone?"

But Waning Moon held its silence. Basuba stood where she was for a long time until she knew for certain that she would be out-waited by that thin cold sliver of light.

The moment she gave up, something stirred in her.

"All right, then. I can feel that the Death has begun, though I know not what it is that is dying. May this leave-taking be gentler than the others, for I am still so raw." Her voice changed from plea to demand. "If it is not to go kindly, then give me the strength I must have to survive it."

Basuba started back to the hold, feeling discouraged, thinking that she knew no more now than when she had gotten up from her pallet. But she had taken only a few steps before she noticed a difference. Yes, something heavy and sad had been left behind. She took a few more steps as she tried to figure out just what it was.

Elinor's words, spoken to her in her herb garden that last night, floated back to her. This time they came as a truth, not as a question: "It's time to let go of the fragments." With them came that very calm feeling deep in her belly.

*Chapter 12*

# Beltane,
# May 1, 1641

*Far better to have loved and lost*
*Than ne'er to have loved at all.*
*Once Love has touched your heart,*
*You listen all life for Her call.*

Once the decks had been swabbed, rigging repaired and tightened, and fallen barrels righted, the sailors were in a mood to celebrate. And Jean-Paul made sure Fiona knew it.

Bad weather had passed, the ship was at midpoint of her voyage, and the passengers were in need of cheering. So what if there would be no moon tonight; they would light torches to set their makeshift stage. Time for the crew to make merry until dawn, if they liked.

The men gathered at the prow of the ship, turned over some buckets to make stools, brought out their music makers—an accordion, a flute and a drum—and began to tune, strum, blow and sing. Before long, their noisemaking attracted an audience, mostly men and adolescents. Seeing that, Fiona and her traveling mates and Barbara Turner took seats off to the sides.

When enough people had collected to satisfy the performers, one of the sailors gave a sign, and they broke into a ballad guaranteed to be familiar to all. That was followed by other songs. Some of them were known by the passengers; at least they could recognize a number of verses, though perhaps the tune would be different or the beat a bit faster. Others were new—ballads and love songs from parts of the world where they had never been, perhaps never heard of.

When the audience was warmed up enough to join in on a few of the refrains, the sailors rested their instruments a while and sat back so that Salty Bill could pull his bucket in close to the passengers and begin a story. He told a humorous tale that poked fun at newcomers to the Americas, and he told it with relish. He knew his timing was perfect; they had been at sea long enough for the shift in attention. No longer spinning only the memories of what they had left behind, passengers were starting to get edgy about what lay beyond the dock awaiting them. Soon the sailor had the looser folks doubled over in laughter, holding their bellies, as he told about his two characters, Thomas and Mary, getting stuck in just the same mire his listeners dreaded for themselves.

Basuba wiped the tears from her eyes. Whew, it was good to laugh about the fears that she found sitting heavily around her on her pallet when she awoke these days.

When the laughter finally subsided, Salty Bill removed his crusty sailor's cap and held it out to the audience like a bowl. "We here on the crew, we're tired of you landlubbers asking 'When will we land?' So, Mates, we're turning the question around to you. Pick a date when we'll first spy land. Make it yours by putting some coins in my cap here. Winner takes all, except for the pittance I take out for wear and tear on this fine cap of mine. Now call your dates out loud. My partners here," he gestured over his left shoulder, "have memories strong as oxen. They'll be our date keepers." More laughter as the cap went around. Marion noticed Biddy Jacobs' husband scan the crowd before he pulled a few coins from his pocket to add to the cap.

More songs, more stories, an accordion solo by Jean-Paul, and a sailor's jig in which some of the men tied bandanas around their waists to take the roles of female dancing partners rounded out the festivities. The evening grew late; the audience began to melt away. The entertainers said good night, but seemed in no hurry to pack up their instruments.

As folks drifted away, a sailor reached for his flute and played a tune with a sad, haunting melody for the small audience that remained. Then Jean-Paul laid his accordion on the ground and stepped forward. He arranged a piece of deer hide on the deck and placed a large feather and a stone on it. He sat on the deck next to the hide in silence for a moment.

Fiona found herself looking closely at her sailor friend for the first time as she waited for him to speak. Jean-Paul's features and his earth-toned skin gave him the cast of a wise elder, even as a child, a visage universal enough to make him look at home in many ports. Born in the teeming port city of Marseilles, France, he grew up speaking enough languages to get himself around the trade routes, often working as a day laborer in this port or that one until he got the urge to ship out again. His work, his curiosity and his natural inclination for observing the life around him allowed him to feel at home with many different peoples. His shyness let him enter a place inconspicuously; his underlying friendliness permitted him to be accepted once he was recognized.

Marion thought it peculiar to have a storyteller sitting right on the deck below his audience instead of perched on a stool at eye level, or maybe standing, leaning against a post. If Jean-Paul knew this, he did not seem to care. He briefly touched the heavy gold cross that hung from his neck and then placed the stone in the palm of his right hand and began to speak in a low voice.

"Five years ago I sailed to the New World for the first time. After a week, maybe two weeks, in the harbor city, I grew restless. I traveled north to the edges of the English settlements. I wanted to know the country for itself. At a trading post, I met Pidianske many times when he came in with hides. We shared food in the woods behind the trader's. He told me names for the food we ate and the trees around us. Pidianske, he is a Maliseet, an Indian. A small man. Strong. With no hair on his face.

"One day Pidianske came with two other men. After we had food, he took me by the arm and pointed in the direction that they were going. I guessed at his meaning, picked up my pack and went along with them. I had no work yet, nothing better to do.

"When we reached a river, the Maliseets pulled their boat out of the grasses. *Canoe* is the name. Such a fine, thin craft it is. Hard to get into at first. One swift stomp and my foot would go right through the bottom, for it was made of tree bark. We moved up the river past a settlement with big log cabins built on a clearing. Pidianske gestured a number of times in a way I took to mean that he had camped on that bank as a child, before the clearing, before the houses. He was looking closely at the riverbanks for what I did not know. Suddenly, he pointed to a turtle sunning itself on a log. More pointing to the turtle, to the log cabins just disappearing behind us, and to his own back. This I took to mean that his people, like the turtle, carried their houses on their backs."

Jean-Paul paused to look at his listeners. He needed a sense of who grasped his meaning. Tonight, he could tell that Fiona and her friends were with him. There were some other folks whose eyes were beginning to wander; he knew that they would leave soon. He did not look far enough over his right shoulder to see the preacher who was listening closely, arms folded across his chest, feet spread wide apart.

The storyteller sighed and continued, "One of Pidianske's companions spoke, and the canoe darted to the bank of the river. The man jumped out and put his arm around a white pine and then ran to a cedar and did the same. Now more gestures, broad sweeps of the arms towards the forests, then the motions of chopping down a tree, repeated many times. Then movements that looked like a fire was being lit, a fire so big that the man jumped back away from it. I believed this meant that the forest once had many more trees than it has today.

"Next, we passed an enclosure that held cows, then one with hogs. My friends put their heads down and looked away from the animals. It was only at the end of my stay with them that I knew them well enough to guess what they would have liked to tell me then: that these penned-up animals had lost their spirits. To them, the animals they know—the moose, beavers, otter, and bears—have spirits and..."

"Blasphemy! Blasphemy! You sin, Sailor, by repeating what those savages, those infidels, believe." George Denton stepped around to face Jean-Paul.

The preacher went on, rage hurtling through his voice. "Yes, those very words rolling around in your mouth, those very thoughts in your mind, they lead you right to the devil. Right to the devil because it is he that those savages worship. God would never allow His people to believe that animals have Spirits. Do you not know the Commandments that tell us there is one God and one God only? No, perhaps you don't. By your skin color, you look to be a heathen. Take notice, Heathen Sailor. Right now I am informing you that there is one God only. This very moment you are being lead out of the darkness of your heathen world into the light. Now you can accept the Grace of God. But should you refuse this time, you will have a much harder time finding your way out of the Darkness later." So spoke Denton, towering down over Jean-Paul, his close-set eyes, pale green now, blazing under his arched eyebrows.

And the self-styled orator would have, no doubt, gone on. But the small group around Jean-Paul began to boo and hiss so loudly that he was drowned out. A sailor appeared on either side of the troublemaker, grabbed him by the arms and turned him around. As they walked him off, he looked back to face the group and could tell that he had no followers amongst them.

"Are there so many like that preacher who hate the natives, or are there more like you who would be friends?" asked Fiona of Jean-Paul after the group had complained about Denton's behavior.

"There are enough like him who fill the pulpits and set the villagers against the natives, and there are many European traders who think them like children who would give everything away. So they use trickery and rum on them. And there's some like me. I don't know how many; we don't seem to leave tracks like the others do."

"And your friends there, what do they say about Christians?"

Jean-Paul took a deep breath and replied, looking Fiona right in the eye, "Different people, they say different things." His voice sank away. "I have heard some say, 'Maybe the Christian God is stronger than our gods. Maybe we must walk after him so that our people will stop dying.'"

"What?" cried Fiona. This was not the answer she wanted. She sat down quickly on the deck close to him. "Whatever do you mean, Jean-Paul?"

Picking up the threads of his story again, Jean-Paul continued, shaken. That was not the answer he had meant to give; it was not the one he wanted to believe. But the story held its teller too close now, and so he had spoken what stood in his heart at the moment.

"When I returned to the Maliseet village the second time, two years later, I saw at once that there were fewer wigwams, little food drying, and I was not greeted as before by laughing children when I approached. All this after I had waited at the trading store for days for Pidianske. The trader said he must be in soon to buy powder and shot for winter hunting.

"One day, I decided to wait no more but to travel towards the place where the village had been. I knew there was no guarantee that it would lie in the same spot, but trusted that I knew enough of the language to be able to find it. What else was there to do? After some adventures I arrived in the village, carrying what hunting supplies I could.

"A woman came to the door of a hut. She called me by name in a weak voice. I had to go very close to recognize her; her face, her stance had changed so much. She asked me if I brought medicine for them. She said, 'The Black Robe has no medicine for us. But you, you are our friend. You have come with medicine to help us.'"

Jean-Paul stared at the stone, living it all again in his memory. "What could I do?" he cried out, looking into the eyes that were locked on him now. "I had no medicines. I didn't know what was wrong. Yes, I had heard talk at the trading store amongst the settlers, but it was so full of hatred that I paid it no heed. They talked of the Indians dying from a disease that God had brought to them because they were unclean. This sickness does not touch immigrants, but it cuts through the Indian villages, killing children, old people, women; even the healers are not powerful enough to withstand it.

"You see, I did not believe any of that. Clean. Unclean. That changes from moment to moment within each person I've known. Not from people to people. No God would pick out an entire people to be destroyed. So, I did not listen.

"But, there are no medicines to be had anyway. The settlers have nothing, and the Indian healers can find nothing to stop these illnesses they do not recognize. The healers have not been given any stories that tell of these diseases; they believe that these sicknesses have never been visited on their people before."

Jean-Paul stopped. The body of Pidianske's son, collapsed on the ground, his skin spotted and blue, blood oozing from his mouth, lodged heavily in his mind and would not leave. He felt his heart tighten again into a knotted cord as he recalled the boy's mother asking one more time for medicine, so sure that he, their friend, could help.

"I—I can't go on," Jean-Paul said, clumsily collecting his things from the deck. He bolted through the gathering of listeners towards the railing where he could be safely out of their line of sight. He shuddered. He had not meant for the story to end up where it did, though each time he told it, he feared that it might.

The folks he left behind sat in silence. Marion got to her feet and went over to where the storyteller stood, his back to the deck. She found his hand and wrapped her smaller one around it. They stood together watching the moonlight play on the ocean surface, saying nothing.

Slowly, various folks stood up, stretched a bit and simply said, "Good night," and went off. Fiona and Basuba lingered, collected the buckets, and put things aright with the remaining musicians.

Fiona was relieved when she saw that Marion was still standing with Jean-Paul. She herself did not know what to say to him. She felt sorry for what he had been through, but she wished he had not showed his pain. The man she was looking for must be brave at all times. Fiona slipped away to her pallet.


For Marion, the dark sky of the New Moon that came the following night was a relief. The chain that was attached to her heart broke away, and, with its weight gone, breathing came easier. She felt like her old self again. The stars, no longer washed out by the Moon, were her grief split apart into tiny fragments; each constellation was a map of a new possibility of healing, a way of starting again. She sighed happily and turned to go inside; she would sleep this night, a full sleep. No allegiance to any moonrise required.

When she awoke the next morning, Marion lay on her pallet for a few moments. She stretched, thinking about the bottoms of her feet, her fingertips, her stomach, the crown of her head. They all felt different. Something was gone—the heaviness, the numbness that she had had to push herself through each morning in order to get up and greet the others and get on with the day. This new sensation was as fragile as the first tendrils of spring when the green is so delicate it makes one's heart ache. She decided not to think about it for too long, just to appreciate it and then start moving.

As the slim curve of Moon showed itself to the sky that night, Marion was drawn to it lightly, gaily. She greeted it like a friend, not a feared master as before. She held out her own hand as though to mime the gentle curve of the crescent that bowed like a baby's cradle on its side. All at once she fancied that she could make out Gwyneth's profile in the crescent. She laughed aloud and squinted again to make it happen more easily. Her mind leapt to the wood carvings and the one that had stayed in Gwyneth's palm: the face on the crescent Moon. She felt a long chord of love come forth from her heart, travel up the sky to the Moon, and move from there back to England to anchor itself in Gwyneth's heart.

Beltane, May 1, came on the second night of the increasing Moon in a cloudy sky. As Fiona, seated by herself on a bench, stared at the slender sliver of light in the sky, her thoughts drifted back to Blue Fens. She could almost smell the damp of the soil that would be freshly turned over in the empty fields, waiting for seeds. Today men would be hoisting into place the Maypole the married women had decorated. Children would carry in water for all the cooking, women would bake for the feasting afterwards, and elders would sort seeds into baskets for sowing. As folks gathered to make the Fertility Blessing for the year's crops, the young adults would be eyeing each other, some shyly and others boldly, wondering how it would be to take a partner.

"Perhaps Matthew is walking hand-in-hand with someone out to the fields this very minute," she thought. Her mind raced ahead to learn who was with him. "One of my friends probably. Nancy, Lucy—or Sally, she's such a flirt. I know that any of them would happily go with him if he asked. Or maybe one of them will reach her hand out to touch his as folks dance in the Commons."

Fiona pulled Matthew's silhouette into her mind and tried to see who was walking there beside him down the lane that led away from the village to the beckoning fields. If she could sense the height of the woman and how she moved, she could guess the name; after all, she had known those three since they were old enough to toddle. Determined to have the answer, she worked at it until her forehead tightened into a fierce wrinkle.

Nothing. Nothing came at all. "What's happening to me? I'm out of practice. I used to be able to see these kinds of things. Oh, bother! What ridiculous thoughts. I don't care a whit about him anyway."

Fiona dismissed the scene abruptly and settled her mind on Jean-Paul. He had to be the one Madame Dora had in mind for her; she had met no one else. She shifted her weight to get more comfortable on the hard bench and tried to picture walking with the sailor out to the fields. No sensations came. She wriggled a bit on the bench and tried it again. It wasn't working. It must be because they were moving along on a ship surrounded by water instead of dancing in a village square that lay in the midst of good rich soil. Once more, she urged her body to come forth with some desire to be alone with the Frenchman. No good. She could feel nothing arise in her body—until the image of Matthew Fields strode into her heart, bringing with it a rush of heat and longing.

By this time, the three women and their friends gathered even for cloudy sunsets. Having watched the sun disappear so many times in a clear sky, it was easy for them to sense where it was during a shrouded descent. They tended to watch the sky more on clear days and to talk more on the gray ones.

One evening Marion surprised everyone by telling them that she had been baptized in Ely Cathedral.

"By The Lady, I thought only fine lords and ladies and maybe a few merchants were allowed in there for church rites," exclaimed Fiona.

"Twice a year the priests hold baptisms and weddings for the likes of us. It still costs a pretty penny, though. It was my mother who insisted on it." She looked over at Basuba who nodded in agreement.

"So you're a Christian then, Marion," said Fiona in a teasing voice. She knew she had her on soft ground here. "Fancy that."

"I'm enough of one to say I've been baptized if I'm ever questioned by the authorities," Marion retorted. It was getting easier to hold her own with Fiona.

Then her voice softened and slowed a little as she slipped into the memories. "When I was little, I wanted to go to services in the Cathedral so badly. I wanted to touch those shiny, big statues on those huge altars with all the candles gathered below them. I watched every movement of those fine ladies, dressed in their best. Watched as they got out of their carriages and were handed in through those tall doors. We, even my mother, would creep as close as we could to look at them. Usually someone would chase us away. In our neighborhood, my mother took me each Sunday to a small church. In one little window there was a saint made out of colored glass. I liked his smile. Wherever you stood in the church, he was smiling at you."

Marion looked at Basuba and grinned sheepishly and went on. "It all seemed more wonderful than the candles you would light, Basuba, in a cave or by your hearth. For a while I didn't want to do that with you."

"I remember that time," said Basuba.

"Then, because I missed you, I decided that maybe God and the Great Mother were married. God must be for the rich and for city folk like me and the Great Mother was for everyone else like you.

"When I got older I wanted to be an altar boy. That's when I learned why they called them altar 'boys'—because girls cannot touch the silver goblet or other special things on the altar below our saint. And he didn't do anything about that. When I prayed to him to make them change the rules for girls, he just kept smiling the way he always smiled. One of the altar boys lived near me. He was mean. He skinned cats alive. When I told the saint about that boy, he just went on smiling." She looked at her aunt. "That's when I ran away from home. I knew that I could find my way to your cottage. I still remember my hand shaking the first time you asked me to light the candles on your altar that first night I got there."

"Basuba, if you're a healer who follows the Old Ways, you must keep an eye on the witch trials," Peter Turner half-asked, half-stated.

"Peter," said his wife sharply, "wait a minute. Marion's just told us a lovely tale from her childhood. Let it settle for a few breaths before you start in, turning the talk to danger. Please!"

"I apologize, Marion. Barbara's right. My mind is always racing on to scout out injustices."

When Basuba did take up the threads of Peter's question a few minutes later, she said, "There've been three witch trials in England within the last ten years. None of those murdered were healers. Instead, they were poor women, mostly old women. One had a large hump on her back, two were beggars who swore a curse on folks who would not give them bread. The poor souls were given over to liquor and fighting, some thieving perhaps, but nothing more than that."

Peter looked at her keenly, his forehead furrowed in wrinkles from thinking hard. "Ah, ha. So you do pay attention to who is being picked up."

"Oh, yes. Many's the night we've talked about it 'round the fire until dawn, wondering should we go to the Mayor or the Bishop and tell them the patterns we see in the arrests."

"And..."

Basuba shrugged, threw her hands up and sighed. "I came close to it once. But my friends counseled me out of it. 'You will have to choose between speaking to the authorities and continuing with your healings. Once you speak out on witchcraft, they follow you like a hawk,' they said. 'Besides, look at you! You're the living picture of a witch to the authorities. Leave that work for women who are young, lovely to look at, wealthy and educated, who have important fathers or brothers or husbands.'"

"I see. I can hear the wisdom in their advice. I'm sorry." After that, even Peter Turner was silent for a long time.

During one of her early dawn vigils, Fiona declared to Jean-Paul her interest in taking a hand at repairing sails. She was feeling saucy; she knew he would oblige her anything that he could, and she wanted the sails.

Jean-Paul, guessing that she would soon tire of the chore, humored her and agreed to set her up with a needle and sail that very day. He and Salty Bill, the sailor in charge of repairs, were more than a little surprised when she turned in some very tight and tidy stitching at the end of the first day. She was there again the next day.

One thing led to another, as it probably always will, and Fiona's work repairing the sails quickly caught the attention of the adolescents on board who were always looking for something to get into. The boys begged to be let in on the work, and three or four of the girls did too. Salty Bill growled about having to depend on sails fixed by landlubbers during a storm, and then passed out needles and thread anyway. He kept a close eye on everyone's handiwork and whittled his new crew down to two or three pretty fast.

Before long, Fiona had cajoled him into giving her extra scraps of canvas that she could turn into poppets for the younger children. The adolescent girls joined her in the stitching, too, and some soon returned from their mother's sewing baskets with bits of yarn for hair and a button or two for eyes.

Once Fiona had successfully designed the first poppet and taught her students how to carry on, she became bored with the task. Dolls had interested her only because Alyona had given them to her.

She said to Salty Bill, "If I could make an animal poppet, I would. I'm tired of working with figures of people."

"You might talk to Hendrik Hanson then, the big Snoose. He's hacking with cough so much these days that he's given up his pipe, but he keeps on carving bowls for them, and he's made lots of animals."

Fiona approached the Swede with her request, and soon he was unfolding the brown cloth in which he kept the pipe bowls he had made. When the cloth was opened flat, Fiona saw eight or nine round knobs of wood, each about the size of a hen's egg, some darker, some lighter than the rest. In his collection of human and animal faces, Hendrik had an eagle, two bears, a deer, three kinds of owls, and a wolf.

The Snoose held up one of the bear's heads and squinted at it hard, turning it this way and that so as to examine it from every angle. He shrugged his shoulders as he handed it to Fiona with the rest of his bundle. "They ain't the best you'll see, Mistress, but carving them sure helps while away time when you're at sea."

He agreed to let her choose three or four of the animal heads. "Let me see those poppets when you've finished. And come back if you want more."

Now Fiona got to work. She carefully cut, stitched and stuffed bodies for the animal poppets. Before long she pulled her pocket of beads out and began to out-line features like wings and paws with them.

The older girls watched her with awe; the sewing they learned from their mothers was purely functional— the darning of a hole in a sock, the lengthening of a skirt hem. Here with Fiona, a squarish piece of plain material became a col-orful creature that their little sisters and brothers would talk to as though it were real. After a while, cautiously and gawkily, they took up beading, too. Fiona moved from one girl to the next, giving a bit of advice here and there. Finally, her patience stretched thin as one of her hair ribbons, she took a break to stroll the deck.

Coming full circle, she picked up her own work again and strung a brown bead onto her needle. She was crafting an arm for one of the bears. "How gor-geous these beads are," she crowed as memories of home and Mother and Grand-mother flooded her. "My stitches are so big and clumsy next to Alyona's, but no matter. This is fun for me and for the young ones, and it gives these restless hands of mine something to do."

Before their very eyes, the part of the deck used for sail repair became the center of children's play. Little ones followed their older siblings around, and a few parents came out to tell stories and teach games. Marion, the lover of books, came each day to share a story.

Salty Bill continued to grumble but never did move his operation away. One day a sailor brought out his accordion and played some songs. He invited others to join in, and soon he and Fiona were making up playful harmonies together.

When the sailor played refrains easy enough for youngsters to pick up, he had more takers.

Fiona was surprised one day when a woman with whom she had never spoken stomped into the group of children gathered around the sailor and grabbed the hands of two of them and pulled them away.

Over her shoulder, the red-faced woman called out, "Simon and Barbara Jane, you'll be coming away from there now, too. Your folks don't approve of that carrying on any more than we do." With that, a small girl and a slightly bigger boy stood up and, keeping their eyes on the ground, ran off.

Fiona turned to Hendrik. "What is going on?"

"Don't you know, Mistress, about them who's against singing and dancing? There's a lot of them sailing these days. We carried a group last spring that was going to the same settlement these folks are headed for."

"What's wrong with singing?"

"Never have been a church-goer. I couldn't tell you," said Hendrik.

"You won't need to ask," chimed in Salty Bill. "Bet my britches on it, that preacher will be ranting and raving about singing by this time tomorrow. You can just listen to him," and he laughed.

"Listening to him won't give me any answers. He'll just say it is a sin. I want to know how it got to be a sin and who decided it."

"You're an odd duck," said Salty. "I never heard anyone ask how come. When it's religion, people are just for or against something."

Next morning Salty Bill chuckled to Fiona as she approached. He pointed to the place on the deck that had become the site for Preacher Denton's daily worship service. "Listen in, Missy. What did I tell you?"

"...any people true to the Lord, any people who walk in His Ways, are most graced when they are swimming in tears and troubles. All those goads keep them on the path of righteousness. And what are laughter, songs, drink and dance? They are sure signs of a people falling away from God. Sure signs of people listening to the Evil inside them. Sure signs of being led astray into temptation, into body lust, into sin. Look around you now, my flock, and see just who it is leading your children down the road to damnation."

So saying, Denton scoured the faces until he lit on Fiona's. He brightened with glee and pointed to her. She bristled and stood taller, her hands balled into fists. How dare he! "There she is now. The redhead. Beware of her!" he yelled.

"We, people in God's community, have the right—nay, even more, the obligation—to keep each other on the straight and narrow. Husbands, when you see wives stepping off the path to fancy themselves dressed in a whorish ball gown; parents, when you see children dallying in the fields of temptation and imagination…"

And so Denton went on, standing on a stairway to provide himself with the stature a pulpit would have given him. Sure enough, close to his feet stood the woman from yesterday with each hand tightly gripping a shoulder of one of her children.

Fiona noted that Denton's group was growing as the journey wore on. There had been three deaths so far, one to small pox and two to tuberculosis, and Denton was the only preacher on board. Each death fed his audience.

When Fiona picked up the sail she was mending two days after Denton's oration, an owl poppet that she had given to little Anne, the go-between at Elizabeth's birth, fell out of the canvas where it had been hastily tucked and onto the deck. She picked it up and thought of the conversation she had had with little Anne.

"Animal poppets! But that's no fun. Animals can't talk to us, Mistress," the little girl had complained.

Fiona had taken up the owl then, half-beaded, still in need of stuffing, stuck her hand inside to manipulate its wings, and said, "Hoot, hoot. I talk, and if you listen, you will understand what I am saying. Hoot, hoot. I'm in a tree now, looking out with my eyes that see so well in the dark for my dinner."

With that little Anne had taken over the owl, swooping this way and that with it, developing a rounded, smooth "hoot" in her throat. She had begged Fiona to finish beading the poppet fast as she could, but would have no stuffing in it; she wanted room for her hand so she could make its wings fly.

Now the owl was back, perhaps forgotten in play. Then Fiona's eyes fell upon a bear poppet lying close by on the deck. She squatted to pick them up.

Salty Bill stood over her, "Two of the girls came over with those. Said their folks told them animals cannot talk, so they're giving them back. Won't be coming by to play anymore."

That afternoon Anne did come back, but not to play. She dashed up to Fiona and said, "My mother says you may have made a doll that looks like me so that you can make me do things that you want. Well, if you did, my father'll tell the preacher." She shook her little fists at Fiona while her whole body trembled fiercely.

"No. You don't have to worry. I made no doll like you. I wouldn't do that," replied Fiona. But the girl was gone before she finished the statement, leaving right after she had heard Fiona say no.

"What a brave mite, that one. Coming up to you when she feared there might be a doll named after her. I'm sorry, Fiona. She takes you for a witch now, doesn't she?" muttered Jean-Paul.

"It seems so. Foolish parents, to put such harmful ideas in the heads of children. Well, she does seem a strong one. Maybe she'll think for herself one day."

Tenderly Fiona tucked the poppets into the sail she was working on, making sure that enough of her handiwork showed to make them easy for little searching eyes to spot. Maybe if she just left them there, they might find their way into the hands of a child.

The next day, when she peeked, she filled with satisfaction to see that the bear poppet was missing.

## Chapter 13

# Two Spells Cast

*Three times 'round, three times 'round*
*Care for what you do.*
*It comes three times 'round*
*Just back to you.*

Fiona took the necessary time to scan the deck before speaking. Three of the traders, liquor slurring their talk and bumbling their steps most nights by sundown, had acquired the unpleasant habit of following her when she strolled at night. She was used to keeping her guard up against them; tonight she did not want anyone else close enough to hear her words, either.

"You are willing to do it then?" she asked her flamboyant companion. Just standing near her puffed Fiona up with importance.

"My dear, your desire ignites my passion. Of course!"

"And you, ah, can do it?" Fiona had her hand on her pouch, rubbing the small bulge of coins there. It was awkward to ask, but she knew this would be a costly venture so she had to be sure.

Madame Dora pulled herself up straight with a snort and fixed her unwavering gaze on Fiona. "Young woman, you offend me to doubt my capabilities in such a matter. Can I do it? Why, I was famous for this work when you were still at your mother's knee." She released her face into a smile and rubbed her palms together. "Let me think some about the fee. Since that despicable preacher has included me in his venomous words, I'll reduce the sum a bit. On the other hand, the Moon is waxing and you want me to shrink his powers. Working a change against the direction the Moon is going is very difficult. That will raise the sum a lot. You are lucky that my gifts are so strong; not many could help you with this task. You are savvy enough to understand that, no doubt?"

"Yes, I am."

"We'll need to work at night. No one must know, including your traveling companion, the herbs woman. That girl who's with you, we'll need her to stand watch while we are at work. And, it is crucial that we have something of his with which to work the spell. Since you are the petitioner, it falls on you to retrieve that article. It may be dangerous. Are you up to it?"

Fiona quickly pushed aside the current of fear that started to rise in her at the question and answered fiercely, "It shall be done. Any article?"

"Something that he keeps close to his person is the best, obviously." She sensed Fiona stiffening and added with a touch of condescension, "If that is too difficult, sweetheart, anything that he has touched will do. Naturally, what you bring back— its proximity to his person—affects my price. The way these spells work, the less an object has been steeped with your opponent's essence, the harder I must work. But, why am I saying this to you? You're no innocent. You're well-versed enough in these ways to know how things work, of course?" She hurried to answer her own question. "Of course! Come to me when you've got it. Good night, my pet."

By the light of day, in the absence of any shadows, Fiona's task looked much harder. Nothing in her daily routines brought her close to the preacher, and nothing ever could without fixing the attention of others, including him, on her. She considered his pallet and the space underneath it where his belongings would be stowed. She made her way as near to the area as she could get without arousing suspicions and stood there, idly, to observe whether one would ever have an opportunity to dig for another's satchel. Her experience confirmed what her mind already knew: the hold was a place of constant comings and goings, and Preacher Denton's pallet lay deep within territory that would make her a trespasser.

Next she studied the mess hall. Once again, boundaries were clearly established there. Since the early days of the voyage, the various camps of wayfarers had claimed their places in the meal line and staked out their tables. She had never seen anyone break the pattern by sitting with a different group of people. Fiona fancied herself standing nonchalantly near the barrels where folks left their used dishes at the end of a meal. Denton would drop his spoon into the barrel, and she would reach in to pull it out with no one noticing. She shook her head ruefully; not a prayer of that working.

She pounded the deck, walking as she thought. There had to be something, something that would impress Madame Dora. Something that might get her thinking about taking Fiona on as an apprentice. It would be too humiliating to return with empty hands and, even worse, to have no revenge on the preacher who made her look like a fish on a hook to the others, flailing feebly this way and that. She hungered to watch his powers shrivel away because of her doing.

The sun pummeled the deck with radiating waves of heat. Distressed that she could think of nowhere else to prowl for a token, Fiona walked absent-mindedly over to where Marion and Basuba sat on their bench in the shade provided by the main mast. Without saying a word, she slumped down beside them and stared idly at the deck. She began to count the floorboards.

Abruptly she straightened her spine. What was happening? She had just caught herself daydreaming about Matthew. In her imagination she had seen him standing in a field of high wheat, beaming and looking at a letter he held in his hands. The letter was from her. She could not read the words, but she knew they told him that her heart was full of him. How stupid! She would never be such a traitor to her people, and where did the idea that she loved Matthew Fields come from? She stood up to shake off the dream and peered over at her companions.

"Marion, I cannot believe that you willingly earn your living by a means destined to destroy the Old Ways." Fiona, with her hands on her hips, moved closer until she was standing right over Marion who was engaged in writing a letter for a passenger. Marion blinked and looked up at her in surprise.

"Fiona, whatever is ailing you?" asked Basuba sternly.

"Let the scribe defend herself," replied Fiona.

Marion swallowed hard and broke eye contact with Fiona. "I don't have a way to answer you," she said slowly. "I love reading and writing. It makes the world grow larger and larger. It teaches me to know myself. When I listen to you, I am troubled by what you say. Still, I cannot see giving up my trade." She moved her hands across a piece of paper, patiently smoothing out the wrinkles. "This is my livelihood and my craft." She looked briefly back up into Fiona's hard face. "I am sorry. I don't want to lose your esteem either."

"The day may come indeed when you have to make that choice, Marion."

"What ails you, Fiona?" Basuba repeated.

"There is plenty in this reading and writing to make a person feel foul."

"Why blame the tool instead of the one who suits it to a particular purpose? Would you take the hayfork from the farmer for fear of the injuries it can cause a body?" asked Basuba carefully.

"I'm going off for a walk. How you can bear sitting in one place for so long is beyond me." And Fiona was gone.

Fuming, arms crossed, she practically stomped her way around the deck. The deck, the ship, the people, all crowded together in this tiny space—it was too much too long. She stopped at a railing and stared out to sea. If she could swim to the New World, she would leap from this prison in a moment. That lucky Matthew Fields! Probably out planting right now. For a short moment, she saw his sun-browned hand in the dark rich soil, clearing away the stubble from last year's harvest. Then she imagined that hand reaching out to hold hers, raising it to the sky in celebration of a new season, new life, new possibilities. She reached her arm up as high as she could and wrapped it around a rigging rope. Suddenly she was aware that her heart hurt. Her eyes burned with hot tears.

She wiped the thumb and index finger of her free hand hastily over the corners of her eyelids. This was no time for tears. She had something huge to accomplish if the spell to bind the powers of Preacher Denton was going to work. Her left hand tightened hard around the rigging rope; she had to come up with a means.

That was when it dawned on her—the rigging rope! She knew exactly where it was that Denton mounted the rigging each dawn; she had learned to turn away from that spot so he would not mar her view. A piece of that very rope! Not a personal item to be sure, but she could convince the Madame that it was a potent one. She would have to be impressed by the novelty of Fiona's solution to a difficult situation.

Her mind raced on. In fact, if it was Denton's power to rile up others that she was determined to crush, what could be better than this, his touchstone for leaping into the sky to get closer to his god? A smile burst across her lips. Securing a piece of that rope would weaken her enemy in many ways: magically, through the spell; practically, for she would not leave enough of the hank he grabbed to make it easy for him to vault to the rigging anymore; and mentally, for he would no longer be able to rescue his restless body from the confines of the deck. What a surprise it was going to be for Madame Dora when she learned that Fiona had accomplished her difficult mission so soon and was ready for the spell to be cast tonight.

Marion was so relieved when Fiona approached her to ask a favor for that night that she did not question either the purpose or the admonition not to tell Basuba.

Late enough in the night for most folk to be bedded down and early enough to avoid the little light the Moon would bring when it rose, Fiona, with Marion in tow, met Madame Dora. They walked in silence to a spot close to the stern. Fiona pointed out the place where she wanted Marion to wait and told her she must keep an eye out in all directions. If anyone approached near enough to hear anything, Marion was to call out loudly to Fiona in a gay voice that would suggest a simple game of hide-and-seek.

"What are you truly doing, Fiona?" whispered Marion excitedly.

"This concoction needs to bake a while in our oven. When it's ready to be displayed, you will be the first to know," replied Madame Dora briskly, punctuating her point high in the air with her index finger.

Marion watched them as they left, her eyes widening as the two women disappeared behind a dinghy that rested against the ship's railing.

"I love surprises!" thought Marion, clapping her hands together. "It could be something for Basuba since she's not to be told anything. That seems odd, though, for I'm sure that they've never even spoken. So why should Madame Dora be planning something for her now?"

Crouched on the deck under the curve of the dinghy, the two women got right to work.

"I've designed a spell that will be as deep as it is short. We do not care to be caught doing this, do we?" The Madame laughed an extended cackle. "It would be hard to explain to the others."

Madame Dora gestured wildly and widely with her arms as though clearing a circular space in front of them. She pulled a small bowl out of her bag and took handfuls of ashes from it which she sprinkled all around the circle.

"Rub these into the deck here, you bold girl. Rub 'round and 'round in a circle. Use both your hands. This will fix our intention."

When Fiona had finished rubbing, Madame Dora called out to three or four invisible forces, speaking in a language that Fiona had never heard. "The money, Fiona. Lay your jolly fat purse right here." The Madame patted lovingly a spot of deck in the center of the circle. "Money's power in the circle makes our spell even stronger."

Touching her precious pocket of coins, Fiona felt the soft grease of the ashes on her palms and fingertips. In spite of herself, she shuddered. For a tiny moment, she thought she felt Alyona behind her, wanting her to pull away. She brushed off the feeling. What a relief that there was nothing to like in Preacher Denton, because something was brewing here that she did not know how to stop. She stared through the darkness at her palms; something was brewing, and she herself was stirring the pot.

The Madame's words called her sharply back to the moment. "Now, we are ready for the token. The token that will bind the powers of that wicked preacher. The token that will silence his lips when he speaks out against the likes of you and me. The token that will ensure that he has known his last day of binding the minds of poor, foolish folks to his will." Madame Dora gestured dramatically towards her customer.

Fiona fumbled for a moment with her pocket and then brought out her prize. The spellweaver's eyebrows shot up into two right angles when she first saw the piece of rope. She bent over to get a better look at it.

She started immediately to wring her hands and mutter, "Oh, poor dear, this will certainly cost you a pretty penny. I'll have to work ever so hard to make something happen with a piece of common rope. Whatever did you have in mind?"

In a stately voice, Fiona replied, "This, Madame, is no common piece of rope." She told her story convincingly in a grand style.

"Ah, ha! No common piece of rope, indeed. Clever, clever! Only we Irish have such sharp wits. You will go far." She picked up the rope, murmuring appreciatively. "And with this rope we make this poppet into the preacher himself."

So saying, Madame Dora brought out a poppet from her bag and gave it to Fiona. "Here, pull the rope tight as you can 'round his neck," she ordered as Fiona gasped and jumped back.

There in Madame Dora's open palm lay one of her own poppets, stitched for children's play, the poppet with the bear's head that Snoose had spent so many hours carving. Madame Dora was asking her to strangle it.

The Madame clucked happily at her novice's reaction. "You see that! My spell works already and I haven't even laid the words on him yet. The power just leapt out to scorch you, and it's not even directed at you. Just fancy how it shrivels the preacher, even as we speak."

She uncorked a bottle and held it out to Fiona. "Dab some of this potion onto the poppet. Just a bit, for it's very strong, very expensive."

The foul-smelling liquid cut into the soft flesh that lined Fiona's nostrils, bringing her quickly to her senses. She felt Alyona's presence beside her. It was as though the old woman lay a firm hand on her granddaughter's shoulder and pulled her back from the scene of destruction in front of her. As if that were not enough, in her mind's eye she saw little Anne's face looking up trustingly at her as she had done in their first days of playing poppets together.

Fiona's hands flew up in front of her, desperate to ward off the effects of Madame Dora's work.

"No, no, no!" she cried, backing away. "You are as evil as he is! You must stop what you are doing at once."

"Ho, ho. Too late for that. I have already unleashed the forces against him. They have almost finished binding his power by now. I can see him thrashing in his bed right now."

The Madame peered off very briefly into the distance as though looking through the wooden walls right into the hold. Then she turned her hawk eyes back full force to Fiona. "Where is your courage, coward? You are a disgrace to your heritage."

Alyona's invisible hand tightened on Fiona's shoulder.

"You said the spell would not work if I failed to pay you. Well, I won't pay you a tuppence for it. It's finished." She grabbed her purse from the circle and jumped up.

"Too late to stop it! Didn't you hear me before? Once a spell of mine has been set in motion, I can turn it on anyone. You," she sharpened her shriek by pointing her index finger right at Fiona's face, four inches from her nose, "and anyone else I choose."

Fiona, speechless, backed away, ready to turn.

"Just watch and see what happens, girlie. You'll be very sorry!" Madame Dora pelted through the air at Fiona as she dashed back to Marion. Fiona took her young friend's hand and pulled her to a run as fast as she could.

"Basuba. We must get Basuba right now," cried Fiona as they headed to the hold.

The midwife, conditioned by years of awakening instantly to tend to a woman in labor, was alert as soon as Fiona gripped her shoulder. Sensing her friends' anxiety at once, Basuba grabbed her shawl without saying a word to awaken others and went with them out to the deck.

Fiona, fearful that Madame Dora's evil forces were tracking her down, dreaded standing anywhere that the woman might see her. Basuba took her by the elbow and steered her trembling friend to a stand of barrels behind which lay an open space where they could talk softly without attracting attention. Fiona sank to the deck immediately, huddling against a barrel. Basuba knelt down beside her, motioning to Marion to do the same.

For a short while, Basuba simply cradled Fiona as if she were a small child. The older woman crooned some wordless tune as she gently rocked her friend and stroked her red curls. Marion, confused and frightened, tucked herself under Basuba's other arm. She patted Fiona tenderly on the shoulder. She had never seen the bold country woman like this. It was strange to be comforting her. It seemed wonderful, too, until Marion remembered that if Fiona was this scared something very bad must be happening.

At that moment, Fiona shook off Basuba's arm and sat upright. "Basuba, there's trouble. I caused it. Big trouble. She says it's gone too far to stop. You've got to help me. I'll do anything you say."

"Start from the beginning."

After she had listened long enough to get the gist of the trouble, Basuba broke in with a command and some questions. "We'll do a protection prayer for you and the preacher right now." She thought a moment and went on, looking Fiona right in the eyes. "Fiona, the prayer will protect you better if you can truly desire that Preacher Denton be protected from harm, too. Can you do that?"

Slowly, very slowly, Fiona nodded her head.

"Whew!" thought Basuba to herself. "She's truly frightened if she's willing to help him so readily." The herbalist took a deep breath and made a silent prayer to the Spirits of her Ancestors to assist her in the work of undoing the damage of Madame Dora's spell.

With the completion of the prayer, Fiona felt her pulse begin to smooth out as her heart stopped pounding against her chest. "You must tell me as exactly as you can, word for word, what you intended for Preacher Denton with this spell."

Basuba's question helped to clear Fiona's head and she was quick to answer. "I wanted to destroy his power so that no one will listen to him when he speaks. I wanted to make him small and weak so that people will not even notice him when they see him. I wanted to take away his confidence that he has been chosen by his god to lead others."

Basuba felt fire rise from her belly to her chest and she flared at Fiona, "Careless woman, do you not know what you ask for? I only hope that you did not call those words into a spell before you left. You know the principle that is the foundation of all spells! You would have all that come back to you three times over? Your own words to fall to the ground, unheard by others? Your person so emptied of the Life Force that others will not even see you when you stand in front of them? And the most hardhearted, that you can no longer hear the Great Mother speak to you, call you her Own Dear Child? All this you would bring upon that man and yourself?"

Basuba sighed heavily, the anger burned out. She shook her head, "tsked" a bit, and said more gently, but very solemnly, "You have failed to take the 'Three Times Over' principle to your heart, Fiona." She swiftly reached out her hand and cupped her sternly under the chin. "If I am to help you now, you will return to take up this teaching when we have put things aright."

Fiona bowed her head and gulped, "Yes, ma'am, I will do that. I had not thought about any of what you've said."

"Madame Dora did not remind you of that?"

"No, ma'am."

Basuba turned her attention to the spell. "What do we have to help us here? You were the petitioner, and so it stands in our favor that you are the one wanting to undo the harm. Now, the question is whether we must destroy what the Madame has done or whether, by luck, we may be able to turn it around by building on it. It will be far easier to build if we can." She mumbled to herself as she mused for a moment. "Ashes. You sowed the circle with ashes. A prayer to destruction, but we can also cast it as a request for Change, for Death and Rebirth. We may be able to work with that. What was actually said by you and by the Madame to bind Preacher Denton? Think carefully. Tell me everything so I can choose best whether we undo or go forward."

Suddenly the words were as clear in Fiona's mind as if the spell were being cast that very instant. She repeated them to Basuba. "Madame Dora said, 'The token that will bind the powers of that wicked preacher. The token that will silence his lips when he speaks out against the likes of you and me. The token that will ensure that he has known his last day of binding the minds of poor, foolish folks to his will.'"

"And the token, did she hold it as she spoke?"

"No. No, she didn't know what it was then. She said all that as the sign that I should bring the rope out."

"Good. An intent spoken, but without a means to make it hold. You did not touch the rope to the poppet, right?" There was no sign of the rope.

Fiona's face fell. Had they touched? Her fear had been so intense she couldn't remember now. Her hands groped for her pockets. She found a bulge. Could it be? Yes, it was! With a victorious grin, her first smile of the night, Fiona whisked out the poppet.

"I have no memory of grabbing it. Thank Nature." She hugged the cloth bear to her heart.

Watching her, Basuba turned away to hide the smile that played on her lips. She would not weaken the healing happening in this moment by reminding the proud Fiona that she was extending love to what would have been the preacher. Instead she turned her face to the Heavens and silently thanked her Spirit Guides for this little gift that was already doing wonders to turn the spell. And she thanked them for the confirmation that they were on a good path.

Basuba turned to hug Marion who had been quiet all this time. "Run back to my pallet and get my flask, Night Star. We need some water for the Banishing. And my Healing Pocket with the special herbs. Fiona, tell her where your largest ribbon is. We need that, too."

Trembling, Marion reviewed her list: flask, Healing Pocket, blue ribbon. She must move fast; she could hear the urgency in Basuba's voice. But how she dreaded to leave her friends when Madame Dora's presence flooded the entire ship. Then, like a shooting star, the memory of Grandfather arrived at her side. There he stood, holding out a hand for hers. She could see better into the shadows. It felt safe to move. Darkness was a friend.

While Marion was gone, Basuba asked Fiona, "Are you steady enough to return with Marion and me to the ash circle? It would be best if we washed it all away as soon as possible. She has left there by now, don't you think?" Basuba saw her friend shudder at the final question.

"What if she has not, Basuba?"

"Then, we will be united and strong when we meet her. I wager that she's sleeping like a baby by now."

"How can you say that after all that has happened?"

"Because I'm guessing that she's as good an actress as we've ever beheld in the ha'penny theaters of Ely Green."

With Fiona carrying the flask of water, the women made their way cautiously to the dinghy. No sign of Madame Dora, but the ash circle remained. Basuba directed them to sit around it.

She said to Fiona and Marion, "We must work fast to attach our visions to the forces that Madame Dora has raised. Do what I ask, and quickly." The other two nodded their assent.

Basuba looked at them closely. "What I ask of you may not be easy. Remember to trust me in spite of your doubts."

Reaching for the flask, Basuba uncorked it. "Fiona, your scarf."

Fiona held out the sky-blue scarf, her last purchase from Ely market. As Basuba lifted the flask up to the skies to bless it and then poured some water onto the ribbon, her meaning dawned on Fiona. For a brief moment, the young woman clung tightly to the scarf. Then, before Basuba had to say anything, she relinquished and placed her beautiful ornament, her first scarf, in the center of the ash circle.

"With this Holy Water and our open hearts, we banish all thoughts and words of ruination spoken against anyone here tonight," said Basuba in a compelling voice. In rhythm with her words, Fiona began to wash the circle clean with her scarf. "We banish desires to bind the gifts of Preacher Denton's speech." And then Basuba said quietly, "Fiona, you carry on now." There was silence while Fiona sat stock still. Basuba guessed that the young woman was regretting her agreement to trust her fully. Would she bolt or stay with them?

Ever so slowly, Fiona resumed washing the circle. After what seemed like an age to Marion, she said, "With Nature's help and this Holy Water, we banish all hopes that Preacher Denton become invisible to his followers."

Another pause. She swallowed hard in a desert-dry throat. "We banish all wishes that he lose his confidence that God speaks directly to him."

She couldn't stand it. This was too much. "Basuba," she whispered bitterly, "have you forgotten what he has said to his followers about you, about me, about the natives of the Americas?"

"No, child, I have not, though it seems to you that I have. Go on. We must carry through with this. The evil work is not yet fully undone. Danger for him and for you still rides this ship with us," she whispered back. Then she added, "Go on. You do well. Follow your open heart. Stay with me."

Fiona looked at the circle. Some of it was gone, but enough remained. She knew that she would have to continue with the banishing of all that she and Madame Dora had intended until every trace of the ash was gone. She swallowed hard. She tried to form the words that would banish all her desire to quench Denton's powers to bind the minds of others to him. But, for all her desire to trust Basuba, she could not go that far. Did she have to give up her fight for fairness to appease the Spirits? It did not seem right.

At that moment Basuba said, "Be true to yourself. Say only those things you can live by. But find those thoughts quickly, for time moves on."

Then something shifted inside her and Fiona was ready.

Images of Denton and Madame Dora waited in her mind. "By Nature and my Ancestors, I banish my desire to harm another by binding his powers, or her powers, be it man or woman. I banish my desire to fight my enemy with the hatred she or he uses against me."

When Fiona looked down at the circle, all traces of ashes were gone.

Basuba felt the forces of evil fall away. She took a large pinch of dried crocus leaves from her Healing Pocket and sprinkled them over the circle, speaking with warmth and gentleness in her voice. All the while she wondered if her brave pupil would be able to follow her next move, too.

"By the powers of New Life, we ask that Preacher Denton's true gifts from the Creator grow and flourish. We ask that our ability to love in the face of doubt be strengthened. Mari?" She offered some crocus leaves to her niece.

Taking the greens, Marion said, "We ask that Preacher Denton stop hating us and the natives of the New World." She passed the leaves on to Fiona.

Fiona sighed as though she were surrendering something. "With this gift of New Life, we ask that all of us, especially Preacher Denton and Madame Dora and myself, learn to know the difference between the voice of Nature and the voice of our own pride," she said forcefully as she tossed the leaves.

It was done. The spell reversed.

Basuba brought the ceremony to a close with a prayer that asked that any harm, unknown to them, that Madame Dora had brought in be banished. Then she thanked Great Mother Nature and the Ancestors, and they opened the circle with a chant.

Soon the three were back in their pallets, sleeping soundly.


"Will our spell work?" The tea leaf reader's hawk eyes darted into Marion's memory. "Can Madame Dora fix Fiona with any evil eye? How can you be sure our spell is stronger than hers? Will we see Preacher Denton change? What if…"

By the afternoon of the next day, Marion was all questions. Fiona, following Basuba as closely as her own shadow would, sat silently and listened to her young friend ask them.

"Enough! That's plenty of questions right there," Basuba chided gently. "Yes, our spell is under way. There were signs of it taking form last night as we cast it. And, yes, it is stronger than Madame Dora's spell. Any spell built on love is more powerful than one built on hate. As for the Evil Eye, Madame Dora may use her mind to try to weaken Fiona, but it won't have an effect. Fiona did a lot of cleansing last night with us. She has very little anger or hate left inside her for any of the Madame's spells to attach themselves to."

Basuba looked over at Fiona. "If you sense her fixing her thoughts on you, you have only to see yourself protected and know that anything hurtful will fail to touch you." Fiona wore such a serious face that Basuba added playfully, "If, however, Madame Dora walks up to you and it looks like she's going to strike you, then duck. That's the difference between thoughts and action."

They all grinned.

"What about Preacher Denton? How will our spell change him?" asked Marion eagerly.

"Ah, Sweet Cabbage, that question draws us into the realm of Mystery." Basuba rearranged her body to get more comfortable, and Marion knew this answer would be a long one. "As you know, we are made out of clay and brought to Life by Nature breathing into us…"

Marion nodded at this tale, familiar from her earliest days. Was it her father who had first taken her little hands in his to pat a lump of river clay into the figure of a person? She let the shadowy memory slide away and returned her attention to Basuba.

Basuba was saying, "We are, then, Spirit living in Body. Spirit is lighter and moves faster. It hears prayers. Body is denser and slower. It hears and sees actions. With our spell, we entered the place of Spirit. Our hopes and prayers went from our Spirits to the preacher's Spirit, carried there by Nature and by our Ancestors."

"Preacher Denton's Spirit is receiving prayers from our Spirits right now?"

"Yes, you can think of it that way. And Madame Dora, too. She was named in one of Fiona's prayers. Will we see the changes? Who knows? Our prayers give birth to change on the Spirit plane. But to 'see' changes, they must show in the actions of the preacher so that we can recognize them through our bodies, our ears and eyes. It takes longer for the changes to manifest there."

"We must watch carefully then," said Marion.

"Yes, and we must train ourselves to see changes that are ever so small, for that's probably how they shall begin."

"And the Madame. If love is stronger than hate, why is she living such a fine life?"

Basuba reached over to tussle Marion's head and smiled. "Is she leading such a fine life? I do not think so. She travels alone, she eats her meals alone. She fears aging for she paints her face against it. When she believes no one is watching her, her face looks quite sad."

"Her mind is mostly on money," added Fiona.

"I guess I've never seen her eyes shine with light the way yours do. And her smile seemed scary the day we talked. I felt a chill around her table when I went close to it," noted Marion, surprised at what she could tell by looking back through time.

"You know much about her, don't you, Niece?"

"Yes. How is it that I do?"

"It's probably your stopping long enough to catch up with what your insides have to tell you," said Basuba.

Marion's face suddenly reflected a sorrowful cast. Basuba saw what was happening and said, "Here you are again, saving the hardest part for last. What is on your mind, Mari?"

This time Marion faced Fiona with her question. Her face blazed red with rage. "You Irish are people of the Old Ways. You're not supposed to do evil like the preacher, like the witch hunters do. What happened to Madame Dora?"

Marion's confusion and anger threw Fiona back to memories of herself at age thirteen. Awkwardly, as though she were a boy reaching out for the first time to hold the hand of a sweetheart, Fiona grabbed one of Marion's hands in hers, a hand hot and balled up into a fist, resisting her touch. Fiona was silent and gave herself a few breaths' time; the hand softened and opened.

Fiona avoided looking into Marion's face too quickly. She said, "I remember when I asked that same question. My story is different, of course, but, underneath the surface, my question was truly a match for yours. My two friends and I were playing in the river, hiding under a stone bridge. Tommy fell in and couldn't swim. Dennis and I weren't big enough to get him out. Just then Lady Nash's coach drove by. She ordered one of her drivers to jump into the river and pull Tommy out. He was saved, and I was glad of it. But I was so angry that it was the Lady who saved his life. I wanted to think that all the nobles were cruel to us field workers and tinkers. That made it easier to know whom to hate and whom to care for."

She paused to give Marion some time to think. Then she asked, "Do you see how our questions are alike, Mari?" Fiona sounded almost shy as she called Marion by her nickname for the first time. Then she smiled into her young friend's face, squeezed her hand, and let it go.

"Yes," sighed Marion. "I guess I was wanting to believe that Christians are the bad ones and that all of us who follow the Old Ways are the good ones. It's easier that way, but confusing, too, because I do know some good Christians."

"Whew! I'm glad you're changing your mind, Niece, because there are not so many of us people of the Old Ways left. If we were to be the only good ones, we'd be in a big stewpot of trouble," teased Basuba. "It's hard enough for us as it is, even with all the kind Christians," she added more glumly.

Basuba turned to Fiona. The sun shining behind her danced in the auburn highlights of her hair. "Are you sad about dirtying your fine blue scarf last night?"

"It pinched me for a moment then. But no more. It's become one of my ceremonial tools, thanks to you." She looked directly at Basuba and added softly yet clearly, "Thanks to you, Teacher."

"You honor me. Fiona, you did fine work last night. You were brave, you were honest, you took action instead of hiding from the trouble. You trusted me even when it was hard. And you made beautiful, strong prayers."

Fiona bowed her head in the face of so much praise. Basuba's words seemed to flow right into the bottom of her heart. Strange, they did not seem to be feeding her hungry pride—rather, they fed her love.

Basuba said, "There's more. Listening to you last night, watching you, I saw you learn the truth of the 'Three Times Over' principle. If you believe that you can let it guide you from now on, I think that you have indeed taken in its lesson well enough."

Fiona raised her head, looked deep into Basuba's eyes, and said with a huge smile, "Yes, I am willing to follow."

## Chapter 14

# Becalmed

*North meet West, let the dance begin.*
*Dance, dance, oh ye winds.*
*What was still, now be aswirl.*
*Dance, dance, oh ye winds.*

Basuba, Marion, and Fiona sat with their friends a couple of days after the incident with Madame Dora. They watched another day drawn to its close by the setting of the sun.

Resting there on the bench, Fiona sensed her body flexible and calm. Something inside her had grown steadier since the ceremony she had done with Basuba and Marion. And she had survived seeing Madame Dora with no bad effects.

"Have you heard the story going around the ship that there are three or four men in the brig who've been indentured against their will?" asked Peter Turner.

"What? I've heard that some of the traders have ended up there for a night or two when they've drunk too much. But folks held against their will for the entire trip? How does that come about?" asked Fiona.

"Oh, some poor fool lets himself be plied with liquor by a stranger in a gin shop, a 'Spirit' they call him near the docks. In the morning, when he comes to, he's on a ship bound for the New World without a cent to his name. Been spirited there, you see. He has to eat, of course, and so he owes the captain a lot by the time they dock. He sits in the brig until his looks suit someone. Then his fare and board are paid, and he owes five or more years to his new master."

"Oh, wretched! Does that happen often?"

"It's hard to know since there are not many who care to tell the tale to folks such as us. And those who might want to, the ones who find themselves in the brig, they need to stay on good terms to finish their indentureship as soon as they can."

"We fear it's quite a big business," said Barbara. "We've heard of letters being intercepted and changed. Let's say my cousin writes me in Boston from England. He asks if I can pay his passage. The letter never reaches me. Instead, a 'Spirit' forges a reply saying 'Yes.' My cousin arrives and no one is there to meet him. No money for the fare. He's forced into indentureship, and some scribe gets a handsome fee."

Marion shivered, perhaps from the cool evening breeze, or perhaps because her hopes for the New World were rent some by the Turners' story.

Basuba gazed absent-mindedly out to sea as her thoughts wandered through her collection of herbs. If the rumor were true, and those men were being deprived of sunshine and fresh air, they must be ailing.

Fiona frowned. Why had Jean-Paul never mentioned anything about any men in the brig to her?

Dawn broke in a still sky as Fiona watched. She had witnessed every dawn but two of the voyage so far. Today she found herself alone on the deck. "No sign of the preacher," she noted after straining her neck to scan the entire rigging for him. How odd that the realization did not bring her glee, but instead left her wistfully imagining what joy it must have brought to start out each day as he had done up in the ropes.

Facing East to greet the morning sun, Fiona thought of her family so many miles behind her. Back home, folks would have risen long before this first light, rekindling the fire, preparing the meal to break the night's fast. The familiar scene ran through her mind each morning like a link on a chain of memories. The strange thing was the way her mind then turned to consider what Matthew Fields might be doing. It had done this so many times that she had a clear picture of his cottage, the table where he sipped his gruel and chewed his dry bread, and his parents. Images for all of them and she had never even been to Plainfield. The young man entered her dreams, too. More and more often when she awoke, she had the sense that he was just leaving her presence.

Fiona hailed Jean-Paul when she saw him and he came over to greet her.

"Not a spit of wind in our sails this morn and a sky clear as a bell. We haven't moved for a minute in the last two days. This'll surely be our third day dead in the water. Captain's worried. Fines to pay when we fall behind schedule like this. Comes out of all of our hides."

"How long could this last?"

"Can't say for sure. Keep scanning the horizon for clouds. That's the sign we need."

"Jean-Paul, is it true that there are indentured men held in our brig?"

The sailor looked down at the deck, his eyes avoiding hers. He busied himself by tightening a rope in the rigging.

"We've not seen them. Do they never get out?" she persisted.

"They get out. Come up to work the night shift." He finally looked over at her. "Never do see the daylight, though."

"Why haven't you told me about them?"

He shrugged and made ready to leave. "Why should I? Not your business. Not mine."

She wasn't finished. "But they've done nothing wrong. And they're held against their will."

"Yes. And you want me to unlock the door and let them out?"

"You and the rest of the crew. There must be enough of you who'd dare to do it."

"What for, Mistress? Do you think that the *North Star* is the only ship that the Spirits work? Hah! Nigh every ship that crosses the Atlantic carries secret cargo of one kind or another. Who do you think loads that cargo, unloads it at the other end? None of us has clean hands." He jumped up onto a barrel, leapt into the rigging, and was gone.


By afternoon, word around the ship was that they were indeed becalmed. A few of the poorer families and some of the laborers held themselves back from meals; they could not afford to build up a bill larger than what they were already accruing. Each additional charge increased the length of the indentureship they would owe to a master in the New World. Fiona noticed that Anne's family stayed away from the mess hall. She wondered how she could get a rusk or two to the girl and, if she succeeded, whether it would be accepted. And she wondered if she knew enough about the ocean wind patterns yet to work the weather the way she could back home.

Fiona was at the railing next daybreak reviewing what she knew of the Atlantic's weather signs. A hazy ring around the sun always brought wind and, perhaps, stormy weather. A great circle around the sun signified storms for sure; if there was a break in the circle, the winds would gust from that direction. The only sign today was a low dawn. That should mean low winds, but, so far, there'd been no wind. The air was so still that the gull flying by a moment ago was reflected perfectly in the glassy surface of the sea. Just as Jean-Paul had predicted, they had moved little the day before, if at all.

At the back of her mind she heard the worried voice that calculated that the *North Star* had been becalmed since Madame Dora cast her spell.

Fiona heard a slight noise and turned to find Jean-Paul at her side. He grinned and looked down at her long green skirt and full apron. "Too bad you don't wear britches. On a still morn like this, I'd dare to take you up to the Crow's Nest if you had the strength in your arms for it."

"I have the strength and I have the yen. Get me some britches and I'll go." Suddenly Fiona saw herself up in the rigging working the weather the way she did at home. True, she could not read all the weather signs yet, but she could make a good guess. Using what she did know would be a lot more satisfying than staying down below on deck, stewing about being becalmed. Besides, how exciting to climb that high and be as free as the gulls.

"You'd do it?" Regret hung heavy in his voice. It had seemed such a simple gesture to get back on the young woman's good side. He had never dreamed she would take him up on it. "Don't you worry about your reputation among the proper folks on the ship?" he asked anxiously.

"I've worked in the fields all my days; I'm sturdy as a youth. If I tuck my hair in a cap, they'll never suspect a woman."

"Well, the captain and the first mate were in their cups late last night, so they'll be snoring now. No one else on the crew to worry about. All right. I'll be back with some britches."

Ten minutes later, a graceful youth emerged from behind a barrel and Fiona was nowhere to be seen. But the youth's suppleness was lost to the tremendous weight of the britches. The only available pair in the right size had been seasoned with layers of tar for protection against the cold, numbing dampness of storms.

Taken aback by the extra weight of the pants she had donned, Fiona almost lost her nerve when she scanned the distance to the Crow's Nest. The thought that the spell she had put in motion through Madame Dora might lie behind the becalming spurred her on like a goad in her side.

Saying nothing about either her fear or her plan to her guide, she started up the rigging behind him, calling on Alyona, and all the Spirits that dear woman prayed to, for assistance now. Step by step, ever so slowly, she moved from one rung of the rope ladder to the next. The distance between each rung, designed with large men in mind, was greater than the widest of her steps. With each upward thrust, she needed all the strength she had in her arms.

She fell into the rhythm of calling out one Spirit Guide's name with each thrust she made. "Help me, Mother Mary." Lunging for the next step—"Carry me, St. Bridget." And the next step—"Stay with me, Alyona."

She could read the concern on Jean-Paul's face when he looked down at her. She must look as gawky straddling the rigging as the preacher had ever appeared to her.

At last she was crawling into the lookout with the sailor's help. "I'm fine. I've brought in too many harvests to be tired out by this. I'm just slow in these heavy britches climbing a ladder made for big men." She grinned at him and he relaxed. "Don't you worry a whit about me falling from here. But now that I'm up here, I'm going to stay for a while and enjoy myself. You need not wait for me."

The Crow's Nest was too tiny for two bodies, so Jean-Paul left her there and climbed part way back down the ropes.

Alone in the lookout, Fiona surveyed the sky. Absolutely clear in every direction.

She prayed to Alyona, to Mother Mary, to all her Ancestors, saying, "Forgive me for my part in bringing about this becalming through asking for a spell to bind Preacher Denton's powers. The becalming serves no one and harms many. Help me now to court the winds, to tell their story so the *North Star* may move again."

She looked down at the deck where she could see the routine activities of the early morning. Then, with surprise, her eye was drawn to the prow where a size-able crowd gathered around a group of four men. One of them waved his arms in the style that she recognized immediately to be Preacher Denton's. Why did that horrid preacher, of all people, have to show up now and disturb her mood when she was finally up in the skies where she'd longed to be since the beginning of the trip? And why were so many folks milling around him, and at this early hour?

Fiona forgot all about the deck as she turned her attention to what she knew about weather. She greeted the Four Directions and called on each for assistance: East, to bring winds; South, for the fire of the sun to heat the air to start the winds moving; West, that the water lend itself to dancing and moving easily today; North, that the solid earth of the New World call out to them, bring them home to it. Then, facing the northwest from where the weather would come, Fiona told the story of what she wanted to have happen: "In your broad reach, cool air from the North and warm air from the West meet, and stir each other up. Your meeting becomes a whirling dance, the dance sends eddies to circle out through the air. The offspring of your union fly towards us. Your loud howling voices fill our sails with wind."

As she told the story, Fiona imagined every part of it happening as vividly as she could. She pretended she could already see the winds swirling, feel them rushing against her face, hear them howling. If only the ship's passengers understood this work the way the Blue Fens weather workers did! Then they all would be envisioning the things she was; making howling wind sounds; moving their arms, their bodies as though they were buffeted by the wind; and the story would have more life to it with a better chance of manifesting.

Fiona began to chant, making up verses as she went along, letting the wind she was calling give her the words that would arouse it. "North meets West, let the dance begin. Dance, dance, dance, oh ye winds. What was still, now be aswirl. Move our wee boat along."

She sang the refrain a number of times. How she longed to move her arms back and forth, making the rhythmic undulating motions that would honor the wind.

A sharp voice of caution in her mind warned against it: "This is just the action that will name you 'witch.' Don't do it. Don't endanger yourself and the others!"

But her will and her self-respect fought back hard. "This is who I am. I do honor Wind. I do dance with the forces of Nature. I have been trained to call them, been given the teachings of lifetimes. I cannot pretend that I do not know what to do."

Common sense told her that some eyes from the deck below might well be upon her. Most might not guess exactly who she was, but she probably did not look to anyone like a member of the crew. If she were daring enough, this could be an opportunity to show Christians what the Old Ways—the gifts that were there for everyone—could do. Certainly, a change in weather would benefit them all. Then they would no longer fear the Old Ways, fear Wicca, as a dangerous practice, but see its beauty.

The face of Anne came to her, and in response Fiona opened her arms to let them move. Her arms danced, they beckoned, they mimed what they hoped the wind would soon do as a child mimes an elder, a friend in play.

Suddenly, the face of Anne's mother pushed itself into her mind. That hard, fearful stare that Fiona had felt fixed on her more than once since the making of the poppets. No, this woman would not be delighted by the gifts of the Old Ways; she would be further frightened by the power. In that moment, the country woman understood in a new way that it was the power the wise women had, not their actions, that had led them to the stake to be burned.

What to do now? Betray her past, or betray the present, and possibly the future? Anger tore through Fiona like a raging bull. She could not—would not—live her life this way like a captive animal. Her mind filled with the memory of a huge brown bear, dressed in a ridiculous red ruffled skirt, moving on its hind legs in front of a crowd at a fair. She refused to live like that. Where would she find a place that would allow her to be herself?

Breaking her pride, the young woman pulled her arms in and imagined that she swayed with the breezes, imagined that she played with the winds.

She sent the images out as best she could and then finished her prayer with "If it be for the good of all, let the winds come."

She put one leg over the edge of the lookout and felt for a foothold. Jean-Paul waited for her just below on the rigging, baffled by what he had watched this strange young woman doing, and more than a little anxious about any repercussions that might come his way.

"With some luck, Captain Billard and his first mate will still be sleeping off their liquor," he wished fervently.

If Fiona had secretly hoped that someone might have recognized her in the Crow's Nest and been a bit awed by what she had done, she must have been disappointed.

Marion came running up to her a few minutes after she was back on deck dressed in her usual garb. Breathless, the maiden flailed her arms in excitement. "I've been looking all over for you. Have you heard the news? Those men who've been held in the brig this entire trip—why, the preacher's just brought them up onto the deck. He marched down there and got them out."

"Let's go see."

The two hurried to join the throng of spectators still gathered around the men. Marion glimpsed Biddy Allen and Biddy Jacobs with baby Elizabeth in her arms in the crowd. Fiona spotted Salty Bill standing back, watching the spectacle, and steered Marion over to join him. She guessed he would have some comment about the goings on.

When Marion and Fiona got a glimpse of the prisoners, they were startled to see how weak and pale the men looked. The three of them huddled together near the railing; the two older ones covered their eyes to escape the sunlight, and the other one, a heavy man even after all this time with few rations, blinked constantly, turning his entire face into a huge wrinkle each time. Preacher Denton stood a few feet in front of them, orating.

"...And God woke me in the night, and he said, 'Son, it's your job to know the sinners on this ship. You think that you know all of them by now. But there are some sinners being held deep in the bowels of this ship. I want you to go down there and bring them up to the light. Bring them back into God's family.'

"And so, folks, I did that. I went down, down into the bowels of the *North Star*, and I brought the Word of God to these men you see here. And they got down on their knees and begged me to bring them back up to the light. And, here they stand before you now—sinners brought home to God."

Salty Bill stood with his arms crossed in front of his chest and his feet planted wide. He threw his head back and snorted. "What a fox! Snoose has sailed with him before. Says the man's always up to something to get folks' attention. First time I've heard of this one, though. Reputation's catching up with him now. Captain Billard let him on only because he brings so many fares with him. And because of those fares, he gets away with this. He's made himself a big hero today. This'll draw more folks to him."

Denton's voice boomed out. He was leading a prayer. "Dear God, with these sinners offering themselves up to you, we beseech you to send the *North Star* the winds she needs to race across the Atlantic once more. God, I have done my part. I heard You, and I have brought these sinners out of the dungeon into the light. Let the rest of your flock do their part. If enough of you join me in prayer, offering your sins up to the Lord, He will hear us. The *North Star* will move again. If, instead, you hold back from God, He too will hold the winds from us…"

Fiona's jaw dropped.

Salty Bill, who had no idea of where her thoughts took her, grinned at her and said, "And he's aiming to be an even bigger hero. I can see by your face that you agree that rascal's pretty clever. He'll win either way, and, if we do get wind, the captain will keep his mouth shut about him bringing the men up from the brig. Got to hand it to him. Clever rascal."

Just then, Madame Dora strolled by. She looked right at Fiona and said in her loud voice, "We've been becalmed ever since I met you on the deck a few nights back, have you noticed?" Then she threw her head back and laughed and strode off with purpose.

Marion looked at Fiona and said, "I'm off to get Basuba. She'll want to make up a tea for those men."


By late afternoon, a mild breeze stirred, sufficient to ruffle the sails and give the sailors some force to work with. By evening, the wind had grown stronger, and they were moving at a plodding but steady speed. By daybreak, the sails billowed full.

## Chapter 15

# Drawing Down
# the Moon

*Blessed Moon, Blessed Moon*
*Come, shine your light on me.*
*As You grow and as You lessen,*
*Teach me to see.*

Tonight was her night. After folks had retired to the hold, Marion would stand under the Full Moon and picture her best friend all those miles behind her in England. Tonight that mysterious orb would link her close to Gwyneth once again.

With keen anticipation, Marion had watched the Moon grow to full circle over the past few nights. She had spent most of this day in silence, calming her emotions and clearing her mind of thoughts. Since sunset of the day before she had eaten nothing so that she would be able to change her state of mind more easily. She groomed herself carefully, brushing the long waves of her hair, and crushing some cedar sprigs to release their aroma to rub into her wrists. She tied her First Blood pouch around her waist in ceremonial fashion.

Fiona agreed to watch as before. Marion stood at the stern with the Full Moon almost overhead. She sang a chorus of songs, and then, when the moment felt right, she held her pouch up to the Moon and reached in for her carving. There she was, the woman with her arms in an arc raised to the sky. Marion kissed the figurine softly.

As her fingers wrapped around it, she was flooded with images and knowing that seemed half-memory, half-story. She suddenly sensed herself, Gwyneth, Basuba, Fiona, Mary, Elinor, and others whose faces she could not make out, standing in a circle in a grassy field, their arms raised in arcs towards the Full Moon, standing just like the figure in her hand with moonlight streaming into them.

Something else was entering them along with the moonlight. What was it? That flow without a name that traveled deep inside her to feed the source of the wisdom

185

that spiraled up in her and settled her mind when it could not reach a decision on its own. She rounded her arms into a curve that outlined the Moon. Yes, that's what was streaming into her with the moonlight—nourishment for her intuition.

When the moonbeams had danced themselves into a staircase, Marion sang her way up it. When she reached the midpoint, a daisy landed on the step in front of her, and a rose drifted by her right side. She looked up to see Gwyneth at the base of the Moon, her arms full of flowers, her face full of laughter. As Marion hurried up the last steps, the flowers kept wafting down over her. When she reached the top, Gwyneth hugged her. There they were as though they had never separated. They hugged and they sang and they walked the Moon. They looked down on England and tossed handfuls of tiny purple heather blossoms out over the island. When they looked down on the New World, they tossed more. Then each Maiden poured a handful of seeds into the other's First Blood pouch. "Beginnings! Beginnings!" they cried.

Suddenly Marion found herself back on the *North Star* with no idea how she had gotten there. She looked up at the Moon with longing. It hung so high above her in the endless sky. But she was all right, complete. She had met Gwyneth. They each had a pocketful of Beginnings.

Fiona lay still on her pallet, her ears primed to catch the changes in her companions' breathing that indicated they were drifting off to sleep. Then, she slipped ever so quietly out of the hold, drawn to the bright moonlight that caressed the deck. Even though it was easier to fend off the advances of the drunken traders with other folks around, she did not want to have to explain herself to anyone right now.

It was watching Marion earlier that brought Fiona out now to meet with the Moon. Something in the way her friend had raised her arms to that golden orb, something in the full rounded arc of her arms, called to Fiona. She would have no peace until she too had welcomed the Moon into herself this way.

"Why?" her mind asked.

"I'll know as I do it, or sometime afterwards," answered her heart.

"You would stand, unguarded, your back to the deck, with your arms raised in a clear sign of worship?" challenged the mind.

"Certainly!" the brave woman within her responded. Then, something shifted inside Fiona, and she found herself thinking of how such an act could endanger her friends. She returned to the hold and gently shook Marion into wakefulness.

Standing alone in front of the Moon, Fiona took a deep breath. Something would change forever when she drew Moon down into her this way. She knew it. Something would be lost, something gained.

She clasped her hands behind her back and considered leaving without going through the ordeal. Why should she surrender something that she could not even name? What kind of cowardice, complete foolishness, would that be? No warrior with any self-respect would agree to such a sacrifice. She hardened her gaze and looked out at the Moon, determined to resist its strange appeal.

As she turned to leave the railing, she stopped in her tracks. What if the cowardice lay in not risking this exchange with Moon? After all, if she was as strong as she believed, what did she have to fear? If she did not approve of what the Moon brought her, she would put a halt to it. Yes, more courageous to explore this mystery than to back away from it.

Fiona raised her arms. They preferred to shoot straight up, to reach as high as they could. With some effort she rounded them, feeling her way slowly to make them into an arc that echoed the curve of the Moon. How foreign this rounding was to her body. She shifted her feet a bit to accommodate the new position and waited.

"Waiting for what?" asked her mind, which always wanted to keep busy. She put her attention on her breath, softening her belly and breathing slowly, deeply. Each time she found herself caught up in a thought, she pulled her mind back to her breath.

After a while, images began to float up from her womb to her heart. Half-pictures, half-thoughts of a field of tall grain waving in the wind; an apple changing from blossom into round, juicy fruit; a ewe tending her lamb; young folks dancing together; folks gathered around a table, plates of food passing amongst them; old folks telling stories; a woman and a man playing with children. As they fell away, an image of herself that she had never glimpsed before came boldly into her mind. There she was, a full-grown woman giving birth while a young Maiden and an aging Crone sang to her, breathed with her, witnessed for her.

Fiona darted through her mind, looking for the familiar image of herself as Maiden. Always before, Maiden had stood right in the center of her mind's eye, close, always drawing an arrow out of her quiver. Now birthing Mother occupied that space.

On the periphery of her inner vision, Fiona saw something move. She looked. There was Maiden, waving to get her attention, laughing, dumping some of her arrows on the ground. "This quiver's gotten too heavy," she exclaimed.

"Where are you going?" asked Fiona with a great pang of longing piercing her heart.

"Not very far. But out of your center." Maiden waved again. "I'll always be around when you need me. And, remember, I'm fast. I'll be there in a flash." She grinned before she faded into Fiona's imagination.

"Great Mother." The thought pulled Fiona's attention back to the birth scene. It was happening—the change. No way to stop it; no desire to stop it. This was Life. This was the Flow. As she formed the word *flow* in her mind, the moonlight poured into Fiona like a river breaking through a dam to fill a waiting lake. Her arms told her how much they had been longing to hold a curve like this.

"It takes as much courage to stay with something through its ripening as it does to begin something new." The words took up all of her.

Finally, it was finished. She knew when she was completely full. Her body told her. She lowered her arms. Like someone leaving a lover, she was coming back home to herself, changed and yet the same. She stood perfectly still in order to sense the vital fullness she now carried in her being. She murmured her thanks to the Moon and left the railing.

Marion said nothing when Fiona came to her. Like she had done with Jean-Paul a few nights before, the Maiden simply slipped her hand into her friend's and they walked back to the hold in an easy silence.

Basuba willed herself to wake in the wee hours when the Full Moon commenced its downward arc. No one would be afoot then, and with the night so fair the sailors on watch would most likely give themselves over to snoozing. More importantly, she knew this was the right time to seek counsel from the Wisdom of the Night at Full Moon.

The Moon had been up for a long time, and it hung low in the western sky. It shone right over to the New World like a bridge for her. Suddenly Basuba knew what she needed.

What must die was her fear—fear that the Old Ways were being lost, fear that the New World would not give her the resources she needed to continue to be a healer. Until the old had died, she would not be able to see what lay ahead for her. She thought about the seasons: about how it seems that most everything dies in the Autumn, about the long, fallow time without any signs of life, about the wriggling of the seeds underground that happens long before any new sprouts are visible. She saw that she had to move past the Autumn in her own heart. She had to give way to the Fallow Time and accept that it was all right not to know what would come next. She had to trust that Spring would come to her as it always came to Earth.

Yes, she would follow the Moon towards new possibilities. Yes, she would bring with her the knowledge she did have, trust that her friends in the Old World would find their way to carry on, believe that she had been given enough tools, have faith that she would meet others who would help her.

All at once she pictured herself dumping baskets of herbs over the stern of the ship and chuckled aloud at herself. She was ready right this minute to toss most of that "field of herbs" she'd brought with her—ready to open her mind to the healing treasures of the New World, ready finally to follow the principle she had blasted the apothecarists for: to heal with plants that grew near where one contracted an illness.

Yes, she was ready to dump a lot overboard, but she certainly could not do it now in the middle of the night because hauling that much stuff around would definitely awaken most of her sleeping neighbors.

Basuba breathed a sigh of relief. Now that she knew what was needed, she could release her fears and go forward. Her mind was so full of new thoughts that she did not notice the figure who slipped out of the hold just before she went back in. She slept better that night than she had in months.


Denton was also too preoccupied to see the figure who entered the hold as he was leaving. He paced the deck hours before dawn, his stride long and firm. Sometimes he stopped and looked out at the sea, clenching and unclenching his belly muscles, fists and triceps. Although he could feel the ship racing along with the winds, he barely gave it any thought. While he should have been jubilant that delivering the men from the brig had gotten the *North Star* under way again, instead he was totally perplexed about what to do next. It was all about the script that God had handed him for this trip: it simply did not make sense.

The three men, they could fend for themselves now. They had shared enough in his hard-won status of hero to be treated well by the captain and his crew. If not, Peter and Barbara Turner, those crazy Seekers, would take them on as their cause. Let them! He had accomplished what he needed with the three men already: freeing the ship from becalming by bringing them to God.

It was the other one he could not get out of his mind.

Like Peter Turner, Denton had heard the story the traders told about men being held in the brig since the voyage began. When he got the inspiration to rescue the poor fools, he assumed that whoever was down in that darkened hole would do anything that was asked of him to obtain his freedom. After all, George was providing them not only with liberation from their sunless prison but, even more valuable, with liberation from sin. It was so perfect, so clear that this was God's plan. He, a chosen one, would lead them up from veritable darkness into the light, from sin to the Lord, their Father. Who could resist?

But one man had resisted. One man heard him out along with the rest and then refused to give himself over to God in exchange for seeing the light of day. So, of course, Denton had to leave him down there in that dark pit. He had to. Surely God would allow it to be no other way. Surely such a man did not deserve to be brought up from the darkness. Surely.

Since that moment, every time George Denton had tried to nestle his head into his pillow, his own memories of being locked for so long in that dark, damp shed years ago by his father rushed to him. No matter which way he lay on his pallet, however he might huddle, they found him. They would not let him be. The darkness came back, the cold clammy air came back, the rotten, splinter-filled boards he cowered against in the far corner of the shed, the smells, the sounds of silence, and his father's cursing came back. And, worst of all, he came back, the devil himself. He was there just as George's father had screamed that he was.

So it was that George could not bear to let the fourth fellow rot in the brig. When he thought of the wretch down there by himself now, he ached to run right down and tear the brig apart, board by board. It was all he could do to keep himself on the deck, appearing to be who he always had been.

He tried to console himself. Perhaps the devil had already taken the fool. But no, the muscular blond youth had seemed like an ordinary enough fellow, eager as the rest to leave—until he had heard the terms. The other prisoners had no fear of him; in fact, he had been the one to speak for them when George first entered their cell. So what was it that God wanted George to do about this? This was not one of God's tests, was it? His loyalty, or his sanity? Surely he would be of no use to God if he lost his mind.

The preacher tried to think about it practically. If he were to release the man, some of his followers might talk amongst themselves about his being weak, not going the last mile for God. If he left the fellow to rot, Peter Turner was bound to hear about him and would certainly demand his release. Then Turner would look like a hero, too.

George's head began to ache and then to buzz, and soon it was throbbing so fiercely that he could not hear himself think. He could hear only the pounding of his heart. He imagined climbing down into the bowels of the *North Star* once again, pulling some coins out of his pocket for the sailor on duty, and thus getting him to unlock the door to the brig. Unlock the brig and let the sinner out, without giving the poor fool a word of explanation, only a vivid gesture towards the ladder and up.

That made the buzzing stop. George shivered. He would be free from the memories now. But what would God do to him?

As triumphant as George Denton's first emergence from the brig was, just that quiet was his second return. It was early morn as he gestured for the prisoner to mount the rope ladder first, and he followed at a slow, detached pace. Part of Denton longed to stay underground, the child in him believing that God would not be able to find him so easily down below. And, he had no words for his followers to justify this rescue that he could not explain to himself. He held back as the pale man stumbled into the sunlight, and when he himself got off the ladder he stayed right where he was.

But Denton's desire to fade into the background this time did not serve him. After all, he had always clamored to be the center of people's attention. The passengers, licking their chops over any excitement having been this length of time at sea, soon swarmed around this fourth stranger from the brig.

Before he knew it, Denton was surrounded by folks hungry for his dramatic interpretation of the event. As usual, a few of the crew ringed the edges of the crowd which, after yesterday's news, soon swelled to include almost everyone on board, Denton loyalist or not. One of the preacher's followers took the bewildered stranger by the elbow and steered him over to the George's side. The crowd fell into silence, all eyes on the two men.

At that moment, Fiona, Basuba and Marion arrived at the fringes of the commotion.

Basuba, her face lit with a huge grin, was saying to the weather worker, "Thanks, Sister, for your part in getting us asail again," when Marion, mouth hanging open, tugged on Fiona's arm with one hand while she pointed to the man who stood next to Denton with the other.

As soon as Basuba saw who it was, she too put a hand on Fiona's arm.

Fiona's jaw dropped and she said, "Matthew Fields! How in Heaven's Name…" She lunged forward to run to Matthew, to call out his name at the top of her lungs.

Suddenly she felt Basuba's grip on her arm, the same signal that Alyona had sent her in the midst of concocting the spell with the Madame: "Hold back. Pay attention. Wait."

Fiona tried to shrug off Basuba's grip but, strong as she was, she failed.

Basuba whispered firmly in Fiona's ear. "It may not serve Matthew well to have the preacher know that he is a friend of yours right now. There'll be plenty of time for greetings in a few moments."

She felt the young woman's body soften and release its resistance.

Preacher George Denton composed himself as best he could. At least his arms knew what to do, his body knew how to move, even if his mouth had no idea what would come out when it opened. He wanted God with him, if that was possible after what he had just done, so he began with a prayer.

"Dearest Lord, I come to You as a confused sinner, just like the rest of the folks here. Sometimes the way to You is clear, sometimes it lies covered in fog. Sometimes a man has to act in the midst of the fog, knowing all the while that You are present, even though Your Way is not visible. Today has been such a day for me." Denton relaxed a bit. His old rhythm was there, his voice was strong; he was sounding like himself—except for his words. His words were weak, wishy-washy. Why had he admitted to his own confusion? He was supposed to be the sure-footed leader.

In spite of his concerns, he turned to gesture towards Matthew and heard himself speaking again. "I found this fourth man in the brig when I went down there yesterday. This man would not take God for his Salvation, would not bend his knee to Our Lord. And so I left him there in the damp and the darkness. Left him there alone. But," here George Denton was as surprised as everyone else by what he said next, "the Lord came to me in the night. He said, 'George, you have always done right by me. You have followed My Teachings closely. But, this time I would have you do something more. I would have you reach out to that lonely sinner and rescue him. We cannot afford to leave him alone with the devil in that cell. Even though he will not have Us, we will not abandon him to Our Enemy.' And so, folks, I did rescue this man from the devil and brought him up into the light, too. Let us thank the Lord now for his Goodness and Mercy."

Denton stopped, aware that his followers expected a much longer speech from him. But he was finished and agog at what he had just learned from his own words. What a tremendous relief to be right with God again.

Basuba could not keep a grin from traveling from one ear to the next, but she waited to hear what her friends might say. Fiona could think only of finding her way to Matthew as soon as possible, so it was Marion who looked over to her aunt and asked, "Isn't this our spell at work? Nudging the preacher to let a good-hearted Pagan out of the brig."

All three of them burst into laughter so gay it matched Fiona's entire ribbon collection.

As for Matthew, he was never able to decide which surprised him most: being released from the brig after all, or watching Fiona half-walk half-run towards him on the deck of the *North Star.*

The Turners championed the indentured men as Denton suspected they would. The couple went directly to Captain Billard and, on the strength of the popularity of the release, secured meals and four pallets for the ex-prisoners in the hold with the other common passengers.

Billard agreed begrudgingly but insisted that he would have to add a surcharge to their bill to cover the improvement in accommodations. "No special favors. Wouldn't be fair to the other passengers, and a man has a right to his livelihood. I have to buy the grub they eat, remember?"

Basuba was there beside Matthew with tinctures and poultices as his eyes readjusted to the sunlight, his body to the freedom of movement and the better food, and his temperament to the bombardment of choices, voices, possibilities, and decisions.

Marion was there to bring him up to date on all that had happened to them, to fill him in on the other passengers, to wonder with him about what the New World would be like.

Fiona was there, taking her time getting used to his being there. She, who was usually so quick to act, needed time for her mind and her dreams to settle down together before she was ready to go forward. And Matthew was in no rush; he was content with recuperating and enjoying the undulating, shimmering waves of gratitude that kept washing through him.

Marion quickly powdered the page she had been writing, scrolled it and put it away in her bag. Whenever she wrote about Gwyneth, her work was cut short by a nagging inside her. For one thing, paper was so costly it was outrageous to use it not for a document, not for a letter, but to record one's own thoughts. Did anyone else do that? Fine ladies, perhaps. She grimaced at her extravagance. For another thing, she worried that it was possible to put too much store in writing. Why, just penning her thoughts, turning them into black images and pouring them across a sheet of paper, seemed to accord them a ring of truth. Here she was, guessing wildly at how Gwyneth was feeling and what she was thinking since they had parted, and then finding that she half-believed she was correct as soon as her ideas became words incarnate.

Matthew walked over and sat down beside her. "Are you putting away your pens and paper? I was just coming over to see if you'd trade me a letter to my folks for a couple of harvest songs? I know it's not the best price you've been offered, but it's my tops," he said with a smile.

Marion laughed back. "Your three best songs and it's done." Then she asked more seriously, "Your family? What is the last they know of you?"

"Between you and me?"

"Yes, cross my heart."

"I told them I was off to London to come home with a wife, so young and sure I was then. And they've had no word of me since."

He fell silent and then spoke again as his thoughts moved on. "Who knows who's been feeding Yellow Hound." His voice was so sorrowful by then.

"Oh, Yellow Hound!" cried Marion, her hand rushing to her heart. She remembered the fun of playing fetch with him. "Matthew, he's such a good dog. I mean, he's friendly and he's also a fine protector. I'm sure he's found his way to a good home by now. But he must miss you something fierce."

Matthew reached for her hand and gave it a squeeze. "Thanks, Mari. What you say helps even though we don't know if it's true."

Fiona walked by a few moments later, expecting to stop and chat. She wanted to tell them that she had just thrown off a shriveling stare that Madame Dora had fixed on her. When she saw Marion and Matthew, heads bent together over pen and paper, she continued her stroll instead.


"Watching the sun go down could get into my blood," said Peter Turner, his face picking up a pinkish glow from the fiery flames of red and orange that spread across the western sky.

"Would that I could live to see the likes of that," teased his wife. "The minute we hit solid ground, Peter'll be looking for a law to rally against. No more dilly-dallying with sunsets. Just you watch."

Even now, surrounded by miles of water, Turner was ready for action. "Let's start with Matthew's story and then we'll figure out what to do about his future," Peter said eagerly. He had been biting his tongue for two days now, waiting for that story.

Matthew studied the deck for a while. When he did raise his eyes, he caught a glimpse of Fiona's long lashes as she quickly lowered hers away from his face.

He released a loud breath and said, "My story has all the markings of my kind. A country youth, new to city ways, new to city ale, never been to the docks before, taken in by a friendly face who insists on touring me by the big ships. The fellow next pours some of the strongest ale I've ever had down my throat and then expects me to buy a round. He was a very big man, hailed by everyone in the tavern, so I agreed. Soon, I'm out cold and when I awake, I'm in the brig. Similar story for the other three; same 'Spirit' in fact for two of us."

Peter Turner was not convinced. He said, "Matthew, that story may work for them. But you seem somehow quicker than that, more like a cat who'd land on his feet. Hard for me to picture the man who could get you to drink when you did not want to. There must be more to your story."

Matthew's eyes returned to the deck. Peter assumed the red glow he saw creeping across the youth's face was a reflection of the fiery sun's last kiss.

Fiona broke the building silence that was weighing heavy on them all by asking "What do you know of the others, Peter?"

He shook his head. "Not much. They still seem dazed. Glad to have a pallet and some food. They talk as though it's hopeless to fight their indentures."

"Poor fools, they follow Denton like chicks do a hen," groaned Barbara Turner. "But it doesn't sound like he's offered them any counsel since he got the credit for putting wind back in the sails with their release."

"I wish we could tell people that it was Fiona!" said Marion fiercely.

"We know all too well what the preacher would do with that," sighed Basuba.

"What about us? What will be our plan to save Matthew from five years of indentureship?"

Fiona felt her heart hit the bottom of her stomach. "Five years?" she echoed weakly, not knowing where to look. She couldn't bear to cast her eyes on Matthew.

"That's what Captain Billard has in his books. That's passage and food both below and above deck, according to what the public will pay for an indentured servant." Wanting to lighten his message with some humor, Peter added wryly, "Would have been four years if he had been content to sit in the brig the entire trip."

"Peter, you've thought about this kind of problem before. What do you suggest we do?" asked Basuba.

"Have you any contacts in the New World? What about your own fare? Is it paid in full?"

Marion's face lit up with a radiance that the setting sun was definitely too weak to be providing.

"I know," she said with a certainty that lifted Fiona's heart right back up to its home in her chest. "We'll stick together, all four of us. Fiona and Matthew can farm, Basuba can tend the ill, I can scribe and teach reading and writing. Together we can work five years off in one. I know we can!"

Peter Turner's eyes were fixed on her. "A young woman after my own mind," he said. "That's some thinking! Never heard of it before, but why not?"

"What about the Hadleys, dear?" said Barbara.

"Jonas Hadley. Of course!" He clapped his hands and told the others eagerly, "Hadley is the administrator of a settlement. A friend of mine from University."

"And he's my second cousin. We've plans to meet him in Boston if our arrival is timely. Which, thanks to you and the preacher, it seems it will be," added Mistress Turner with a wink in Fiona's direction.

"Hadley's coming to the city for supplies and the hiring of any extra hands. He'll meet us at the dock."

"May the Spirits be with us!" crowed Basuba.

Marion looked shyly at Matthew, "Is my plan all right with you?"

Matthew looked back just as shyly. "I need to stretch my legs. Give you a chance to talk about this scheme when I'm not here. If we were family, it would be one thing, but you hardly know me. This is too much to ask of you," he said gruffly. He was off.

Fiona looked with wonder at Marion and Basuba. "You would truly consider giving Matthew such a gift? A gift of a year of your life to someone who's almost a stranger."

Basuba put a hand on a knee of each of her friends and said, looking at her niece, "Mari, it's a wonderful plan. Born in the center of your heart."

Then she widened her view to include Fiona and the Turners. "It is a huge vision that carries the four of us in its arms for the next year. It would have been easier for us all if it had first hatched out of Matthew's hearing. But here it stands, wings and all, in front of us. I say, let's sleep on it. Ask for a dream, maybe, and talk again tomorrow. From listening to what seems true and right for each of us, we'll learn how to move forward from here."

The others nodded. It was a huge plan indeed.

Matthew made himself scarce for the rest of the evening. He ate his stew with Jean-Paul and some of the crew he was getting to know, then retired with them to their quarters to play cards and music.

## Chapter 16

# Shifting Worlds

*The circle is open,*
*Yet never broken.*
*Merry meet, merry part,*
*Merry meet again.*

With the next sunset beckoning them, the Turners and the three women gathered on their usual bench and packing crates to witness it. Matthew was absent as expected.

Fiona allowed herself to notice how she missed the young man's presence. At first she tried to push the soft, warm feeling away by recalling his story and being disgusted that he had gone along with the Spirit's demand that he buy the next round of ale. When she was calling the disgust up, it just disappeared and was replaced by a simple, quiet understanding that he was a good person who had made the best choice he could at that time.

Basuba had just seated herself and was still arranging her skirts when Peter Turner asked, "Well, what's being decided here?"

"Husband, hold your horses," commanded Barbara. "The sun takes a long time to go over the horizon. There's no rush."

Turner grinned at his wife and eased his body back against the wall behind him.

The silence that fell then lingered. Basuba checked herself, not wanting her opinion as the elder of the group to carry too much weight. But as she looked her friends over, she guessed that Marion would not go first since the bold idea had come from her and that Fiona would hold her tongue since it was Matthew at the center of the deliberations. Eventually Basuba said, "I dreamed last night, as I hoped I would. I always feel easier about any decision that comes with a dream." She couldn't resist pausing just at this point.

When Fiona could stand it no longer, she begged, "Basuba, please go on. Tell us your dream."

"I am walking through misty land. And I know that I am carrying something, something fragile and already damaged. I look down to see it's a cooking pot—whole still, but with a long crack down the outside that, luckily, does not run through to the inside. Once I see the pot, my eyes are locked on it. Because of that, the walking gets harder. I nearly step off the edge of a high cliff. At the last moment, I look up and see that if I stretch as far as I can, I can reach over to solid ground."

After taking as much of another pause as she could handle, Fiona asked cautiously, "What do you make of your dream, Basuba?"

"It's a 'yes' to us banding together with Matthew."

Fiona felt her heartbeat speed up as a giant sense of relief gushed through her. Marion lit up, and Peter asked, "How do you read it so, if I may ask?"

"Something like the pot being us standing together. The crack, perhaps, is the danger to Matthew and all of us if we don't look out for each other. The mist, a warning to pay attention to what is around us. The leap to safe ground is the promise that the New World holds for us all."

"And that dream's enough to settle it for you?" continued Peter.

"Yes, funny as that may seem." She chuckled and poked her face in close to Peter's. "Remember, I'm in my Crone Years and I know which signs to trust."

"I'll respect that, Mistress Hutchinson." He turned to Fiona and Marion. "That's one voice cast. What about yours?"

Marion studied the ground for a moment. She rubbed her hands along her thighs to smooth out her excitement. She looked up and said, "Even though it was my idea, I still think it's a good one. Friends should stick together. We would all worry if we didn't know what was happening to Matthew. And how terrible for him to wait five years to be free!"

Marion looked at Fiona expectantly. Then everyone's eyes were on her. Fiona opened her arms in what started out to be a shrug and ended up looking a lot like the beginning of her greeting to the Full Moon. She felt like she belonged somewhere at last—even though it was only the people she was sure of and not the place at all.

"Let's do it!" she said joyfully.

The Turners beamed.

"Mari," Fiona continued, "since it was your idea, do you want to go find him and tell him? Hurry. Bring him back here." Fiona's voice was practically in song.

It took her a few moments to recognize that the new feeling in her body was shyness; it didn't feel nearly as awful as she had expected it would. In fact, there was something incredibly sweet about it.

That night, amazingly enough, Fiona and Matthew found themselves each approaching a place on the deck that gave a lovely view of the rising Moon, which they chatted idly about for a while. When that topic had been thoroughly combed, neither one of them seemed to be able to think of anything else to say.

Fiona caught herself looking down at their two hands on the railing. How close they lay to each other! Two strong hands, different in size, each holding the railing instead of each other. Then she gulped, wondering if Matthew knew what had been holding her gaze for so long. She cleared her throat and looked back out at the moonlight cascading onto the ocean surface. There was only one thing she had on her mind, try as she did to cull up something else they might talk about.

"Matthew, you did not tell us the whole story of how you were spirited away." Her voice was more strained than she wanted it to be. "I saw it in your face."

"You're right." He paused, then in a brusque voice asked, "Fiona, are you asking me to tell you it all now?"

"I guess so," she said slowly, and then added quickly, "but I fear that I will have to apologize at the end of it." What a relief to have admitted it! Now it would be that much easier to listen to him fully.

"First you have to promise that you won't change your opinion about helping me work off the indentureship," he said lightly.

They both laughed and looked at each other in a way they had not done since that night ages ago when John Carter had left them for the tavern.

Her voice was tender, caring, as she said, "Matthew, you didn't have a chance to try out your petition, did you? Who knows what has happened since we left? And, you had no choice about leaving, either. Here you are, with at least the next year of your life accounted for."

"Funny, isn't it? You did have a choice about leaving, but the next year of your life is accounted for, too." They looked at each other, shrugged, and laughed. "When I was in the brig, I had lots of time to stew about the petition—when I wasn't stewing about you. One day, I saw that there was nothing I could do about it anymore. There are either enough people to carry it forward, or there are not. I've had a sense of peace about it since then."

By story's end, Fiona had placed her hand on top of Matthew's, and he had turned his over so they were palm to palm.

Coming out of the privy next day, Basuba found herself face to face with Madame Dora.

"So, your young fox has found a mate. Ask her if I did not tell her early on that she would find her man on this ship."

With that, Madame Dora released Basuba from her piercing gaze and moved out of her path.

Basuba went on her way to her favorite bench. She looked down at the satchel at her knee. Only half as full as it had been last night. It had been hard to release her beloved herb friends into the ocean, but the Full Moon had taught her that that was what she must do in order to be ready to enter into the new life that awaited her on shore. She smiled as she thought about the rake and salmon who had discovered a delicious breakfast treat.

"Funny how much lighter I feel, too," she mused, "though it was my bag that I emptied into the ocean."

"Have something here for you, Mistress."

Basuba recognized Jean-Paul's voice and looked up to greet him. They had been chatting more frequently since she had successfully remedied some of his crew mates.

As he sat down beside her, something wriggled under his shirt. Then a furry little head poked out and gave a meow awfully big for its size. A second little head popped out and looked around.

"Their mother is an excellent mouser. Even takes down a rat now and then. They're for you. Maybe they'll help you get better employment," he said with a grin as he pulled the two kitties out and placed them in Basuba's lap. "Healer with two mousers available for indentureship!" he called as though he were a hawker at a county fair.

As soon as Basuba touched the little balls of tumbling fur, tears of delight and lonesomeness for Blackie and Grey Cat sprang to her eyes. She looked up to the heavens and felt Jimmy's presence. Silently she thanked him for being here with her on this side of the ocean.

Jean-Paul had been watching her the whole time. He shook his head slowly from side to side and said, "You're an odd one, Mistress. Strange as it is, you and yours—but especially you—bring to mind my Indian friends before most white settlers. You'll take the cats then?"

"Most certainly. Which one can I name for you, Friend?" she asked playfully.

"The one who likes to wander the most, I suspect. You'll have to wait a bit to learn which cat that is."

"And you'll have to come visit us so you can watch them grow. Will you?"

"In the fall, yes. Once the shipping stops, I'll spend the winter here in the Americas. Yes, I would like to visit you. And, if you wish it, I'll teach you what I learned from Pidianske about the healing greens that grow here."

"Jean-Paul, you know I'd love that. I'll wait for you."

When he had gone, the herbalist looked up at the heavens again. "Thank you, dear Moon," she said, squinting to find the whitish orb in the blue day sky. "What a gift from the Creator," she sighed, then laughed. "Why, the very day I let go of the old, just look at all the new things that come into my life."

She snuggled the kitties and said to them, "I see now that the knowledge of the past can never be truly lost. If a person follows her path, the Great Mother will continue to provide her with new teachings." Then she gently squeezed the tiny balls of fur and laughed again, for they looked so wise when their whiskers twitched that it seemed as though they understood her and agreed.

Matthew stood looking over the prow of the ship to watch the waves as the dauntless wedge of the *North Star* parted them. So good to feel the breeze in his hair, on his face again; he would never tire of that.

He smiled wryly at his fortune. He who could think of only Fiona, his fields, the trees and the petition for the King a few months ago was now facing a whole new world where customs and laws and property ownership were still fresh fields waiting to be sown for the first time.

His thoughts were interrupted by the arrival of Fiona and Marion. The women took a place on either side of him. Fiona reached up to untie the red ribbon that held her hair back in a braid. How she loved to wear it free to be picked up by the wind.

"How did the meeting go?" she asked.

"It was heated from beginning to end. But we came out all right, if Captain Billard stands by what he agreed to at the last. When I told him our plan, he took his nose out of his account book and slammed it shut. 'Never!' he said. 'I've never heard of such poppycock. Folks dividing an indenture. And women to boot.' Other things like that."

Matthew looked at each of his friends with a grin, "Apparently, he doesn't believe you're strong enough to do a man's work."

"Go on. Then what happened," Fiona urged.

"Peter jumped in, rubbing his hands together like you've seen him do when he's excited. Said as a man of business, he thought it was a brilliant idea."

"A man of business? Peter?"

"Well, we haven't heard his whole life's story now, have we? Anyway, he told the captain that new settlements need many hands for a short while; after that, a long indentureship can be a drain. He went so far as to let on to Billard that this idea was so good and so new that perhaps he, the captain, could profit from being the first to push it."

Matthew poked Marion in the ribs and said, "You must have a good head for business, being the one to dream this plan up." She blushed.

He continued, "Peter named some Boston folks who are friends of Hadley's. Whoever they are, it impressed the captain. Then Peter said, 'I know what price you could have gotten for five years' work from this man. We shall see that you get no less—and no more—under the new arrangement.' The captain nodded and we left. That Peter! I've never seen the likes of him before."

Marion said, "Now it all seems real. Before, it was just a dream."

"Oops! Don't go changing your mind on me now, Maid Marion."

"I'm not. Not at all. It's good to know we'll be together." She looked over at Fiona. "I was half-afraid you'd take off on your own once we docked. Now we're almost family for a year. That's good."

"Yes, it is good to feel like family," mused Fiona as the pleasant sensation that accompanied that thought settled in around her shoulders. She looked from Marion to Matthew and said, "I guess if I have a year in the fields with you, Matthew, we will find out who's stronger. You may be surprised."

"If you're stronger than I am, I won't have to work nearly as hard as I'd planned," he said with a chuckle.

When the first mate called all the passengers who had indentured themselves for their fare to assemble, George Denton stood by, curious to see who would come forth. The four men he had rescued would be there, of course. He knew who some of the others were from conversations he had had with them during the voyage. The preacher could scarcely believe his eyes when the three Ely women appeared. Indentured? About to become servants, these uppity women who stood in line straight-backed, sure, proud?

He did not envy the master who would have to contend with them. Or did he? "What a feat to break the Spirits of those three. That immoral redhead who refuses to cap her hair and flirted with first a sailor, then a fool; the old scold who interfered with a birth in my community, who kept a sinning daughter of Eve from her well-deserved pain of childbirth; and that young wench who dares to earn money from reading and writing, using skills that belong only to men as God declares in the Bible, and so mad she was singing to the Moon that night I strolled by," he muttered to himself. "Oh, to make those women bend and bow, to speak only when ordered to, to do the work no one else would dirty their hands with, to eat only table scraps."

Where might they end up? A coin in the first mate's pocket would buy him that information. If it turned out to be near enough, once he had delivered his recruits he might just have to stop by and watch it all. And wasn't it his duty as a God-fearing man to find out more about these three proud women? They could be dangerous to any Christian community—Pagans or worse. Witches, if he was lucky. After all, it was possible that the young one could have been praying to the Moon. A person could gain a lot of respect, a lot of power, an important job, if he uncovered a witch.

Denton clenched and unclenched his arm muscles in anticipation of such a scene. Suddenly he flinched. Why was Letticia's face filling his mind now? No! He shook his head fiercely to chase her away.

Next morning, shortly after dawn, the call they all had been waiting for came from the Crow's Nest: "Land ahoy!"

George Denton, in his perch in the rigging, was awash in rue. This was the very day he would have chosen, had he been a gambler. But, of course, he was not one, for gambling was a sure pathway to hell. He squinted hard at the ocean, as though he could see down to its floor and way beyond into the realms of hell itself where his tormentor abided. That was just like Satan to plant the correct date in his mind so as to tempt him with gambling, to make him feel the pinch of not adding that purse to his pocket.

Then George scanned the crowd milling around the main mast that held the Crow's Nest. Who amongst his flock was gathering there? Who for him to stand in front of later on today to fix with his firm gaze while he spoke of the wages of sin? The crowd grew until it surpassed any that he had pulled together, even when he brought the men up from the brig.

Old Salty walked into the center of the bow when he sensed the tension had built enough to put the crowd in his palm. He sauntered over to the mast and put his arms around it as though shaking apples from a tree and called up to the sailor who had given the notice, "What do you see, Man? Pretty maids waving their handkerchiefs at us from Boston's Widow Walk?"

The sailor guffawed and looked out again at the narrow thickening he had caught sight of on the horizon. "It's no bigger than a quill line drawn across a paper, but it's land," he called down.

With that, six youths raced to the prow and strained to see. Soon they were outdoing each other with their claims.

Off-duty sailors lazed around the deck and laughed. This was one of the best days of any trip for them.

Fiona looked up at the Crow's Nest., a rush of fond memories washing over her. How she'd love to be there now, tracing the dark horizon line of the New World with her eyes. She said to her friends, "Perhaps we'd have been wise to wager. Did you consider it, Basuba?"

The older woman laughed, "No. What I can see of the future has more to do with paths and the forks in them. I've never had a gift for dates." She scratched the marmalade kitten she carried under its chin.

Old Salty made his way slowly around the crowd, stretching the cap out to someone here, then someone there, only to veer off at the last minute.

When he passed by a fuming Madame Dora, who stood with her arms tightly crossed, he folded his own and pretended to execute a do-si-do with her. She snarled at him and stepped quickly back into the crowd. How humiliating! She had bragged to many of her customers that she would win that bet. She had banked on that success, expecting it to bring a flood of nervous passengers to her tea table, willing after that proof to pay her new, higher prices.

"She's absolutely furious not to have won," exclaimed Marion to Basuba. The black kitten with one white paw was climbing cautiously across her shoulder.

"Her reputation for fortune-telling just dove to the bottom of the sea," replied Basuba. "She ought to be glad it's the end of the trip and not the beginning."

At last Salty Bill stopped in front of the tinker, a man stooped over from endless hours of repairing tools. The sailor saluted him and made to pour the money out as soon as the tinker's hands were in place to receive it. In the twinkling of an eye the man's hands were full of coins. The mender of pots and pans grinned, "Well, there's a few rainy days for me and mine in this cap. I'm a satisfied man."

Old Salty winked at the crowd. "The tinker's not the only one deserves a grin on his face today. You'll all be strolling on dry land so soon you'll be homesick for this ocean before the week's out."

The sailor began to walk with an exaggerated tilt and wobbly, bowed legs, just as he had seen so many folks do when they first got back on dry land after all the weeks of accustoming themselves to the roll of the ship on the sea. The crowd laughed long and hard. Then folks began to mill and chat ravenously about what they would do first when they finally docked.

By the next day, the deck had been transformed. Crates and barrels that had disappeared on the first and second days of the voyage now emerged from stowage. The larger items of baggage, the trunks and heavy boxes, were carried to the stern.

"Say, Fiona, Marion, have either of you seen your satchels in that pile yet?" asked Matthew as they surveyed the growing mountain of gear. After searching carefully, the two saw nothing of theirs.

"I suspect they keep the possessions of us indentured folks locked away in stowage so we won't escape in the commotion of docking," said Matthew.

"Smart of them," replied Fiona. "The thought of disappearing like that has already crossed my mind more than once."

"What they've got of mine is not enough to keep me here," laughed Matthew.

The sharp voice of the first mate cut in from behind them. "Be assured we plan to watch more than your gear when we dock. In fact, you won't even see us dock. You'll recall, Master Fields," he served up Matthew's name with sarcasm, "that the brig has no windows. Expect to be there from dawn tomorrow until you leave with your master. Whoever that might be."

They had all turned to face the sailor by now. He leered at them before he went off.

"Can they do that to us?" asked Marion incredulously.

"Oh, yes. The captain rules this ship like a king rules his kingdom," said Matthew grimly.

"Thank Nature we've got the Turners helping us," said Marion, clapping her hands together.

"And Jean-Paul and Salty Bill," said Matthew, lightening a bit. "Besides, Fiona can play peek-a-boo with the cats and her poppet down there in the dark. Those kittens'll get their first lessons in mousing in that brig, believe me."

Fiona could not take her eyes off the mail satchel that one of the sailors lashed to the mast mid-afternoon. She watched folks carefully tuck into it the letters that would travel back to England on the next eastbound ship. One woman held her small parcel close to her heart and then kissed it before she let it go.

Fiona's mind filled with an image of Alyona working her way ever so slowly to the top of the hill outside Blue Fens and looking off in the distance towards where she'd watched her granddaughter disappear so long ago. An old woman out of breath and forlorn.

Suddenly Fiona had to find Marion and Matthew. When she did, her eyes bounced back and forth between them. Which one to ask? When she could bear it no longer, she turned to Matthew and the words raced out, "So, did you mention me in your letter to Plainfield?"

"Oh, and what would you give to know?" he answered, a smile flashing in his eyes.

Fiona leaped over the river of hot pride that burned in her at his taunting. She surprised herself when she said,"It's worth one kiss when our feet first touch the grass."

"A kiss if I did mention you? Or a kiss if I didn't?" He couldn't stop teasing.

"A kiss either way. I just want to know…oh, the truth is, two kisses if you did write something about me."

"Two kisses it is then. Maybe you'll even give me three when you hear what I did. I asked them to send word right away to Blue Fens that you are in good health and great cheer—and as comely as ever."

"Three kisses it'll be."


Of course, the passengers of the *North Star* were as good as glued to the bow of the ship as the sun fell on that final day of their journey. Since the moon was a sliver only four nights short of darkness, the setting sun would take the last light down with it. Luckily, the friends managed to find a place together at the railing. They heard a sharp whistle and looked up to see Jean-Paul grinning at them from the rigging above.

"Now, Fiona, don't you go getting any wild ideas about your last night on the ship, about britches, crow's nests, and things like that," he called down.

She laughed and said playfully, "You'd indulge me one more time, wouldn't you?"

In return, he dashed away as quickly as he could across the spider-webbed rope. When he had reached a safe perch, he stopped and made a face at her, and they all laughed again.

As she looked around at the milling crowd, Fiona's eyes landed unexpectedly on Anne. She could just glimpse the little girl through the pack of bodies that lined the bow. Fiona did not mean to stare, but the sight of her old friend held her gaze. She was silently wishing her "Godspeed" when the child turned and looked directly at her. Keeping her face still, Anne flashed a quick good-bye wave to Fiona. It was the briefest, tiniest wave of a hand, but it was a wave. To Fiona, that little message of good will seemed to crumble a thick wall that had stood between them since the incident with the poppets. Even though she would probably never see the girl after landing, something important had come to life between them once again. She turned away before her attention to Anne would alert the little girl's mother. She turned away with a satisfied feeling.

Peter Turner cleared his throat dramatically, took a long look at his indentured comrades, and said, "Captain Billard and I had a talk and, in the end, he agreed that it's not necessary for you to visit the brig. He's a smart man. Came around to seeing how a cheery indentured servant finds a master faster than a grumbling one who's spent a sleepless night playing pinochle with the rats."

"This way, we can introduce you to Jonas Hadley properly," added Barbara.

"It is all falling into place. Thank you, Friends," said Fiona, reaching out her hands to the couple.

"Time for celebration," said Basuba. As they all watched, she plowed her left hand into her pocket. When she pulled her palm out and opened it, she held a small pile of tan, oval pumpkin seeds. "We're landing just in time to put these into the soil. They come from my garden across the sea. Take some, each of you. Plant them wherever you settle. With these bright orange pumpkins as their guides, the Spirits of our loved ones will have an easier time finding us on All Hallows' Eve."

She winked at Marion who nestled against the kitten she cuddled as she thought about her father. Then Basuba offered the seeds to her companions.

Seeds in their pockets, minds on the days to come, hearts full of anticipation about the future, the small group fell silent. A comfortable quiet, the kind that often descends on folks who care about each other and are soon to part.


Marion's fingers wrapped and rewrapped themselves around the beloved wooden figurine of the woman drawing down the Moon. At the same time her sharp eyes picked out the features of the coast they were approaching. Everything she saw was cause for wonderment. Her mind swam with questions about what they would find, where they might go, who they would meet.

Suddenly the pain of completing another leg of the journey tugged at her heartstrings; once they landed she would be even farther away from Gwyneth physically and mentally. She'd gotten used to the ship and all it contained; here her memories of Gwyneth knew how to find her. But the New World would brim with a million new things. She was scared. She clutched at her wooden carving.

Then, in her mind's eye, she saw the letters that she would write each month. One after another the papers appeared and formed themselves into a bridge that spanned the ocean from one continent to the other. She relaxed. The choice was hers and Gwyneth's: as long as they kept the link between them alive, there it would be. Images of the New World flew into her mind again, crowing like a large flock of birds. What fun it would be to share with Gwyneth all the adventures that lay ahead. Yes, she was ready to open the circle that had been her life on the *North Star*. Ready to open the circle of what had been and go on to her new life. "Let it begin!" she thought eagerly.

Fiona stood with her hands on the railing, enjoying the feeling of the solid weather-smoothed wood in her grip. Ah, to walk amongst living trees soon, to close her hands around a trunk and listen. To her surprise, when she focused her attention on the image in her mind, Fiona saw that her hands were holding a willow. In her imagination she listened hard for the pulse of this tree. It was new to her, for she had never bothered to hold a willow before. The rhythm was strong and steady, yet light and fluid. The pulse seemed to have many strands to it that were bound together in a special harmony, a harmony that drew her to it.

She turned to Basuba on her left and asked, her heart filled with strong desire and her voice less sure of itself than usual, "Will you," and then she turned to Marion on her right, "and you, take me as a Willow Woman? I still love Oaks and Elms, but I understand about Willows now. They're the reason we'll all be together this next year."

"I thought you'd never ask," said Marion with a whoop. She threw her arms around Fiona in the first hug they had shared.

"All right by me. But we'll have to think of a very difficult initiation for one who's been so partial to those big Oaks as you, my friend," teased Basuba before they hugged.

"If you're all Willows, I want to be one, too," said Matthew.

"We're a little short on Willow Men here, so that's fine," declared Basuba. "Don't you agree, Mari?"

Marion nodded vehemently, but Fiona scarcely saw her. Already the young woman was staring off into the future, dreaming of a village in the New World where everyone could worship as they chose, where folks would come from different parts of England, Holland and France—anywhere that Nature was adored—and share their customs and holy days. A village in the midst of open wild land that belonged fully to Mother Nature. Her strong will surged through her and she knew that together she and her friends would either find such a community—or build one.

Basuba looked up into the heavens as a wave of freedom rolled over her. It was true—when she threw her blessed herbs overboard, she had thrown away her need to be able to do things the way she had always done them before. She was ready now to follow the path that opened in front of her and to notice the forks in it, to leave something behind when she went on. Her left foot tingled and she looked down at it. "Yes, I'm ready to walk that solid ground. Ready to follow where Life takes me—truly ready to follow the Moon."

Then the herbalist threw back her head and laughed with glee, for just as the Moon came into her thoughts, she glanced up and there it was, that slim silver arc, smiling down on them. It called out to her a loud "Yes!"

# *About the Author*

Photo by Dagny Bilkadi

Kaia Svien obtained a Bachelor of Arts in Art History from Pomona College and a Master of Science in Curriculum and Instruction from the University of Wisconsin at Madison. She practiced as a Learning Disabilities Specialist for many years. Kaia has studied with excellent guides in the Wiccan community and participates in community and ceremonial life. Part of her work today is to design and facilitate rituals and to mentor those who want to base their spiritual practice in their ancient European-American cultural roots. She develops and teaches classes on this ancient culture at a local Cultural Wellness Center. She lives with her beloved in inner-city Minneapolis.

To order additional copies of this book,
please send full amount plus $4.00 for
postage and handling for the first book and
50¢ for each additional book.

Send orders to:

## Galde Press, Inc.
PO Box 460
Lakeville, Minnesota 55044-0460

Credit card orders call 1–800–777–3454
Phone (612) 891–5991 • Fax (612) 891–6091
Visit our website at http://www.galdepress.com

Write for our free catalog.